Reviews

I finished the book because I couldn't stop reading. I love the story, I love the characters, I love the message, I love the writing style, I love it all. I want to go back so I can better appreciate the character development and story arc. I cried multiple times throughout the book.

—Betty, missionary and missionary wife in Kenya

A good read! Very realistic about the messiness involved in trying to help and love people who find themselves in difficult circumstances.

—Leslie Walt, missionary and missionary wife in Austria

I love to read books that bring me into the story and I ask, "What would I do in that situation?" I found myself thinking—do I only spend time with people who are "like" me? Or do I want to help others, but only a certain amount, so that I don't get uncomfortable? These (plus many more) were questions that came up from this book and are excellent questions to ponder and respond to. Well done, Christine!

—Jill, Plains, MT

The book was hard to put down until it was finished. Dorothy is an empty nester, encouraged by her son to volunteer at a pregnancy center. She does, but struggles a bit since her gifts to help are not typical of other volunteers. She connects with one woman, Bailey, who has made some bad decisions and needs a role model. The book answers the real question about what is more important in life. It shows how both family and church work together through the difficulties of helping others.

—Carolyn, Austria

This book was one of the quickest reads I have ever had an opportunity to enjoy. The day after finishing this story, with all of the meaty, fun conversations, my son came over for lunch. As we talked, I found it helpful to consider Dorothy's (your?) example of how to listen to, trust, and respond to an adult son. For one thing, I was reminded to ask God for His wisdom before speaking. *Dorothy's Gift* breathes with compassion and practical wisdom in a modern setting. I also found it true to reality regarding much of what it takes to help damaged women. At the same time, it offers a lighter approach to addressing serious matters lovingly and matter-of-factly.

—Rona, Las Cruces, New Mexico

DOROTHY'S
Gift

CHRISTINE C SCHNEIDER

CHRISTINE SCHNEIDER

Publisher: Keybobby Books, PO Box 1770, Plains, MT 59859

Book Cover by Rebeca-Ira

ISBN: 978-0-9630214-4-1

1st edition 2025

DOROTHY'S GIFT

Showing compassion is always right. We may have to show it wisely, but compassion is always right. —Connie

· 1 ·

The questions did not seem to bother her.

"Bailey Austin. I'm twenty-one."

The questions bothered me. It was the thing I liked least about working at the pregnancy center. I tried to be gentle, but the questions were so personal.

"Bailey, do you smoke?" *None of your business!* I would say.

Her answer was soft. "Sometimes, but probably not now."

Check. "How 'bout alcohol? Drugs?" Would she honestly tell *me*?

She shook her head, the auburn twist of hair wobbling precariously on the top of her head.

Check. "Are you on medication for anything?"

"Sometimes for allergies, but only in summer."

Check. "What makes you think you're pregnant?"

She told of her nausea, tiredness, and insatiable hunger.

The only way for me to continue was to blame the questions on someone else. "I need to ask you these questions. I know they seem very personal, but we want to help you."

She nodded, and the haphazard twist of hair unwound and fell down around her face. A friend of mine once said he could tell if a woman was pregnant or not by the dullness of her hair. I'm not that astute.

She ran her fingers through her locks and then folded her hands neatly in her lap.

"Have you ever been pregnant before?"

She took a deep breath to aid her hesitation. Ah, if I had only known that our future was written in Bailey's past! She deliberately looked me in the eyes. "No."

I smiled, my lips feeling stiff and mirthless. "So you've never had a miscarriage or an abortion."

She said nothing, and I wrote a question mark.

Next question: "If this pregnancy test is positive, what would be your plans?"

"Oh, I'll keep the baby," she said with a cheerful lilt in her voice. "I'd never have an abortion." I crossed off the question mark and wrote "no."

I explained to her that she would conduct the pregnancy test because the nurse wasn't here today, and I wasn't authorized to do the test. I handed her the cup for the urine sample, and she went into the bathroom, while I wrote impressions and comments on the clipboard.

I had told Connie, our director, just how I felt about the intrusive questions.

"The girls expect it," she assured me. "When they come in for help with something so intimate, they know there will be questions. Besides," she added as encouragement, "You haven't a threatening bone in your body. These girls look at you like a favorite aunt."

I shook my head, unwilling to be flattered. "I would never answer questions like these. I'd say 'It's none of your business.'"

Connie shrugged. "If a girl ever says that, then just give her the test."

Bailey returned. Her trembling hands held the dropper as she squeezed five tiny drops of urine into the tester.

Four minutes is a long time to wait for your life to be permanently and irreversibly changed. I read again from my clipboard. "Does the father of the baby know you might be pregnant?"

She picked at her fingernails and admitted, "I don't know who the father is."

Before I could say anything, she continued. "I work at the casino and . . . well, you know."

At least my imagination knows.

We both bent over the tester.

"Nothing's happening," she murmured.

I looked at my watch. "We have to wait the whole four minutes." I glanced at my clipboard again and decided to ask my own question. "This is kind of nerve-wracking, isn't it?"

She tried to giggle, but her eyes strayed back to the tester.

Ask another question. "If the test is negative, what changes might you make to keep this from happening again?"

"Changes? I . . . I don't know."

"There are worse things than being pregnant. Like STDs: sexually transmitted diseases." I looked again at my watch. "Can I give you some literature?"

She nodded, but her gaze stayed fastened on the tester.

I rummaged in the cupboard, choosing appropriate leaflets: "How to Avoid STD's". "The Secret to a Happy Relationship." I closed the cupboard door and returned to my seat on the sky blue chair. "Do you have any religious beliefs that might give you support or comfort during this time?" Perhaps I could reword the questions so they don't sound so stiff and sterile.

"Religion?" She looked at me suddenly.

"Like church or a Bible study. Have you ever read the Bible?" My question. Better.

"No. My life's been much different than yours." Surprisingly, her eyes suddenly filled with tears.

I did not need to be reminded. Every time I counseled someone, I was confronted with my trouble-free life. Guilt always wrestled with gratitude. My life was probably smoother than this girl could ever imagine. I glanced at the tester, where two faint pink lines were forming.

Suddenly embarrassed, she blinked the tears away, and took a deep breath. "Looks like I'm pregnant." Determination strengthened her voice. She marked her form and signed and dated it. "Now what?" A hardness had come over her, probably a mechanism for coping alone.

I helped her figure out approximately when the baby would be due.

"A Christmas baby," she said without expression.

"You ought to go to a doctor to get this confirmed and to begin prenatal care. You need to take care of yourself and the baby. Can we schedule you for an ultrasound in a couple weeks?"

She shrugged as she stood and fished around in her purse. "I s'ppose so. Could you throw these away?" She handed me a partially empty pack of cigarettes. "I won't be needing them anymore."

"My pleasure." I sat at the desk and scheduled her ultrasound. "Would you mind if I called you next week to remind you?" Standard question. A girl's standard answer: please don't call.

She surprised me. "It would be nice if you called."

I would. We would talk once on the phone. A few weeks later, she'd borrow some maternity clothes from the clothing center. The baby would be born, and we would give her a pretty layette. She would come in for a few teaching DVDs to earn disposable diapers and her child's wardrobe for the first year. That's what we're here for: to help and support. When you volunteer once a week, that's all you can do.

Bailey buttoned her coat against the March wind, "Thank you, Dorothy," she said, actually remembering my name.

I always wished it wasn't legally risky to give hugs. She needed a hug badly.

That was Tuesday. On Thursday, I was at home, putting the finishing touches on a bridesmaid's dress, when Connie called.

"We just got a rather incoherent call from Bailey Austin. We got her file out. You talked with her on—"

"Yes, I remember her. What did she want?"

"She wanted to speak with you, but of course I didn't give her your phone number."

"Did she say what she wanted?"

"She wanted you to meet her at 14 Green Street."

I looked at the billows of rosy satin on the ironing board. "Connie, I can't go right now and meet her. I'm in the middle of things."

"Do you know what's at 14 Green Street?"

I had a sudden, sick feeling that I did. "No."

"I think she's going to have an abortion."

I didn't know what to say, so I just held the cell phone to my ear and listened to the silence.

"Dorothy?"

"I'm here." More silence. My brain would not kick in. "I won't know what to say."

"That's part of your charm - you're quiet."

Really?

Connie spoke again. "Do you have the car today?"

"Yes."

"Turn off the iron, get your coat and keys, and go get the girl."

I'd never fainted. Was this how it felt to faint? "I'm not a brave person, Connie."

"Did you like Bailey?"

"Well, yes, but—"

"They'll ruin her for the rest of her life if they kill her baby." She paused and then delivered her final word: "She asked you to come."

My hands were shaking, but this was why I had volunteered in the first place. "Fine. I'll go." The brain finally began to function again. "Any legal details I need to know?"

"Don't go in. Wait for her across the street. I told her Aunt Dorothy would come."

I had to laugh. "Pray for me," I said as I hung up.

Turn off the iron. Get your coat and keys. Go. I went.

I parked the car across the street from the clinic and decided against the umbrella, although the drizzle was fairly heavy. What a miserable day to be out rescuing people! On the pavement in front of the building were parallel lines drawn to keep protesters the correct distance from the entrance. Heart thumping, I reminded myself that I was not a protester. I took a deep breath and marched between those lines to the front door.

A bell jingled as I opened the door. I took in the room at a glance because there wasn't much to look at: simple furnishings, burgundy walls, dim lighting, the smell of incense, and fake candles flickering from alcoves in the wall. It seemed peaceful enough.

A young woman behind a desk smiled. "May I help you?"

I glanced around the waiting room. Not peaceful. Two girls waiting on a corner couch looked frightened and unhappy, or was it just my imagination?

Bailey had been sitting opposite them, and she was already on her feet. "Aunt Dorothy?"

I went to her and took her hand. It was cold and trembling.

"Sorry I'm late," I said, surprised at how strong my voice sounded.

"It's okay, but I think I've changed my mind."

From behind her, a young man stood up, his dark, Italian head looming over both of us. "Now Bailey, honey," he soothed, "we've been through all of this. Let's just get it over with."

Bailey, honey?

"Aunt Dorothy, I want to go home." Her misery caused my throat to close, and I swallowed to clear it.

"You live with *me*, Honey," the young man protested.

"Not always!" Bailey's sudden volume startled everyone in the waiting room.

The receptionist came out from behind her desk. "Is there a problem?"

I shook my head and pulled Bailey by the arm toward the door. "None. She just needs to talk first." I waved in the direction of the desk. "Can we just leave the papers here?" The receptionist glanced around. "Well, yes, but you'll have to make another appointment."

"By phone?" I asked, hoping to convey unconcern.

The girl sat down again. "That'd be fine."

The young man had other thoughts. "But we've already filled out the papers for the . . . the . . . this."

Ever helpful, the receptionist suggested, "I have it all in the file.."

He looked at Bailey and me, my hand on the doorknob. "I think I'd like the papers back," he decided.

We closed the door behind us. The rain was coming down hard and it intensified my shivers. Bailey had looped her arm into the crook of mine, and in matched strides we crossed the street.

She ran around and slipped into the passenger's side, and then nodded at the clinic. "Here comes Kent."

"Will he follow us?" I suddenly thought of all those horror movies I had never seen. Where could I go to be safe? "I'm not a good driver, Bailey. You'll have to watch him to see if he follows. I have to concentrate on driving."

"He won't follow us." She turned around. "He went the other way."

I pulled into a supermarket parking lot and left the car running to warm us. "Bailey, what's this all about? Who's Kent?"

"Kent's my boyfriend."

"I thought you said you didn't know who the father of your baby is."

"I don't. It ain't Kent, though." She talked at the windshield wipers, avoiding my eyes. "I thought maybe I could pass the baby off as his, but it turned out he don't want a kid." She dared a glance at me. "Thanks for coming to get me. Thank that other lady too."

I still did not feel up to driving, but I said, "So where should I take you?"

"Here's fine," but she didn't move.

"Here's fine?" I echoed. "It's raining. Where do you live?"

"With Kent."

"Don't you have family or friends or . . .." A plan was forming in my brain.

"I'll be fine."

"*I'm* not fine!" I exploded. "I hate to drive, and I'm a coward. I just came and got you, and now you say you're fine? I'm not going to put you out on a rainy parking lot. It's suppertime. I need to make supper. Do you drive?"

Her eyes widened in disbelief. "Of course."

"Would you please drive me home?"

Looking slightly amused, she traded places with me, and I directed her to our house. She was a remarkably good driver.

Bailey did not, however, know how to cook. She told me so, but after I watched her dissect an onion, I excused her to look around the house. I didn't want blood in the spaghetti sauce.

She returned to the kitchen quicker than I expected.

"What's with the pink satin?" she asked with challenge in her voice. She pulled up a stool to the counter.

"It's a bridesmaid's dress."

She rolled her eyes and made a face. "I'd never be, like, caught dead in something like that."

I said nothing and poured boiling water over the teabags.

"I went to a wedding once, where the bride wore jeans. Now that makes sense."

I smiled. "I'm glad some people like satin; otherwise I'd have no job."

"You sew dresses? For money?" Her astonishment was surpassed only by her embarrassment. "Sorry. Didn't know you sewed it. You can, like, sew?"

"I can. Real people sew."

She fiddled with the cucumber, picking off the tiny prickles. "I crocheted an afghan once." Her voice grew soft with the memory. "My grandmother helped me. It was bright red and royal blue. When it was finished the colors rocked."

"I never learned to crochet," I admitted. "Sewing usually goes faster. But my grandmother taught me how to sew."

She nodded and reached for a sharp knife. "I think I can cut up the cucumber if you like. How would you like it cut?"

"Peeled, in slices."

Her shoulders sagged. "Peeled?"

I took the cucumber and knife and nodded at the lettuce. "You tear up the lettuce, and I'll do this."

Later, we drank tea, and I had the feeling tea was not a familiar part of her life, either, although her grandmother had given her tea once. I invited her to supper.

As we sat down, Daniel, our twenty-four-year-old son, pulled out a chair so Bailey could sit down. My husband, Gary, said grace, and we began to eat. My family was used to young women—brides-to-be, prom debutantes—staying for dinner. My volunteer work had always stayed neatly at the pregnancy center, a topic of conversation, censored by confidentiality. Bailey fitted into none of the usual categories, and I had had no way of warning them before they met her.

"Nice to meet you, Bailey," said Daniel. "Is mom making your prom dress?"

"No, Daniel," I said quickly, "She's just a friend, staying for supper."

Daniel politely refrained from giving her another once-over, but his curiosity had not been satisfied.

My husband was equally stumped. "What happened to the salad?" Gary asked, serving himself some very limp, bruised greens.

Bailey stopped chewing and gave me a look filled with self-disappointment.

It was obvious that any deviation from my normal routine confused my family.

Gary, ever hospitable, though, tried to make conversation: "So, Bailey, is Dorothy doing your wedding?"

Bailey swallowed her food. "No. I doubt I'll ever get married." Her emotionless answer silenced all further conversation.

Later, I explained to Bailey that my clients sometimes stayed for supper; therefore my family had just made the obvious assumptions.

"It's okay," she reassured me, "Your family's not used to people like me."

I couldn't argue with her. I was having trouble myself.

I kept our conversation on the weather and the city's new bridge project while I hemmed the rosy satin, and she chipped the nail polish from her nails. At seven she glanced at her watch. "I have to go to work. Could you take me back home?"

I looked around for her jacket and thought about Kent. "Will you be all right?" I didn't know how to phrase my fears for her. "I mean . . . Kent . . . will he. . .?"

"He's at work too," she assured me with a nonchalant wave of her hand. "We have these spats, but we'll be okay."

On the way to Kent's apartment, we were silent, as I couldn't drive and talk at the same time. The apartment was not in the nicest neighborhood; next time I would bring Gary – if there were a "next time." I gave her my phone number. "If you need anything, please call."

"Don't worry. I won't let him talk me into an abortion." She got out and then leaned back into the car. "Thanks for coming to get me. Drive safely."

And she was gone.

· 2 ·

A few days later, our son, Daniel, popped in between classes. I was finishing the details on the sixth – and last – rosy satin bridesmaid's dress. "Weren't you in this very same position the last time I saw you?" he asked.

I had to squint to bring him into focus after so much close-up work. "Probably. I'm definitely sick of pink."

He dropped his backpack by the door. "I needed a break."

I looked at the backpack. "I assume there's not a computer in there."

He shrugged. "It's padded. What I really need is some hot chocolate and pistachios!"

"And lunch?"

He grinned and hugged me. "That, too."

He grilled tuna salad and cheese sandwiches while I assembled hot cocoa from a package. The pistachios were hidden in my sweater drawer in the bedroom.

When we sat down to eat, Daniel peered into his cup as if a frog were swimming around in it. "What, no marshmallows?"

"Nope. There's this little boy who keeps coming to my house and eating them when I'm not looking."

"Oops."

I watched him crunch into the grilled sandwich. Daniel, the computer geek; Daniel, the law student; Daniel, the little boy I used to cuddle. I would kiss the top of his head, and his hair smelled spicy, like windy days at the beach or cozy evenings in front of a crackling fire. I would beg God to guide him to a godly wife someday. Now, of course, when Daniel hugged me, he could rest *his* chin on the top of *my* head. How blessed I am!

"I love you," I said, out of the clear blue from his viewpoint.

He laughed. "Love you, too."

"So how's the computer business?"

"Slow. I need to find more clients." He sipped his cocoa and then added, "Although, I'm not going broke."

"And your studies?"

"A lot of work. I may have to take a break from computers when I begin studying for the BAR exam. I hope I can find a law firm to hire me before then."

We ate in silence for a few minutes, and then he asked, "So besides looking at pink dresses, what have you been doing?"

My life was so ordinary that it was usually difficult to tell even my family what I did all day. "This is an early May wedding, so I'm pretty much just sewing pink stuff. Of course, on Tuesday, I was at the Pregnancy Center, and – "

Daniel snapped his fingers. "I just remembered." He went to the living room and brought his backpack into kitchen. "I saw something in the newspaper a couple of days ago. I meant to show it to you sooner." He found the spot and folded the paper to a manageable size. "Isn't this the girl who was here last week for supper? The one from the Pregnancy Center?"

POLICE:

City police reported the following:

Kent Smalley, 32, of 1588 Willow Street,
was arrested Sunday on domestic assault charges.
Smalley allegedly assaulted Bailey Austin, 21,
of the same address.

"Mom? Are you all right?" Daniel's voice penetrated the sickness that had surged over me.

"I'm fine," I assured him. "Yes, that's her. She told me he wouldn't hurt her."

Daniel sighed. "People really mess up their lives."

"So many bad choices," I pulled the crust off my sandwich. "You wouldn't believe the bad choices. The worst is the girls who keep coming back. You'd think they'd learn." That sounded terrible, even as it came out of my mouth

"I'm sorry, Mom."

I shook my head. "No, it's okay. I need to – want to – know."

"I mean, I talked you into this in the first place."

That was partly true. He had encouraged me to step out of my comfort zone to avoid empty-nest syndrome: "You need a new cause in your life, Mom," he had told me at Christmas break two years before. "You need people in your life."

"I have people in my life," I had protested. "I have brides and bridesmaids and mothers-of-the-bride and flower girls and –"

"Now that I have my own apartment, you've got a big empty house. You need something that has more meaning than sewing fancy dresses for people who can afford you."

He was right. "How'd you get so wise?" I asked.

He grinned. "I had a year of college."

I chuckled. "Yeah, well, that's why I can't stop sewing fancy dresses for people who can afford me."

"Don't stop. But find a cause. Maybe you could buy a telescope and start hunting for new comets."

That would be his dream.

"Or you could volunteer at the library. Or be a teacher's aide. Or start helping at the kid's club at church." He ran his fingers through that beautiful blond hair. "I don't know. Isn't there something you feel passionate about? Like politics or –"

He kept throwing out ideas, but I already knew, and the idea scared me. I hoped it wouldn't occur to him.

"You and dad have a great marriage," he went on. "You could do marriage counseling. You also raised two fantastic kids. You could go back to college and become a child psychologist. Or –" I could tell by the look on his face that it had occurred to him.

When I mentioned the idea to Gary, he thought I was sick of sewing. "The Pregnancy Center? Are you looking for a different job?"

I was wrapping Christmas presents at the time, and he was handy to hold the knots in the ribbon. "The Pregnancy Center doesn't pay its volunteers," I reminded him.

"Well, we've got a kid who's in law school. We need your paycheck."

"I know. I'll keep sewing, but I love being a mother, and I don't get to do it much anymore, now that Abby's married and Daniel's on his own."

"So you want to smother – I mean, mother – the girls who come in to the Pregnancy Center?"

He grinned at me, and I tightened the knot around his finger with a snap.

"Ouch!" He pulled it away. "What makes you think they are going to let you mother them?"

"Why not? They probably have horrible mothers." The moment those words popped from my mouth, I was sorry I had said them.

"That sounds pretty chauvinistic."

"I didn't mean it that way."

Gary carried the stack of presents to the tree. "You're a great mother. The girls will be lucky to have you."

"So you don't mind?" I had almost hoped he would think it was a bad idea.

"Just don't get too much on your plate."

"It'll only be one afternoon per week."

"Oh. Well then," and it was settled.

"The girl's not your problem." Daniel said, dragging my thoughts back to the present. He carried the lunch plates to the sink.

"No, there's nothing *I* can do."

"Nope."

"Pray. I can always pray." Even as I said it, I cringed. Think about that later.

Daniel tucked a handful of pistachios into his pocket. "Gotta run." He bent and I kissed his cheek. It still smelled spicy. Some girl is going to just *swoon*!

"Have a great day," I told him. "See you on Sunday."

"Sooner."

And he was gone.

I wiped up the crumbs and picked up the folded newspaper. Pray. *Oh, Lord, I'm so bad at praying, so undisciplined and lazy.* I threw the newspaper in the recycle bin.

· 3 ·

Human beings are so self-centered that they don't realize that earth-shaking things are happening to others. Bailey's life was careening out of her control, even as I was feeling sorry for my poor prayer habits.

It had been a long night at the riverboat casino. Bailey let herself into her apartment building and threaded her keys through her fingers as a nasty weapon against any attacker. The stench of the building intensified her nausea.

The landlady, Mrs. Angeli, lived on the ground floor, and although it was after 2 a.m., no one was asleep. Bailey could hear her shrill voice, scolding – more than likely – her son, Mark. Every time Bailey had paid the rent, Mrs. Angeli would once more pour out her annoyance concerning her good-for-nothing son, who took drugs and probably sold them as well. Bailey had never understood why she would let her good-for-nothing son still live at home. It was, of course, because of Mark's son, Arlie. Mrs. Angeli doted on the little boy, and she was usually his babysitter by default.

Bailey tiptoed past the door. There was a large crash, as if someone threw a soup kettle, and two men were yelling obscenities at each other. She hurried up the stairs, being careful to step over the board that seemed on the verge of disintegrating. She never touched the walls because of the filth, and two tiny piles of plaster dust on the steps warned of the unstable banister. Bailey reached her third-floor landing, out of breath and trembling. Her keys were ready to unlock her door,

A light burned in the kitchen. "Kent?" A quick glance around reassured her that Kent was not there. She turned the light off and went into the bathroom. *God, I feel awful,* she thought. The light in the bathroom revealed that she looked awful, too. She leaned her aching head against the doorframe, feeling as if she would vomit, but knowing the relief would not come. She got ready for bed and then glared at the front door, trying to decide if she should hook the chain or not. If she did, and Kent came home, she'd have to wake up to let him in. If she didn't, there were probably drug dealers downstairs. She chained the door.

Once in bed, she buried her throbbing head in the cool pillow and tried to rub away the pain. *Stupid baby.* She needed a cigarette, a beer, something that would relax her. She couldn't even take an aspirin for her back and headache. Eventually, she dozed off.

Morning came before sun-up – much too early. It arrived with loud voices and banging somewhere in the lower levels of the building. Red and blue lights flashed against the walls of her room. She had not heard sirens. Bailey crept from her bed and stood beside the window where she could not be seen. Several police cars were parked in the street. In the eerie, changing light, police personnel, dressed in protective gear, moved about slowly like mustard-colored moon-walkers.

Bailey looked at her watch. Four a.m. *What's going on?* An officer led someone – she thought it looked like Mark – from her building. After them came her landlady with another officer.

Where's Arlie?

Just then, another officer – a woman – emerged from the building, carrying the little boy. Someone fetched a blanket from one of the cars and wrapped it around him. Were they arresting the landlady?

Bailey realized that her heart was pounding hard and that she felt hot and breathless. The headache persisted. Slightly disoriented by the confusion of lights reflecting off her walls, she found her way to the kitchen and poured a glass of water. She sat at the table in the semi-dark and pressed her head into her hands. Would the pain never stop? The aspirin bottle was amongst the clutter on the table, and she fingered it, wondering if the risk was really that great.

A knock at the door saved her the trouble of figuring it out.

"Police here," called a woman's voice. "We need to evacuate the building."

Evacuate? Bailey pushed herself to her feet, turned on a light, and unlocked the door, although she kept the chain hooked. She squinted into the light on the landing.

The officer was the same one who had answered her call last week after Kent had roughed her up. "Hello again," the woman said, "We need to clear out this building. It's not safe to stay. Do you have anyone you can stay with?"

Bailey sighed and nodded. "Yeah. My mother." She had a key to the mobile home. "What's going on?"

"We have arrested the man and woman downstairs. You need to get dressed. You may take your personal I.D., but for now you'll have to leave everything else."

Bailey could hardly think. "Um. What about my clothes for work tomorrow – I mean, today."

"Bring them. But hurry now."

Bailey could hear the police waking the other tenants on her floor as she dressed herself. Her hands were shaking, and she could hardly manage the buttons. She glanced around the apartment, wondered if she should take anything of Kent's, and then gave up the idea. At the moment she couldn't even think of what she needed. Kent would be so angry!

Once outside, one of the police officers took her name and cell phone number, and then the same woman drove her to her mother's house.

Her mother was grumbling about Bailey's bad timing when she had to get up to unchain the door. "It's so early, yet. What are you doing here?"

"I had no choice, Mom; the police made me leave."

Her mother turned on a light and before Bailey could shield her eyes, she caught a glimpse of her mother in a huge pink negligee with feathers and sequins.

"You're not in trouble with the police, are you?"

"No, Mom. They made everyone in the building leave. I just need a place to stay – just for a while. I have a roaring headache."

Her mother enveloped her in a large, feathery hug. "Poor dearie," she cooed. "You can sleep on the couch. When I get up, I'll clear out the guest room, and you can stay there."

Bailey nodded, her eyes still closed.

"Do you want an aspirin?"

Bailey shook her head.

"Josie?" A man's deep voice called from the hallway, and Bailey's eyes snapped open. He was as round and dumpy as her mother was, and he was tying a robe around himself. Bailey wished she were anywhere else on the face of the earth except here.

"Go back to bed," her mother snapped, "I'll be there in a minute."

He ignored her command. "Who's this?"

Her mother sighed and made the introductions: "Carl, this is my daughter, Bailey. Bailey, this is Carl. She's staying here because the police cleared out her apartment building."

"Meth lab?" he asked.

Bailey shrugged.

"Leave her alone!" her mother barked, "She's got a headache." To Bailey she coaxed, "Are you sure you don't want some aspirin?"

"I'm positive. I just want to sleep."

"But if you take something, you'll sleep better. I've got sleeping pills. Why don't you try them?"

"Josie, you leave her alone," grumbled Carl. "She said no."

Bailey had never thought she'd be grateful to one of her mothers' loser boyfriends.

Her mother twirled around in a swirl of chiffon and perfume and shoved open the guest room door. "The blankets and pillows are in there."

"Thanks, Mom. I'll get the lights." She went into the cluttered guest room and pushed enough of the junk from the bed so she could sleep there. She had no intention of sleeping in the living room with a boyfriend in the house. She turned off the lights, locked the guest room door, and lay down on the bed still fully clothed.

Whatever am I going to do? She pulled a blanket over her, turned on her side, and let the tears flow.

· 4 ·

I actually took the flower girl's dress with me to the Pregnancy Center on Tuesday. I hoped to have time between clients to sew the hand-gathered rosettes onto the neckline. When I had first volunteered at the Pregnancy Center, I had had too much time on my hands. Connie, whom I already knew from Christian Women's Club, seemed to understand my fears right from the start and scheduled me for Friday afternoons. By spring, I was ready to quit.

"But we need you."

"No," I had told her. "All you need is a recorded message and a bulletin board. Hardly anyone comes in on Fridays. I volunteered because I thought I could make a difference in a girl's life. I rarely see any girls, except the few that come in to watch a DVD to earn disposable diaper and baby clothes points."

"Do you talk to them?"

"They don't talk to me. They walk in; I say hi; they tell me their name and that they're going upstairs to watch a DVD. They watch it, come back downstairs, and tell me the name of the DVD. I mark their file; they leave. That's Fridays."

"I didn't want to overwhelm you."

"Honestly, Connie, I'm so scared of what God might ask me to do if I switched days, but Fridays are a waste of time."

"You'll need more training," Connie warned.

Training and another year's experience, however, had not prepared me for rescuing Bailey from the women's clinic.

Instead of sewing on pink rosettes, I told Connie about my afternoon with Bailey, while we sorted and packed the children's winter clothing for storage. When it was finished, we would sort and hang up all the summer clothing for the new mothers to choose from.

Connie seemed only to be half-listening to me until I described my fear as I stood at the front door of the clinic. "You went *into* the clinic?" she interrupted with a sharp edge to her voice.

"I did."

Still holding a yellow snowsuit, she rested her wrists on the edge of a box and looked at me for a moment, obviously choosing her words. "Very risky." She seemed visibly shaken.

"Why? All of my fears didn't happen."

"For that we can be thankful." She folded the snowsuit and then shook her head as if something had finally been revealed to her. "Your brain really does freeze when it hits new situations, doesn't it."

"It does."

"Do you remember me telling you on the phone to wait for Bailey across the street?"

Suddenly, I did.

"There are legal reasons for that. You're lucky we didn't have to get your husband to bail you out of jail." She held the box flaps closed while I taped them. "Did they ask you to leave?"

"No. Bailey called me 'Aunt Dorothy,' and I guess they believed it."

Connie laughed. "Thank goodness for small blessings!" She piled mittens and hats into the next box. "Let me explain: If they thought you were in their building to interfere with their business, they could accuse you of trespassing. We might do the same thing if they came here and tried to take a girl away."

"Oh."

"Yes: oh." Connie took a deep breath. "So. What was it like inside?"

"Very different from ours: deep red wall, candles, incense, leather furniture. Lots of money there."

She nodded. "I've been thinking for some time that we need to redecorate here. We could paint the walls.

"Not red."

"No. Soft colors. Maybe a furniture store would donate some decent chairs. You could make curtains, and we could get rid of those office building blinds."

"We could hang pictures – maybe prints of little children and mothers."

She shook her head. "No," she said slowly, "I think that would be hard on any woman who's coming to get counseling after an abortion."

"Right. Well, then, flowers and gardens – something pretty and peaceful."

Suddenly she changed the subject and reached over to squeeze my wrist. "Don't *ever* go into the clinic again. Okay?"

"Okay."

The rosettes would have to wait. We unpacked and sorted children's summer clothing – such brightly colored, cheerful little things. We had so much fun imagining the joy some young mother would have, dressing her child in the pretty summer outfits. In between our unpacking, we took turns answering the phone and helping some of the clients who came in for advice. We doubted that pretty little outfits could fix the difficult lives of some of the young women.

It was almost closing time, and I had just hung up the phone, when the front door bell jingled. Bailey stood before my desk, looking gray and ill.

"Hi. Are you all right?"

"Well, no-o." She drawled, as if I were an idiot.

"Have a seat?"

She flopped onto the chair and pushed her limp hair out of her eyes. "Are you a nurse or something?"

"I'm sorry I'm not. Connie is. Shall I get her? What's wrong?"

She looked at her hands in her lap. "I just feel horrible. And I know I shouldn't take any medicine." She looked up suddenly and said forcefully, "I *haven't* taken any medicine!" Her gaze returned to her lap. "But I need something for my head and my stomach."

"Have you been to a doctor yet?"

"Not yet."

"You need to go to the doctor." I pulled out and gave her a sheet of paper with the names, addresses and phone numbers of medical clinics. "Choose one near where you live. They'll help you."

She read the list for a minute and then asked, "They won't make me have an abortion, will they?"

"No. And if they bring it up, let us know and we'll cross them off our lists. We like to save the lives of babies."

Bailey looked at me for what seemed a very long time, a smile playing around one corner of her mouth. I had no idea what she was thinking. Finally, she said, "You're a very nice person."

I laughed, embarrassed, yet realizing that I might, at least, be the nicest person she knew – which was very sad. "What do you need, Bailey?"

The smile faded. "Nothing. I'm staying with my mother at the moment, although I'm looking for another place to live."

"Kent?" The question was very courageous for me.

"It's over, I hope."

"Did he ask you to leave?"

"No. The building's been condemned. There was a meth lab downstairs."

Words failed me. That reckless idea flitted through my head again, but I discarded it quickly.

She continued. "I think it's all a big hoopla about nothing."

"Maybe. But it's safer for you and the baby to be with your mother."

"Yeah, right." Sarcasm dripped from her words, but I got her point: staying with her mother was not a good thing.

We sat through another bit of silence. Then she stood and waved the list. "Thanks for the help."

I knew I had been no help at all. "If there's anything else we can do." My words trailed to a halt, as I heard how useless they were.

Connie breezed into the reception room. "Hi," she said with a cheerful lilt to her voice.

Sullen again, Bailey muttered, "'Lo."

"Is there anything you need? Clothing? Toiletries?"

Bailey perked up. "Well," she admitted slowly, "I could use a few clothes."

"Come with me." Connie led her upstairs to the little nook with maternity clothes. I followed with the cordless phone, feeling relieved that we really could do something.

There wasn't much that fit Bailey for she wasn't very pregnant, and she wasn't overweight. We found a few things, though, and Connie promised that we had more coming in the end of the week. That meant that Connie would be shopping for Bailey with some of the money that the center had for just such emergencies. In a dresser, Connie found a gift bag of toiletries, normally given to new mothers.

Before Bailey left, she seemed mildly cheered. "See ya on Friday," she called. The bell clanged, and she was gone.

I sat back down at the desk and punched buttons on the phone so the answering service would pick up automatically for the night. "How did you know I wasn't doing a very good job helping her?" I asked Connie.

She grinned. "I was listening at the hall door."

"I'm sure glad you came in. I didn't know what to do."

"You were doing fine. She's not very friendly."

"No, but you knew how to help her." I felt my throat tighten with frustration. "I can't help her. I don't understand her. What am I doing here? I'm just a – another useless, self-righteous Christian, who's so out-of-touch with the world that I can't even grasp what her life is like. She came to me for help – and I want to help – but she knows that I don't know how. She didn't even tell me what she really came in here for."

"She came in for clothing, but she's too proud to ask. I just read between the lines."

"I wish I could."

"You're learning." Connie went back to her office, and I straightened up the desk for closing. That reckless thought returned to my head, and I wondered how stupid the idea really was. I didn't know where I would start, and besides, it might not even be legal.

As Connie and I walked to our cars, I decided to approach the subject from far away. "Are there any places in the city where girls like Bailey can go to live when they can't afford anything else?"

"There are."

"Do people ever open up their homes to women whose family rejects them? I mean, like a teenager, or somebody like that?"

"They sometimes do, but it's difficult." Connie got into her car and then tipped her head out the window. "Dorothy, what are you thinking?"

"Nothing," I said. "Maybe I'll come in on Friday."

I sat in the car for a while, thinking. I realized that I ought to talk to Gary. *Dear God, please help me – us – to know what you would have us do.* I really needed to start praying more.

· 5 ·

My thoughts were still not very well organized when I sat down to dinner with Gary that evening. Perhaps I should have waited to mention the subject, but I did not have a choice, for Gary knows me.

"How was your day?" he asked after we had prayed over the baked potatoes and chicken.

"Let me ask first."

He shook his finger at me and then helped himself to tossed salad. "Tuesdays are always hard on you. I'm trying to be a good husband, taking notice of these things."

I sighed. "Yeah, it was hard. Bailey came in again."

"Do I know her?"

"She came to supper the other night, and you and Daniel both asked about her wedding. The girl with the chip on her shoulder."

He nodded and chewed.

"A few days later, her boyfriend beat her up badly enough that it was in the newspaper. Daniel showed me the item in the paper. And then this week, she was – um – exiled, I think. "

"Evicted?"

"No. There was a meth lab in the building."

"Hers?"

"Of course not." I wondered for a moment why I was so sure. "Anyway, she had to move out of her apartment and in with her mother, which, I gather, was not a great arrangement."

"Not everyone can be you."

His compliment only depressed me more. I shrugged it off, for I wanted him to understand. "Mothering comes so easily to me, Gary. What I'm having trouble with is counseling and helping people who live outside my sphere of experience."

"So what happened today?"

"Bailey came in to ask us for some clothing – at least I think that's why she came in. Connie figured it out, and she's buying a few things for her to pick up on Friday."

"So what's the problem?" His dinner was almost gone, and I hadn't even tasted mine.

"She came to me for help, and I was too – too ignorant to help her – to read between her lines. Worse: she knows how clueless I am. It's as if she can see right through me, and she knows how sheltered and naïve and – and *stupid* I am."

"There's nothing wrong with being naïve of sin."

I disagreed. "Jesus was sinless, but He wasn't naïve. He knew what sin had done to Mary Magdalene and the woman taken in adultery, and He knew how to help them." A sob broke from my soul, surprising both me and Gary. I finished in a whisper, "I want to help Bailey."

Gary sighed and pointed at my plate. "Eat."

I obeyed, trying to swallow a piece of dry chicken around the lump in my throat.

"Why Bailey, in particular?" He asked.

I looked at him through tears and shrugged. "I don't know."

Again he told me to eat, and then his logical mind began to combine my thoughts with reason and common sense. "Rock bottom: Bailey doesn't need clothes and toothpaste. She needs a change of heart which only a genuine relationship with Jesus Christ will give her."

I nodded and ate another bite.

"The pregnancy center offers Bible groups and also tapes, books and DVD's to the girls that come in. Have you mentioned these to Bailey?"

"I've only known her for three weeks. It seemed a little pushy."

"You could invite her to church," he suggested.

I tried to imagine her on Sunday morning with all of the nicely dressed Christians, who would be shocked – shocked! – by her lifestyle, job at the casino, and the area of town in which she lived. Before I could veto the idea, Gary did it for me. "On second thought, I can't imagine her talking to Eleanor McGill."

The thought was so funny that I choked on my iced tea. Gary had to come around the table and pound on my back.

Once I had recovered, I decided to just dump the idea on him without any more preliminaries. "No one's going to really help her, except us, Gary. What if we asked her to live with us until the baby is born."

He lowered himself back into his chair, but the look he gave me was not of surprise. "Are you sure you realize what you're saying?"

"No. I know nothing about this sort of thing. But I can't just say to her 'Be warm and filled' and then go on with my comfy life as if she's all taken care of."

"How long have you been thinking about this?"

I looked at my watch. "About five hours."

His mouth spread into a wide, toothy grin. "That long?" It wasn't really a question. His grin had melted my heart thirty-four years ago. While I finished my salad, he cleared the dirty dishes and piled them near the dishwasher. I don't suppose he'll ever actually put them inside. "Ice cream?"

"Hadn't planned on it."

He looked in the freezer and discovered what I already knew: no ice cream. "Coldstone™," Gary announced. "Come on. We need strength."

I agreed. I was the frugal one. Splurging was Gary's forté.

We drove to the ice cream shop and split a ridiculously huge bowl of vanilla ice cream and chocolate sauce, with all sorts of crunchy things in it. It seemed to lubricate our brains.

We made a list of people we needed to talk to before we would do something so irreversible: Daniel, our daughter and her husband, Connie, our pastor, and one of Gary's best friends who attended the businessmen's early morning Bible study. Then we made a list of potential problems and the steps we could take to prevent or solve them. Finally, we made a list of our expectations and any requirements we would lay on Bailey. We decided to talk to Abby and Will first.

There is something so amazing about your grown child inviting you over to her house to celebrate your birthday. Although Abby and Will had been married for three years – and had invited us over many times – I was always filled with wonder at God's goodness. When Abby was born we prayed that God would be raising up a wonderful husband for her. My little girl was now happily married to a man much kinder than we could have ever found for her. The two of them were running a household – in spite of the fact that her room at home had always looked like an explosion in a thrift store, and in spite of the fact that he had begun the marriage deeply in school debts. With his MBA degree, Will had opened a used bookstore in a storefront that Gary had bought years ago for a bargain price. It's not the job we would have chosen for them, but they lived from thrift stores and garage sales and seemed happy. The house sparkled (at least the part we saw), and the debts were being paid.

Although it was only the beginning of May, Will had cooked fish outside on the grill, and Abby had made noodle and vegetable salads. Her cooking glory was desserts, and once we finished the unimportant part of the meal, she brought out a beautiful lemon meringue pie, my favorite.

They sang Happy Birthday and then Abby announced, somewhat breathlessly, "We're celebrating too!"

Gary and I looked at each other, and we *knew*. Gary managed a simple "Oh?"

"Yup," Will said, unable to suppress a grin. "Abby's pregnant."

My eyes filled with tears, which was my normal reaction to extreme happiness. We gave hugs all around and then settled down to savor the moment and the pie.

"When are you due?"

Abby patted her flat stomach. "It'll be a Christmas baby."

The phrase reminded me of my first talk with Bailey: Two Christmas babies and such different circumstances. It seemed a bit of bad timing to mention our intentions to take in an unwed mother-to-be, so we didn't bring it up.

Daniel was easier, since the pregnancy center had been his idea in the first place. His first reaction, however, was guarded. He looked at Gary for a clue as to how he was supposed to react. Then he turned to me and said slowly, "Golly, you'll need a lot of wisdom."

"We know that." I dismissed his caution and asked, "But do you think we're nuts?"

"You? No. I think your compassion for those girls has made your brain squishy. However, I do think Dad is nuts, for sure. He's the one who's going to have to put the pieces back together when things go wrong."

Gary disagreed. "Your mother is the one who'll have to cope with the day-to-day difficulties."

I took Daniel's side. "That's right."

Daniel shook his head. "Have you two dusted off the list of rules you made for me after I graduated from high school and still planned to live at home?"

"Actually, we've added to the list," Gary told him. "Things like: no drugs, smoking, or alcohol. She'll have to pay a small rent and also put away a percentage of her pay check every week."

"Does she even have a job?"

"Yes. She works at the casino," I said as gloomily as I could. "I wish we could ask her to quit, but Gary thinks it's better that she has a job."

Gary elaborated. "Bailey's going to have to take care of a child until he – or she - is grown. It's going to be a long, hard, lonely road. She needs to learn discipline and stability."

Daniel chewed on his lower lip and then said, "You're assuming she has none?"

"She's gotten herself into a mess because of a lack of self-control. She thought she loved that guy, but obviously he didn't love her. If she had waited for marriage, she would have been a lot better off."

Daniel had another thought. "You aren't going to be too good for her, are you?"

I felt as if he had slapped me, and I retorted before Gary could stop me. "I can't help it that my background is so smooth. Yes, I get frustrated with the girls who come into the pregnancy center for another pregnancy test a year after their first baby is born. You'd think they would at least learn how to prevent it, but somehow I think that I'm missing the main point."

Daniel looked properly scolded, so I calmed down. "Connie says that it's not about sex. She believes that we who try to help the women are grossly underestimating the longing these girls have for love and acceptance. Some of them have never had it and have ended up sleeping with unscrupulous men to try to fill the void."

Daniel leaned back on the couch and crossed his right ankle over the left knee. "It could make you wish for nice young men to marry all these women who have never been cared for properly – men who could show them God's love."

Gary punched Daniel gently and said, "Well, son, there aren't very many around like you and Will." He paused and then added, "Seriously, your mother and I just want to give her a home for a short time, with an opportunity to see God at work in our lives."

"One of our ideas," I told him, "is to require her to attend a Bible study – either at the pregnancy center or at church. It's not really a string attached, but we hope she'll see its importance to us and will be willing to try it for a while."

"So are you asking my permission?" Daniel asked.

"We just wanted your opinion and suggestions," Gary answered. "You seem to be saying: 'Watch out for super-spirituality.'"

Daniel nodded with a smile. "I think you two are very brave, but if you think God wants you to do this, I say do it. And pray a lot."

Pray a lot.

"I thought I saw a crazy look in your eyes when you left on Tuesday," Connie told me. She pulled the stylish maternity clothes out of the shopping bag. "D'you think Bailey'll like these? I actually went to a more 'hip' shop first before I bought things at the cheaper store. Maternity clothes aren't as pretty as they used to be."

"I think she'll like them," I assured her.

"So when would you offer to let her move in?"

"Maybe next week. Gary's talked to his best friend, and he thinks we could do it. We just have to talk to our pastor and his new wife; they're coming to dinner on Sunday. What warnings or suggestions do you have for us?"

"Remember that you signed a paper saying you would not seek to adopt any baby that was born to anyone we help."

"I do remember, but at this point, I think she means to keep her baby."

"Dorothy," she said, her voice suddenly soft, "I'm going to talk to her about adoption. It really could be better for the child."

I nodded. "All we want to do is smooth her way a little bit until the baby's born, and maybe for a while afterwards. Do we have a Bible study going here?"

"Not at the moment, but we have a woman in one of our supporting churches, who's always ready to lead one if we need it." She folded the clothing back into the shopping bag. "What do your kids think about it?"

46

"Daniel thinks my brain is squishy. Abby and Will don't know yet. Did I tell you Abby's expecting?"

"Granny Dorothy!" Connie exclaimed. "Aren't you excited?"

"Very. They just announced it this week, though, and we didn't feel free to overshadow their joy with our nutty plans." I stood up. I really did not want to be in the office when Bailey came today for her clothing. "Daniel is always supportive. He thinks we need to find nice men for all the girls who come in here; that would solve their problems."

Connie laughed. "It might solve some of them." She paused. "You're leaving?"

I turned to go. "Yeah. I might say something stupid if I see Bailey today."

"Have a good afternoon."

I stopped at the door. "Do you think we're crazy?"

"No," she answered gently, "Showing mercy is always right. We may have to show it wisely, but mercy is always right."

· 6 ·

Dale, the pastor of Evergreen Church, had been my pastor for so long that I still wanted to call him Pastor Browning, as I had in my teen years. After Gary and I had been married a few years, we had decided to invite him and his wife to dinner one evening. They had come with the younger two of their four children, who played happily with our baby and toddler. During that evening, Pastor Dale's wife had let slip a longing that put me under a strange kind of obligation. "It's so nice," she shared, "to spend an evening with a happy family who doesn't want us to solve a crisis."

After they had left, Gary reasoned that a pastor is often isolated from "normal" people by his ministry. Gary thought that Pastor Dale and his wife needed a few friends without enormous problems. It was a great idea, except that we just didn't "click." Despite that, Gary and I continued to give them a private appreciation dinner every year or so to encourage them.

Then, ten years ago, Dale's wife had died of skin cancer, and our dinners became man-to-man talks between Dale and Gary. We still were not best friends – the age difference was too great – but the two men chatted about golf and the church building and seemed comfortable with each other. This year was the first year Dale would come to our house with his new wife, Meg. It was also the first year we would be asking for advice on an important decision.

We'd all passed up dessert in favor of our waistlines, so I brewed a flavored coffee while Gary introduced the subject. "Dorothy has volunteered at the Pregnancy Center for several years," he told Meg. "It's generally been a ministry that she could leave at the office, but lately she's developed a new burden, and we wanted to ask your advice."

I poured the coffee and passed milk and sweeteners. "There's a young woman who is expecting a baby, and she needs a place-a better place–to live."

"So what are you thinking?" Dale probed, glancing at Meg as if to see what her reaction was.

Gary answered cautiously. "We have a big empty house, and we have enough money to be able to help the girl. We were thinking of offering her a room with board and a few strings attached."

"What a wonderful thing to do!" Meg exclaimed, her eyes sparkling.

Dale seemed less certain. He smiled at Meg and patted her knee to quiet her. Then he turned to me, the smile gone. "Have you thought this through?"

"I-I think so." It was so unlike me to go for something so radical, that I had just assumed that God was removing the hesitancy that usually overshadowed everything I attempted.

Our pastor looked at Gary. "This could really change your life, you know. How well do you know the girl?"

"Not very."

I didn't like it that Dale was making Gary look unwise. Gary was the wisest person I knew, and until now, I had assumed that his willingness to go along with my idea was because he thought it was a good idea.

"This was all my idea," I told him, "and believe me, I've gone through every possible problem in my head. Maybe she'll take drugs or get drunk. Maybe she'll rob us. Maybe she'll build a meth lab in the basement. Maybe she'll bring her boyfriends into our home. Maybe they'll murder us in our beds." Why didn't these things seem as large and difficult as contemplating a drive across the city during rush hour traffic?

Gary grinned. "Yup. Dorothy thinks up the problems, and if they happen, I solve them."

"There are more serious things to contemplate," Dale said.

More serious than being murdered in our beds?

Meg spoke up again, "I think it's very noble. The girl – what's her name?"

"Bailey."

"Bailey might even allow God to turn her life around."

Dale had another horrible thought: "Isn't she a Christian?"

I answered that she wasn't.

"Were you planning to bring her to church?" Before we could answer, he pressed on. "Because she might not feel very comfortable."

Remembering Gary's comment about the hoity-toity Eleanor McGill, I opened my mouth to say we'd not bring her anytime soon. I glanced over at Gary, whose eyes had gone dark with what I recognized as anger. I snapped my mouth shut and waited.

"I guess," Gary explained in a tense, even voice, "we weren't really asking permission. We wanted to know if you had any advice for us – any pitfalls we might not have seen. We're going to take the girl in. We just want to do it like Jesus would have. Thank you so much for your insights."

Dale was suddenly jovial. "Now, Gary, don't get your back up. I'm just trying to alert you to a few things you might have overlooked. We wouldn't want your friend's life style to rub off on our teenagers in the church."

"No, but their clean, fun lifestyle and love for God's word might rub off on her," Gary countered.

"I'm not sure that's a chance we want to take," Dale said. "I have to think about my whole flock."

Gary suddenly picked up the coffee carafe and peered into Meg's cup. "More coffee?"

Dale pushed away from the table. "Actually, we need to be getting home. Eh, Meggie?"

She nodded and stood, retrieving her purse from the floor near the couch. "Thank you for the delicious dinner. It was so nice to get to know you a bit. And it's nice to spend an evening with a happy family who doesn't need us to solve a crisis."

Stunned, I looked at Gary, who just shook his head. We saw them to the door, awkwardly muttering polite phrases until they were halfway down the walkway. I suspected this was the last dinner we'd ever have with them.

Gary cleared the table, and I loaded the dishwasher, the kitchen choked with silence, as we both struggled with huge implications.

"Well," he said finally, refilling his coffee cup. "That was unexpected."

We sat again in the living room.

"I guess we're on our own," I said lamely.

"Oh, Dottie, honey." It was obvious that a great burden weighed him down. "It's so much bigger than that."

I didn't understand. It was as if Gary had heard a conversation I hadn't heard. "I heard you say that we're going to take Bailey in."

"Yes, if she wants to live with us, she may. We'll figure out the details as they come."

He leaned back and sighed, and his chin tightened as if he were fighting tears. "I saw myself tonight like I've never seen me before, and it was ugly." He sat up and seemed suddenly energized. "Do you realize how many people have come in and out of our church in the last ten. . .twenty years. . .well, since we've been married? Our church never grows. Other churches in town are growing like crazy, but we've always thought we were being more faithful than they. But Dottie, we go to a church that doesn't welcome people like Bailey."

"Is that what he meant?"

"Well, he wouldn't say it quite that way, but he doesn't want trouble with Eleanor McGill, nor does he want to have to explain why an unwed mother is in our midst."

"But Jesus worked with a lot of difficult people – tax collectors, prostitutes."

"And they crucified Him for it."

"But Pastor Dale wouldn't – "I broke off, unsure what I could say. I felt betrayed and confused.

"Never mind him." Gary dismissed him with a wave of his hand. "I'm one of the people who would reject sinners and tax collectors. You've already been feeling this as you volunteered at the Pregnancy Center. And you've tried to reach out to Bailey. This evening just opened my eyes to be able to see what you've been seeing and trying to explain to me. I've been supportive of your crazy idea, and I figured that I could handle any problems that Bailey might deal out. But I wasn't really in tune with your burden for her. Even less did I understand your frustration with how to reach out to her, and not knowing how."

"I felt quite supported by you," I assured him.

"Well, I really do think that what you want to do for Bailey is pleasing to God. We'll figure this out together – with His help."

· 7 ·

Bailey turned us down.

She had popped into the Pregnancy Center to bring us a thank-you note - *a thank-you note!* - expressing her appreciation for the clothing. That was definitely a first. She had an appointment for her ultrasound and went upstairs to see the nurse.

When she came back down, she seemed excited. "I heard my baby's heartbeat today. He - or she - is very tiny but has, you know, a tiny beating heart!" She sighed and hesitated beside my desk.

"That's wonderful! Babies are such a miracle!" I agreed. Since no one was in the office, I decided to ask her. "I think you told us that you don't have a good place to live. Have you found anything yet?"

"I'm okay, I guess."

"Well," I didn't want to sound like the wealthy benefactress. "My husband, Gary, and I were talking, and we were wondering if you would like to stay with us until you can find something more permanent."

She sank into the chair on the other side of the desk, obviously taken aback. "You're serious." It was not a question.

"We are."

"It's very nice of you, but I'm doing fine. I'm moving in with my boyfriend."

My stomach turned over. "Kent?"

She smiled, "No, I have a new boyfriend, Patrick."

That didn't help my stomach a bit. What was she thinking? Was she thinking at all?

"He's Irish, you know," she added. "Much nicer than American men."

How I wished I could say the appropriate thing at the right time, like Connie could, and Gary and Daniel! Finally, I managed, "Bailey, do you think this is a good idea?"

She shrugged off my doubts. "I'm not going to sleep with him."

I searched for something wise to say without sounding judgmental.

The silence got longer, and Bailey stood up. "I guess I disappoint you."

I shook my head. "I think you're making a mistake. Please be careful."

Boredom framed her answer. "Yeah, sure." She headed for the door and tossed over her shoulder, "Thanks for the offer." The bell rang, and she was gone.

I sat for a while, trying to figure out what went wrong. Maybe it was in how I presented it, or maybe she couldn't imagine living with a couple of old people. Maybe Gary and I were lucky to have the matter decided for us. Did we really want a stranger living in our home? I couldn't, however, spend much time brooding over my verbal clumsiness. I had a wedding that weekend.

Formal attire may be uncomfortable to wear, but there is no one handsomer than your own son in a tuxedo. Daniel's best friend, Johnny was marrying his college sweetheart, Eva. Daniel performed his duties as best man with a calm that did not surprise Gary and me, but did soothe the nerves of the bride, groom, and many relatives.

I arrived at the church in the afternoon, armed with safety pins, sewing needles, and spools of black, white, and rose-colored thread. Gary hauled in my smaller, portable sewing machine and set it up in one of the Sunday School rooms. The bride's dress had been finished for weeks, but one of the out-of-town bridesmaids had not been able to come for a fitting of her dress. When she arrived, Daniel brought her to me, and I made the necessary adjustments to the dress and then put in the zipper.

The family joked about me being "Fraahhnk," the eccentric wedding planner in the film, *Father of the Bride*. In reality, I was merely a panic-preventer. When the maid-of honor hooked her heel on the hem of her dress, pulling out twelve inches of thread, I sewed it back. When the father of the bride popped a button off his tuxedo while wrestling with his son, the usher, I came to the rescue with black thread and needle. I also kept double-sided tape for preventing low necklines from revealing too much. I washed and bandaged the flower girl's knee when she skinned it on the carpet, and I loaned my sparkly sweater to the groom's grandmother, who was shivering in the air-conditioned hall.

Over the years, Gary had fallen into assisting me, if he wasn't busy with buying and selling houses. He would wait in the back room with the men, straightening ties, cummerbunds, and vests and freeing pants legs trapped by socks. He even started bringing a pair of black socks in his suit coat pocket after a groomsman at one of the weddings years ago showed up in sandals and had no socks to wear with his tuxedo shoes. When a girl's family hired me to sew their dresses, they certainly got their money's worth.

Once the bride reached the front of the church on the arm of her father, her dress arranged prettily, I slipped into a seat at the side with Gary. "Beautiful wedding," he whispered in my ear.

I snuggled into the crook of his arm. The truth was that Gary and I liked weddings. Each one gave us the opportunity to remember our first expressions of love. Every wedding was a glorious merry-go-round of emotions: we were happy for the new couple because we hoped they would be as happy as we were, and we were reminded of how happy we were now and could continue to be.

We were used to Daniel (and Abby) being in weddings. Multiple times, they had been ring bearer, flower girl, candle lighters, usher, guest book attendant, groomsman, and bridesmaid. Over the years we had discovered - sadly - how many girls spend money on a big wedding but don't have good enough relationships with relatives to include them. Our children often substituted for the bride or groom's estranged nieces, nephews and siblings. This wedding was not that way, but our Daniel, so tall and strong, suddenly looked as if he were ready to be a groom. Scary!

The reception dinner was served in four courses at the Plum River Resort and Country Club. After the cake was cut, the band started playing. I escaped the loud music and wandered out into the damp, cool night to join Daniel on the wrap-around porch. He was star-gazing.

"See anything unusual?" I asked him.

"Nope. Too much light pollution."

I scanned the sky for a minute before asking, "So where's the Big Dipper?"

He swung around to face the building, bright compared to the dark night, and pointed at the peak of the roof. "Right about there."

I turned around again to face the stars. "So are your duties done?"

He sighed. "Just about. I need to get them ready to drive out of here." He squinted at his watch. "Three more hours," he added gloomily.

"Aren't you enjoying yourself?"

"It's too rich for my blood." Then he corrected himself. "Actually, it has nothing to do with riches." He paused to point out the bright star Arcturus, coming up just over the trees to the east. "If you and Dad ever want to give me a wedding like this, just give me the money. Johnny and Eva could have bought a brand new car and made a down payment on a house. It's – it's obscene."

"Shhh." I looked behind us to make sure no one could overhear us. "Actually, the next time this family has a wedding, it's the girl's parents who are going to pay."

He lowered his voice. "Eva's parents will be paying it off for years. They should have made her marry him two years ago when he asked, but, no, she wanted a big wedding."

I tried to calm him. "I know, I know."

"It's insane to wait so long, when you're in love. And the money is criminal!"

I gave his cuff-linked wrist a playful slap. "Stop it! Your mother got a piece of that money."

His voice softened. "That's different. Every girl needs a dress. But she doesn't need six attendants, a four course dinner, a live band, and a honeymoon in Hawaii." He thought a moment and then contradicted, "Well, the trip to Hawaii would be nice – save money on the wedding and splurge on the honeymoon."

I chuckled. "Good idea."

Gary came up behind us and put one arm around each of our shoulders. "What are you two whispering about?"

I glanced back at the ballroom. "It was that obvious?"

He laughed out loud. "You really are plotting something?"

Daniel seemed to shake off his annoyance. "I'd better get back in there. Since I don't dance, I have to mingle."

"It's late," Gary said. "Your mom and I are going home."

"Drive safely." Wasn't the parent supposed to say that?

I could hear the smile in Gary's voice, as he said, "Sure, Son."

Daniel hugged Gary and kissed me and trudged back into the ballroom.

"So what's gotten him in a funk?" Gary asked.

"Obscene spending, outrageous debts, and waiting too long."

"Aha." We wandered back into the crowd to find Eva's parents and to thank them for the beautiful day.

"It's you, we should thank," they assured us. "Your dresses were so exquisite, and we were really thankful for your ready needle and thread."

I was ready to take my needle and thread out to our car. Gary and I enjoy long drives because we generally talk the miles away. I filled him in on Daniel's gripes, and then our conversation roamed through memories of Abby's wedding.

Abby was a modest girl with modest wishes. Our small church had been too large for her. They were married in our back yard on a perfect July evening. Two attendants, some taped music, a simple candlelit dinner, catered by the local grocery store. Both sets of parents gave them a lot of money. They bought a second, beat-up car, and some basic used furniture for their tiny apartment. The rest they applied to Will's school debts. They honeymooned at a lakeside beach, using a time-shared condominium owned by a friend of Will's family. Simple life, wise children. Daniel would be wise too.

It had been a long day, and soon our silences between thoughts grew longer. Although I fought it, my eyelids felt heavy, and I finally allowed them to fall shut.

Then suddenly, I was awake, as Gary swerved for some reason. "Sorry I woke you up," he said. "A couple of deer were thinking of crossing the road."

"It's okay. What were you thinking about while I was snoring?"

He laughed. "You snore so sweetly! I was thinking that I'm glad no one is waiting at home – that we can just go home and go to bed without any obligations."

"Mm."

"I mean, I was glad to offer our home to Bailey, but I can't help being glad she decided not to move in."

"It'd be a change, that's for sure. What made you think of that?"

"Oh, I was thinking about the wedding. Daniel sure did a good job today. Did you hear him tell us to drive home safely? I suppose somewhere down the line, we will become the responsibility of our children, as they used to be to us." He sighed before continuing. "And then that led to thinking about having people that we are responsible for, and that led to your burden for Bailey."

"Well, I'm not planning on becoming anyone's burden anytime soon. I think we have a few more years in us."

"Yeah."

Silence enveloped us again. Finally, I agreed, "It's sure easier that she's not there. I'm still not sure I would have known how to deal with her anyway. God must have known we weren't right for her. Maybe her visits to the Pregnancy Center will be enough."

We pulled into the driveway. "Home again, home again, jiggety-jig," I quoted from a nursery rhyme. "Safely."

· 8 ·

Months later, Bailey would tell us about the night that brought her to our doorstep.

She had felt like the luckiest girl in the world! How could she ever have thought that she loved Kent? Never had she felt such happiness as she did, sitting beside Patrick. She glanced around the table at the collection of her friends and his. No one was as great-looking as he was. He made her feel so special, with his arm protectively around the back of her chair. She leaned back into his embrace, and he hugged her and kissed her ear.

"Tired?" he whispered, his tongue twirling around the "r", as only an Irish tongue can.

She sighed happily. "My feet are a bit sore, but being near you is healing." Actually, the healing had begun the moment he walked into the casino at her quitting time. She had served him a drink, waited on two other customers, and then told Jen that she was leaving. "Well, I'm not exactly leaving quite yet. Patrick came to pick me up. He'll have a few drinks and then we'll be going home." She paused to savor the word. "Home. Doesn't that sound wonderful?"

"Lucky girl!" Jen had exclaimed.

Lucky, indeed. Her suitcase and a box of DVD's were in the break room. She met him at his table, and he seated her and ordered her a soft drink.

Soon, a couple of Patrick's friends joined them after a mildly successful time at the slot machines. "Tequila bangers, all around! We're rich!"

Jen came to take their requests and returned with the drinks and apple juice for Bailey. She didn't need alcohol to make her heart light; Patrick was all she needed. The evening flew by in a blur of laughter, flirting, and the occasional trip to the slot machines.

At one point, Bailey yawned, and Patrick leaned over to ask, "Do you want to go?"

"Only if you want to. I'm fine." But she was tired and was glad when he announced they were leaving. They gathered her belongings and lugged them to his car.

The trouble began the moment Patrick unlocked the door to his apartment. "We can unpack in the morning. Let's go to bed."

"I can't," Bailey told him. "I thought you understood that."

"Understood what?" He raised his voice to announce: "You're living with me. What did you think that meant?"

"I'm pregnant with another man's child." She tried to speak calmly, but she felt fear building in her rib cage.

"So, it's another man's child! That doesn't stop us."

"It's too weird. Can't we just wait?" she begged.

"'Til Christmas?" He shoved her suitcase at her. "You've got to be bonkers!" His Irish accent sounded threatening.

Bailey looked at the suitcase and DVDs. "I have nowhere to go," she whispered.

"Fine." He stormed to the bedroom door and then turned to shout, "Sleep on the couch; but you'd better be gone by morning!" With the addition of a few choice words to make her feel like dirt, he slammed the door.

Bailey's whole body was shaking. She was no longer sleepy, and it did not take long for anger to replace fear. How dare he threaten her! She didn't need this! She pulled out the handle of her rolling suitcase and left the apartment, slamming the door as hard as she could. The sound echoed through the building. She trundled the suitcase to the end of the hallway and then bumped it down two flights of stairs. The noise expressed her rage wonderfully, and she hoped that all his neighbors would complain to the landlord the next day.

She banged out onto the street, and headed toward the center of town. The suitcase, heavy with her belongings, rolled easily behind her, but after a couple of blocks, she faced the fact that she really didn't have anywhere to go. She looked around and tried to come up with a plan.

The door of Kenny's Pub opened, and dim light poured out into the night. A man and woman hurried down the steps and to their car. The scent of cigarette smoke trailed after them, and Bailey tried to inhale enough to make her feel better. The night smelled mostly of damp trees and summer. It wasn't fair! After all evening serving drinks, and not tasting even one. Bailey dropped her suitcase on the sidewalk with a thump and then kicked it over, swearing at the night, the heavy suitcase, Patrick, and finally at herself. *When will I ever learn?*

Three men walked around her, glancing back at her out of curiosity, and then entered the bar. The door clicked shut and she yelled at them, "I want a drink too!"

She held up her watch so she could see it in the light of the streetlamp. The bars would close in less than an hour. Surely she couldn't drink enough in one hour to harm her baby.

"Stupid!" she whispered and shook her head. "I think I'm schizophrenic," she murmured just as two women walked by

"Are you all right?" one of them asked.

Embarrassed, she muttered, "No, just nuts."

Inside her head, the battle continued. Someone had told her that the most harm from cigarettes and alcohol occurred during the first semester – or was that quarter? No, that was college. It would be better not to drink anything. "Better t' be safe than sorry," she told the pub door. She bent and picked up her suitcase, but her purse swung off her shoulder and cracked the hand that gripped the suitcase handle. She cursed again, and tears came to her eyes. "Where'm I gonna go?" she asked the night. "What'm I gonna do?" It was easiest to give in.

She pushed her purse strap further up her shoulder, picked up the suitcase, and marched up the steps of Kenny's. Once inside, the battle was over. The familiar sounds and scents of late evening in the city surrounded her, and she settled onto a stool at the bar, her suitcase propped against it.

The bartender was an older woman, who rubbed the back of her neck and asked, "What can I get for ya?"

Bailey hesitated. If she was going to drink – but only a little – she wanted to make it worth it. "Um, could you make me a Margarita?"

"At this hour?" Before Bailey could change her mind, the woman put up one hand in defense. "Sure. The customer is always right, pum, pum," she sang, snapping her fingers, "'And all that jazz!'"

In a few minutes, Bailey had her drink in hand. She licked the salt from the rim and swallowed the sharp liquid.

Business was slow, and the barkeeper wandered back to Bailey. "Your drink okay?"

Bailey licked her lips. "It'll do the trick."

"Good."

Bailey felt like talking and she remembered what she was trying to forget. "He said he loved me," she whined.

"They usually do, honey."

"No, I mean, really," Bailey protested. "He even said he didn't mind waiting."

"Waiting." She shook her head in disbelief. "As if any of 'em would wait."

Bailey gulped at her drink. "He had to, though, 'cause it would have just been too weird."

"Of course." The lady nodded at her glass. "You gonna to want another?"

Bailey scrutinized her glass. "Well, maybe just one more. But I'd better make it something less expensive." She finished the last swallow, surprised at how fast it went to her head and knees.

"Less expensive," the lady muttered. She reached under the counter and pulled out a shot glass, which she filled with amber liquid.

Bailey tasted it. "Thanks."

"Don't mention it." The lady went to wait on another customer, but she eventually wandered back to Bailey. "You gonna be all right?"

Bailey followed her gaze to the suitcase. "Oh, yeah. Terrific." As the alcohol took effect, her sarcasm spilled out. "At least I hadn't unpacked yet. Didn't even have my toothbrush on the sink."

"You got a place to stay?"

Bailey answered automatically, "Oh, sure." Her thought process – muddled though it was – marched on to confront her hurt and betrayal. "You know," she confided after a gulp of the cheap whiskey, "He actually told me once he liked kids. I thought for sure he'd like mine."

"You got a kid?"

Bailey wrestled with an answer. "Sort of."

"Boy or girl?"

"Don't know yet. Want it to be a surprise."

The bartender snatched the glass from Bailey's hand.

"Hey!" Bailey grabbed for it, but the woman stepped out of her reach.

"Are you pregnant?"

"So if I am. I don't need any lectures on morality."

The woman snorted. "I'll sell almost anyone a drink, but I won't sell you another. I drank through my first pregnancy, and now my baby is thirty years old, but he's still a baby – big, pug nose and no brain cells. They wouldn't even let me raise him, 'cause his handicaps were so severe. Should've had an abortion, but – "

"Nope," Bailey interrupted, "Already thought that through." She sighed. "Give me a Ginger Ale?"

The barkeeper poured out the whiskey and fetched the soft drink after serving another customer.

Bailey had been thinking. "What's your name?"

"Mary."

"I'm Bailey. Do you love your son, Mary?"

Mary's breath caught in her throat. "I – I don't know him, but I guess I do; at least as best I can."

"Abortion's never right. You were meant to have that baby. I love my baby already. I shouldn't've had a drink. Don't want to hurt her – him. That's why Patrick was so stupid. Shouldn't've had that drink. Poor baby."

Mary, although stunned by Bailey's statement, was not drunk. "Honey, you need to go home."

Bailey's eyes suddenly filled with tears. "I can't."

"Did he kick you out?"

Bailey sniffed and wiped her nose on her hand. "Nope," she said with a bit of pride, "I walked out on him."

"Where're you going to go tonight? Motel?"

Suddenly, Bailey felt sleepy and sick. "I don't know," she admitted and dropped her head onto her folded arms on the bar. Her hand knocked over her glass, which spun off the bar and shattered before Mary could catch it. Bailey's head popped up again. "I'm sorry."

"Never mind." Mary's answer was once more businesslike and gruff. She swept up the glass and called someone from the kitchen to mop up the sugary soft drink. It was closing time, and Mary had things to do. "You need to think of a friend or somebody. You can't stay here."

Bailey tried to think, but her brain was sluggish and her stomach queasy.

Starting at the far end of the bar, Mary gathered up a few glasses and wiped the shiny surfaces. When she got to Bailey, she prodded, "So. Out you go. Closing time."

"I don't know where to go."

"There's always the women's homeless shelter."

It struck Bailey funny and she giggled. "I'm hardly homeless. That's for people with problems."

Mary stopped wiping and just looked at her for a few seconds. "Fine. Don't you have a friend you could call?"

"At – " Bailey tried to focus her eyes on her watch but gave up and held her wrist out for Mary to see. "At this o'clock?"

Mary sighed and waved her arm, indicating the empty room. "Everyone's gone home. If you don't leave, I'll have to call the police."

"Can't do that." Suddenly, the memory of Dorothy's face drifted into her mind's eye. "Well, there is Mr. and Mrs. Goody-Two-Shoes. They asked me to live with them. Real nice folks – too nice. Don't know what to do with me."

Mary reached under the counter and plunked a cell phone in front of Bailey. "Call them."

"Don't know their number. Threw it away."

The phone book thumped onto the counter.

"Don't know their last name. Aunt Dorothy, I call her." Bailey pushed the phone book toward Mary. "Find Aunt Dorothy."

Mary made a decision and sighed. "You know where they live?"

Bailey closed her eyes and visualized the way she had driven Dorothy home that rainy afternoon. She opened her eyes again. "I do!"

"I'll take you. Let's go."

The fifteen-minute ride passed silently, punctuated only by Bailey's abbreviated instructions. The motion of the car and the bright lights along the roadside aggravated Bailey's nausea. She tried to roll down the window to get fresh air, but the handle was broken on Mary's rattletrap car. After a couple of wrong cul-de-sacs, they finally arrived on the correct street, and Mary stopped at the curb.

Bailey thanked Mary and pulled her belongings from the car. She staggered up the walkway with her suitcase in tow. Her head was spinning, and the paving stones seemed to move under her feet. She finally arrived at the front door. Without a thought to the late hour, she punched the doorbell, which echoed through the sleeping house. *Oh, why wouldn't they hurry?* She rang it again and heard movement inside. The porch light went on, a bolt was turned, and the door opened.

Gary and I stood in our robes, puzzled and sleepy. "Bailey?"

"I'm gonna be sick!" and she was – all over our front step.

The next morning, I called the physician's assistant at my doctor's office to ask what to do about a hangover.

"Drink too much, did you?"

I suddenly realized that this conversation would be entered into my records. "No!" I protested. "It's for a young woman who is staying with us – and she's pregnant."

There was a short silence on the other end, and then she said, "Tylenol® and some toast. Give her lots to drink." Again, a pause. "Non-alcoholic, of course."

"Of course." I hoped she couldn't hear my smile. "Thank you."

It was almost lunchtime. I carried a tray of tea, juice, toast and pain killer to the guest room in our lower level. When a knock on the door brought no response, I turned the knob quietly and peeked in. "Bailey?"

The pile of blankets on the bed moved slightly. "Mmm?"

"I'm meeting my daughter for lunch, so I thought I'd bring you a bit to eat before I leave." I set the tray on the nightstand.

She didn't move. "Not hungry," she mumbled.

"I need to talk to you before I leave, in case I don't see you before you go to work."

Bailey turned over and opened her blood-shot eyes. "What's so important?" she grumbled.

I abandoned my speech and my plans for the day and reached for the painkillers. "Something for your head, for starters."

"Oh. Thanks." She propped herself up on one elbow and washed the tablets down with a bit of juice. "Anything else?" Resentment poured from her, and I decided that I had done enough for now.

"Nope," I answered as cheerfully as I could. "Feel free to come upstairs when you're feeling better. I'll give you a key to the house before you leave for work."

Without another word, she flopped back down onto the pillow, her face toward the wall. I knew the audience was ended, so I went upstairs and called Abby to invite her to our house for lunch. She came gladly.

Over squares of leftover lasagna, I told Abby about Bailey-in-the-Basement. "She arrived last night, sick as a dog. Threw up all over the front step. Your poor father was out there at three in the morning, cleaning it off."

"Why ever did she come to you?"

For a moment I felt silly, as if I'd done something stupid. "Well, last week your father and I invited her to stay with us for a while, only she had turned us down. We don't know why she changed her mind. We couldn't ask her last night because she was too ill."

Abby put down her fork and reached for a banana. "I still don't get the connection."

"She came into the Pregnancy Center. I stumbled upon the fact that she had nowhere to live. She's expecting a baby." I paused, annoyed that Abby and Bailey would have anything in common. It couldn't be helped. "At Christmas."

Abby stopped peeling her banana and looked at her stomach. "Wow," she said softly.

"Dad and I were going to talk to you last week when we came to see you, but you had your own news. We weren't about to spoil your happiness. We were actually going to ask for your advice: if you thought we were out of our minds or not."

Again, all she said was "Wow," but there were tears in her eyes.

Suddenly I thought this was too much for her. "Honey, I'm sorry. Are you all right?"

Her crooked smile blossomed onto her face, and she blinked away the tears. "You and Dad are amazing. What kind of advice could we have given you?"

"Oh, maybe: 'You're nuts; take a vacation.'"

She wiped at the tears with the back of her hand and chuckled. "My advice?" She took a deep breath and broke off a bite-sized piece of banana. "Don't let her mess up your life. It's one p.m. Make her get up when you do. Don't coddle her. Rules, Responsibility, Respect. Treat her like..." She gulped. "Treat her like a – a daughter. That should be good enough."

I am blessed with wonderful children.

We spent part of the afternoon looking at magazines pictures of maternity clothes, so I could get an idea of what I could sew for her. Then Abby fixed tea and found some cookies, while I worked on a red taffeta prom dress for one of my customers. Just as we poured our tea, Bailey hauled herself up the stairs and stumbled into the kitchen.

Her blond hair hung limply around her face, and her eyes were still blood-shot with dark circles under them. She had washed off all the makeup, and she looked older, yet somehow vulnerable. "Oh," she said, obviously surprised to see us. "I thought you were going out."

"I was, but Abby came here instead." I made the introductions.

Bailey murmured, "Hey."

"Would you like some tea?" I motioned to a chair. "Or maybe something more substantial?"

Bailey eased slowly into the chair, as if a change in altitude – from standing to sitting – affected her headache. "I ate the toast downstairs, but more tea would be nice. I still don't feel so great."

Abby fetched another cup from the cabinet.

Bailey glanced from me to Abby and back to me again. "Does she know?"

Now was the time to start: Rules, Responsibility, Respect. "We have no secrets in our family, so yes, she knows. That is, she knows as much as we know."

Bailey stirred several teaspoonfuls of sugar into her tea. "It was a bad night."

Obviously, that was all she planned to tell us. Then she nodded at the red dress. "What's that?"

"A prom dress."

"Hm!" Disgust wrinkled her nose.

Abby pushed the plate of cookies nearer to Bailey.

"No thanks. I don't want to gain any weight."

I continued to push the needle through the red taffeta, and Abby leafed through a magazine. The only sounds were the rustling of the fabric and the soft sound of pages turning. I felt very uncomfortable, but it was my house.

Finally, Bailey spoke: "It was a bad night," she repeated. "You know that guy I told you about?"

I looked up at her and nodded.

Suddenly it all poured out of her, ugly and profane. She had no place to stay because her mother had her loser boyfriend staying with her. Her friend, Patrick, had offered to let her stay at his place, but he was a crud. How could he have possibly thought she would sleep with him? Duuh! She was pregnant with another man's child! But he didn't kick her out of his apartment. No, sir! She left with her pride in place, but then the lights of the bar had lured her in. It was the first drink she'd had since learning that she was pregnant. Surely, one drink wouldn't hurt the baby, would it? And then the woman at the bar wouldn't give her any more because her own baby was an alcohol baby, and the woman was mean to her, but then she offered to drive her home. But Bailey had no home, so she came here because Dorothy had offered.

Bailey finished with a final: "I tell you, I didn't mean to hurt my baby!"

I didn't know what to say. I reeled from the barrage of swear words and the unhappiness she had caused herself.

Abby, however, said softly, "I don't think one drink will hurt your baby. You did the right thing by coming here."

Disarmed by Abby's kindness, the hardness vanished and tears filled Bailey's eyes. She looked at me and begged, "Would it be all right if I stay here with you and your husband for a while?" She sniffed. "Just until I can get back on my feet? I'm sorry I was so sick last night. I hope I didn't make too much of a mess."

I finally caught my breath. "You made a terrible mess, but it's all cleaned up. Of course, you may stay. We thought maybe you'd like to stay with us at least until the baby comes."

"Really?" Her voice squeaked in disbelief.

I glanced at my watch. It was time to get things rolling. "When do you go to work?"

"Four. Is it that late already?"

"No. We want you to feel at home here, but we do have some rules and suggestions for friction-free life in our home. I'll get them written down, and I'll give you a key to the house."

Suggestions for Peaceful Long-term Co-existence in the Household

Rules, Responsibility, Respect

1. If you make a mess, clean it up.

2. If a garbage container is full, take it out to the garage.

3. Dishwasher: if it's full, run it; if dishes are clean put them away.

4. Washing machine & dryer: Use the equipment properly. You are responsible to do your own laundry. We don't want to see it.

5. You must begin prenatal care for yourself and the baby.

6. No drugs, no alcohol, no cigarettes, no pornography.

7. You may invite friends over, but they will be entertained in our living room or family room. And for the time being, all visitors will have to be cleared with us. You are never to be alone in the house with a man.

8. Music and entertainment – Please be thoughtful (and ask your guests to be thoughtful) with the noise level. Remember the sleep preferences of others in the house. Follow our movie guidelines.

9. You can watch TV, but no Pay-Per-View. If others are home, they have a say in what we'll watch. If you watch late (or

listen to music), we don't want to be disturbed. You can't use our computer. The public library has one.

10. If you are the last one in at night, turn off lights, inside and outside, and lock front and back doors.

11.If you break something, tell us first; maybe we hated it and don't want it replaced!

12. $200 rent. This includes room and board, and it will not be adjusted, whether you are asked to buy pizza on your way home or you never eat here at all. We would like you to eat at least one meal per day with us if possible. Adjust your schedule accordingly.

13. We'd like you to put a percentage of each paycheck in a savings account. We'll help you decide how much. This account will help you once the baby is born and you are on your own.

14. Communication makes for good relations. Communication demands honesty. Don't lie to us, even if you think we will be shocked.

15. We would ask you to go to church or a Bible study once a week. We will help you choose one.

· 10 ·

The first Sunday with Bailey started off shaky, when she appeared at breakfast in tight, low-slung slacks, revealing her underwear and a tattoo on her lower back when she sat down.

Gary raised his eyebrows at me, and I sighed.

"I'm sorry, Bailey, but those pants won't do for church."

She set her juice glass down with a thump and pursed her mouth. "They're the nicest ones I have."

"Church is a place to think about God," I explained. "The people behind you will be looking at your tattoo and underwear."

"I could wear a longer sweater," she protested.

I shrugged. "If it covers you up, do it."

She left to find the sweater and didn't come back upstairs until we were ready to leave.

"You look nice," I told her.

"Do I look pregnant?"

I surveyed her slim - almost gaunt - figure. "Not yet."

"Good."

I don't know what other people do on Sunday mornings, but I can't imagine doing anything except worshiping God with others who love Him. We arrived and were greeted by a few skeptical looks, but most of the women were too busy to say anything they did not usually say.

I took Bailey with me to the kitchen, where I made coffee. She seemed willing to help, so I let her arrange cookies on the trays. When we slipped into the auditorium to sit beside Gary, the congregation was on its feet, and the music team had already begun singing.

I joined in and sang for a minute or two, before I noticed that Bailey was not singing. The words to the song had been projected on the wall, but she wasn't looking at them. Her gaze was directed away from me toward the carpet on the center aisle, and her arms were crossed as if she were annoyed. Suddenly, I realized that in all of our insistence that she attend church, we hadn't asked if she even knew what church was. I stopped singing and grasped the back of the chair in front of me, hoping that my silence would somehow communicate understanding to her.

The music dragged on and on. Songs that I usually loved sounded foreign, as I tried to hear them through Bailey's ears. I wished they would stop. Sacrifice became a word with no 21st century meaning. They sang of bowing down to worship. I had never actually bowed down to worship before; no one ever did.

It was the longest church service I have ever endured. The Lord's Prayer, recited by the whole crowd, sounded like the motto of an exclusive club. At least the special music was up-beat and entertaining, as the Sunday School children sang "Lovely Noise." Bailey actually relaxed and watched the children, smiling at their antics. But when the sermon began, she re-crossed her arms and focused on the back of the chair in front of her.

I did not open my Bible. Somehow it seemed that the ability to find Micah 6 would further shut Bailey out of our exclusive club. I listened to the sermon and tried to remember why Pastor Browning was preaching through the book of Micah. Why do we have a sermon every week? Why do we do the things we do in the order we do them?

Finally the pastor closed in prayer. Bailey jumped up and strode down the aisle and out the door before I could say anything. We saw her a few minutes later beside our car, arms crossed and drenched from the downpour that had begun during the service.

Gary unlocked the car from across the parking lot, and she was already in the back seat by the time we opened our doors.

"You do this every week?" she demanded.

"Every week," Gary told her calmly.

"What's the point?" Before we could answer, she rammed on: "I mean, I'm, like, a Christian, but all that stuff about, like, sin and repentance and adultery – now, there's a word for you. Nobody does that stuff anymore."

"What: adultery?" Gary asked in amusement. He started the engine, and we headed toward home.

"You think I committed adultery?" she shouted.

Shouting is not a part of our family, but I didn't want to lose her, so I said, "Bailey, this conversation is going nowhere any of us want to go. We thought you ought to see where we go each Sunday. Now you know. You don't have to go to church." I glanced over at Gary and asked, "What do you think?"

He didn't look as if he agreed with me, but he said, "That's fine."

Bailey sighed, and then seemed to pull her good manners from somewhere deep. "Okay, then," she said perkily and turned to watch the rain-soaked streets pass by.

Lunch was awkward and quiet, punctuated by observations on the weather and the slow cooker lunch. After we finished, Bailey disappeared into her room, presumably to sleep. Gary and I sat down for a second cup of tea.

"I thought we had agreed that Bailey go to church with us if she's to live here," Gary said.

I nodded and added milk to my tea. "Church was like a foreign country to her."

"She still needs God."

"Did you see how people stared at her?"

Gary shrugged. "I think you were imagining it."

I wanted him to understand, to see things from Bailey's viewpoint. "She was under-dressed, she didn't know any of the songs – or the Lord's prayer. And the sermon was completely irrelevant. What does Micah have to say to an unwed mother?"

"She'll get used to it."

"Used to it?" I felt annoyance rising. He wasn't even trying. "No one at that church is going to accept her – ever."

Gary rose from the table and dropped his spoon into his empty cup with a clank. "So what are we supposed to do about it? Find a new church?"

The thought was appalling, and tears sprang to my eyes. My friends were there. Well, they weren't really friends, but I knew them. They would never understand. "I don't know. I don't know."

He went into the living room and turned on the television. I felt badly for Bailey, and I was pretty certain that Gary was wrong about this, but I knew I would never be able to change his mind. I also lacked the courage to find Bailey a church on my own. I knew I could only figure it out if I really prayed about it, but I felt so weak. I didn't really know where to begin. I was so tired of avoiding prayer, however, so I went into the bedroom and sat on the bed and stared at the closet door.

"Lord," I whispered, "I don't know what to do. I don't know what we should do." Tears came to my eyes, and I stood up to fold Gary's sweater, put it in the drawer, and then sat again. "I'm so easily distracted. Bailey is such a huge responsibility. And she needs you." I thought of the bridesmaids' dresses I had to make before the end of the month. "I don't know how to pray, Lord. I'm so lazy. Please help us with Bailey." I blew my nose, washed my face, and went out to the kitchen to clean up the lunch dishes. I knew my prayer was inadequate, and I felt guilty that I couldn't do it better."

I sighed and then turned to a job I knew I could do well – I laid out pattern pieces on sheer lemon-yellow chiffon.

I had been working at the dining room table for about an hour when Bailey came back upstairs, I thought, to see what was on television. She paused to watch me cut a curved armhole.

"That's a really awesome color," she murmured.

Awesome. I smiled. "Would you like to see the pattern?"

She rolled her eyes. "Nope. Is there any more tea?"

"You're welcome to make some. Would you make me a cup too?"

She clattered around in the kitchen for a while and finally emerged with two steaming cups of tea.

We sat at the kitchen table so we wouldn't spill on the chiffon.

"Do you work tonight?" I asked to make conversation.

"Nope. But I came up to, like, thank you for letting me live here."

I didn't know what to say. "It's okay."

"I mean you're, like, such a good person, and I don't know how to behave myself. Like, I get cranky easy. I know I'll have to work really hard to be good enough to, ya know, fit in. I'm not a very good Christian."

I usually don't think of the correct response to important statements until too late, but for some reason I knew I couldn't let her think that she could ever be good enough to please God.

"Bailey, fitting in is highly overrated. Pleasing God is really the only thing that matters. If people don't like us, we just have to put up with it or not care. But, if God is not happy with us, we are in big trouble."

She sipped her tea and peered at me over the rim of the cup. "If God exists."

I nodded. "If God exists," I echoed. "But I can tell you in my experience that He does exist. I could also tell you many things about Him, but you can't know until someone introduces you to Him."

"Is that what you're doing?"

"I'd like to try."

"Well, if everyone who says they are Christian were as good as you, no one would have trouble believing."

The pedestal she put me on wobbled. "That's really nice of you, but I have to be honest. I'm not 'good.' I have sins."

She snorted. "Not very big ones."

"I still have sins that need to be forgiven."

"Like what?" She challenged.

Her bluntness sent my brain into neutral. I didn't want to tell her my sins, but I knew that if I didn't say anything, I would have missed an opportunity.

I stalled. "Most people don't like being asked questions like that."

"Sorry. I won't ask your friends at church."

"It's okay. I'm going to tell you," I told her. "'Good' church people have sins that are hard to get rid of – things like gossip and bitterness and suspicion. Things that are not so obvious and are easier to ignore because we come up with reasons why they are not so bad."

"My sins are bad!"

"It has nothing to do with how big or little the bad things are that we do. God doesn't compare us with other people. He compares us with Him, and he is so good - it's called 'holy' - that no one can measure up."

"So it is hopeless," she stated gloomily.

"It would be if we had to figure out how to get out of the mess, but God deals with each one of us individually and He made a way for us to get our sins forgiven and to stop sinning."

"I can stop, if I want to!" Bailey declared defiantly.

I just looked at her.

"Well, I could," she protested a bit more quietly.

Finally I shrugged. "Most people can't. I can't. I need help."

Suddenly annoyed again, she sputtered, "You don't need help. Any bad things you do couldn't possibly be as bad as Hitler."

"Well, I don't compare myself with Hitler; I compare myself with God. But," I added lightly, "You asked what some of my sins are, so I'll tell you and expect you not to spread it around."

"You don't have to tell me."

"I hardly ever pray. I know I should, but my attention wanders and I never get it done. I also feel sorry for myself a lot, and – "

"That's a sin?"

"For me, it is. It shows that I'm not trusting God with my circumstances."

"What's wrong with your circumstances?"

"Um." She had me there. "Nothing, really. The Bible says we should be content and when I'm not content, I'm wanting something other than what God wants to give me."

Bailey looked worried. "Too many sins."

"We each need to take care of the ones God shows us personally."

She stood and picked up her empty cup. "Well, everyone knows what mine are."

I reached out and grabbed her wrist, holding it when she tried to pull away. "No, they don't. We have not told anyone except our children, and they will not tell anyone." I let her hand go.

I returned to the yellow chiffon, and Bailey took a taxi to work. It wasn't until I crawled into bed that night that I realized that God had answered my prayer. He heard me! He gave me words to say that might help Bailey.

11

The lemon-yellow chiffon bridesmaids' dresses were hard to finish. One of the bridesmaids lived in another state and couldn't come for a fitting until the day before the rehearsal dinner. I was used to problems like that, but I was not used to Bailey being around. She usually worked afternoons and evenings at the casino, and as she came to feel more comfortable in our home, she hung around a lot in the late morning, making it hard for me to concentrate solely on my sewing.

I had been fighting a headache since the day before, and I hoped to work quietly with my cup of tea before I went to the Pregnancy Center in the afternoon. I had barely gotten the needle threaded when I heard Bailey calling me from the laundry room.

"Dorothy! I need help!"

I was pinning pattern pieces on the lining, and a pin flipped out of my fingers and into the carpet. I had to find it so someone wouldn't step on it in bare feet.

"Dorothy! I can't figure this out!"

I left the pin - heaven knows where! - and hurried down the stairs.

I found Bailey sitting on the floor of the laundry room, surrounded by heaps of damp clothing. She threw up her hands into the air and sputtered, "It won't dry the clothes! The damn dryer doesn't dry clothes anymore."

I pulled the lint filter out, and it was matted with a good quarter inch of lint. "You need to clean this every time you use the dryer. Otherwise, you could start a fire."

"How was I supposed to know that?" she challenged.

How, indeed?

I let it drop. "Well, let's try again." We started to put the clothes into the dryer when I realized that there were far too many clothes for one load. "Did you try to dry all these at once?"

She gave me her you-must-be-an-idiot look and murmured, "Well, duh!"

"You know," I informed her, "I really don't need to be treated like I'm stupid. You put too many clothes in the dryer, and the air can't circulate. Only put one load from the washing machine in at a time."

"I did!" she snapped.

"Then you put too much in the washer. You need to load the washer loosely; otherwise, the clothing won't get clean. And too much in the dryer, and it won't dry."

"Nobody told me." Now she was pouting.

"Who normally does your laundry?"

"I do, of course."

Suddenly, the light went on: "Have you been using the coin laundry?"

"Yeah. Why?"

"Well, you're not paying per load here, so you don't have to put as much in the washer and dryer to make it worth your coins."

She put the other half of the damp clothes in the basket and turned on the dryer. "Sorry I get so freaked out."

"It's all right; I should have explained it to you. When you are ready to vacuum your room, I'll show you how ours' works."

I left her standing in the laundry room and trudged back up the stairs. My headache was worse. I looked at my watch: lunchtime. Maybe food would help.

This might have been only a tiny blip in my life, if Gary hadn't come home for lunch, shortly after. He kicked off his shoes and found my pin!

"What in the – ! Dottie, why is there a pin my foot?"

"I'm so sorry, Honey." And I told him about the laundry and my headache. Bailey wandered up for lunch, and over tuna sandwiches and carrot sticks, I admitted that I was not looking forward to my time at the Pregnancy Center

"Don't go," was his solution.

"I can't just not show up. Someone has to answer the phone."

"Isn't Connie there?"

"Yes, but – "

"You're a volunteer, not a . . . a . . ."

"An employee?" I suggested.

"Actually, I was thinking of a slave."

"I'm not a slave," I groaned. I glanced over at Bailey, who had been watching this brief back-and-forth as if at a tennis tournament. "Can't we talk about this later?"

"Later is too late." he said. "You'll be gone. I'd like you to stay home today. You can rest and then sew. You've said that you need more time to sew."

Bailey spoke up. "Sewing's not rest."

We both looked at her, and Gary cleared his throat and turned back toward me. "Dottie, I really think you ought to stay home. In fact, I think you ought to consider giving up your volunteer post at the Pregnancy Center. You have too much on your plate right now."

I didn't want to argue in front of Bailey, and she obviously was not going anywhere. I also didn't want her to think that she was part of the "too much on my plate." I resisted putting my hand to my aching head, but I muttered, "Fine. I'll call Connie." I stood and stalked down the hallway to our bedroom.

Connie actually did not seem bothered when I explained that I had a headache.

"Get some sleep. I've got a client. See you next week." And that was that.

Cell phones are so inadequate; a person can't slam them down when she's angry. I pushed my bedroom door closed – loudly – but that was as much anger as I could muster. I could hear the faint sound of Bailey and Gary talking, but I didn't care. After taking a couple pain tablets, I lay down and closed my eyes. "Lord," I said to the ceiling, "I really want to do something that matters. I hate to disappoint Connie. Why can't Gary understand? Why does he have to be like that?"

Self-pity.

I sighed, tears prickling behind my closed eyelids. "I know Gary cares about me. And I'm thankful. I just don't want to let Connie down. Please help me, Lord."

About an hour later I awoke when I heard the sound of someone leaving our bedroom. I sat up and saw a cup of steaming tea on the nightstand. I slid out of bed, opened the door, and looked down the hallway just in time to see Gary before he left the house. "Thank you," I called.

He turned and smiled. "How's your head?"

"Better," I admitted. "How's your foot?"

He looked at his shoe. "Fine. Take it easy. I'll bring home supper tonight, and a surprise," and he left.

I married a good man. I sipped my tea, washed my face, and returned to the yellow chiffon. Yellow, like sunshine. Yellow, like buttercups. Yellow, like scrambled eggs. My life is good, I thought. Why am I feeling so out-of-sorts?

I moved the fabric pieces to my sewing machine in my sewing room and prepared to put seams together. Sewing was enjoyable, relaxing (usually), and satisfying. With Bailey gone for the afternoon (I thought), I made a lot of progress. Eventually, though, Bailey wandered up from her room and propped herself against my sewing room doorjamb.

When I came to the end of a seam, I looked up. "Do you need something?" I asked reluctantly.

"No." She looked at the sewing machine and asked, "Are you feeling better?"

"I am. Thanks for asking."

"Yeah."

I arranged the next pieces of fabric on the machine and lowered the presser foot.

She cleared her throat. "Can I ask you something?"

"Of course."

"Why do you let him push you around?"

"Him?"

"Gary."

"He doesn't push me around."

"He did today."

I wasn't going to get any more sewing done. "Why do you say that?"

"Well, he told you, like, not to go to the Pregnancy Center, and even though you wanted to, you let him tell you what to do."

Her voice rose to emphasize: "I'd never let a man tell me what to do!"

How could I explain this to her? "He wasn't telling me what to do. He was giving me the benefit of seeing things as he sees them. He thinks I am too busy. The spring and early summer are always busy months for me. He cares about me and thought I ought to take a break." Was I listening to myself? Did I really mean this?

"That's not what he said."

"What do you mean?"

"I asked him after you went to bed why he was so bossy."

I didn't want to smile because she was so serious, but I wished I could have seen Gary's face. "And what did he say?"

"He said that a husband has a right and a responsibility to take care of his wife."

I did smile. "And what's wrong with that?"

"You need to learn to assert yourself. Be your own person. You don't need a man to take care of you."

Oh, I sensed her longing and disappointment. How many men had let her down? "Don't you think Gary does a good job of caring for me?"

"I suppose."

"I care for him too. And I care about what he thinks. Or maybe I should say I actually respect his thoughts and ideas on things."

"Well, okay, but to let him tell you what you can and can't do?"

"I choose to listen to his advice." Hypocrite! I amended my statement: "After my initial outburst . . .." I didn't know how to finish the sentence.

Bailey finally looked at me and grinned. "You gave in."

"I did not. I felt I knew what was best, and Gary felt he knew what was best, and the two ideas clashed. When we clash, I have decided that I will give up my right to have my own way."

"You gave in," she repeated.

"Say it any way you like. The Bible calls it submission and tells us that God loves a submissive, humble person."

She rolled her eyes and snorted, "The Bible! So old-fashioned!"

"Probably. We decided when we got married that we would try to live according to what God wrote in the Bible even if some people thought we were old-fashioned. I didn't do a very good job of it today. I was angry, and I had my pity-party in the bedroom. But I knew what was right."

"So he gets to boss you around, and you have to do everything he says."

"No. Each of us brings everything we are and do and think to our marriage and then together we make decisions. The Bible actually says that the husband has the harder job because God is going to hold him responsible for how he treats his wife."

She thought about that for a bit and then burst out, "Boy, God's going to be pretty mad at an awful lot of men!"

I knew what to say! "He is. There aren't very many men who treat their wives – or girlfriends or daughters – the way God wants them to be treated. The way Gary treats me."

She shrugged. "It's your life. I wouldn't let him push me around." She glanced back down the hallway. "I'm going to watch TV."

"Okay."

It took a few minutes before I realized I could sew again. I had just started the next seam when the phone rang. I looked at the caller ID and saw it was Will. Before I could even say hello, he blurted out, "Mom, can you come?" My heart contracted to match the fear in his voice. "Abby's bleeding bad, and is having a lot of cramping."

"Where is she?"

"Um. She's at home. I'm at work. I called the ambulance, but. . .." His voice trailed off, as he tried to figure out what to do.

I opened my mouth to say that I would go to Abby, but he rushed on. "I'll go home and go with Abby to the hospital. Can you meet us there – at the hospital?"

Suddenly, I felt strong. "I can. I'm on the way." I clicked off the sewing machine light, turned off the iron, and headed for my sweater and purse. As I dashed through the living room, Bailey turned off the TV.

"Is something wrong?" she asked.

"Yes. Abby's going to the hospital. I need to go there." I whirled into the bedroom, grabbed what I needed and came back out into the living room.

Bailey was standing by the door to the garage. "I'll drive you," she said firmly, holding out her hand for the keys.

"You don't need to."

"You can't, like, drive very good, as I recall," she insisted with a small smile.

I handed her the keys, and she calmly drove me to the hospital, chatting to distract me. "I just saw online that my baby can suck its thumb. Isn't that amazing?"

"Amazing," I muttered, but I was thinking about Abby.

At the hospital, Bailey followed me into the admittance area.

"I can wait for you here," she offered.

"You can come with me, if you like."

Bailey shook her head. "I'll stay here and read magazines."

After the initial confusion of threading my way through all the sick and injured people, I found the right waiting room and found Will pacing.

"Mom." He moved in for a hug, although he seemed strangely strong at the same time. "Abby miscarried. The doctor says she's going to be okay, but she's weak from loss of blood."

I wrapped my arms around him. "I'm so sorry, Will." I didn't know what else to say. The death of a baby – even one we hadn't met yet – was so sad. Abby's child, our grandchild. Will's shoulders suddenly shook with sobs, and he pulled away and looked at the door behind him.

"You need to go back to Abby," I told him.

"They made me leave."

"Let's go talk with the lady at the desk."

She had us wait a bit, but finally we were allowed to see Abby. She looked pale and tiny in the hospital bed.

"Mom?" she whispered in a voice that cracked into a sob. She held out her arms, and I went to her and hugged her gently. She held onto me for a bit and then remembered that Will was there as well. She held out her other hand, and Will took it and leaned in to kiss her forehead.

Then she sighed and smiled through her tears. "Will and I never thought our baby would be the first one in the family to see Jesus."

I had been strong up to that point. Or perhaps I had just been in shock. But her sweet expression of faith broke through my effort to be strong for her. I looked back at the door, wondering if I should leave before I broke down completely. Tears poured down my face, mostly sorrow that my daughter would have to bear this.

"I'm sorry," I managed to say.

Abby handed me a tissue. "It's okay, Mom. We all need to cry."

I sat in the nearest chair and mopped my face. A nurse came in and told us that Abby could go home after the doctor came in once more. I wanted to call Gary, but Will had already done that. We sat quietly for a bit and then we began to talk about other things.

"What were you doing when Will called?" Abby asked.

"Sewing yellow chiffon." Suddenly I remembered Bailey.

As if she read my thoughts, Bailey knocked timidly on the door and peeked into the room. "So sorry to bother you, but I need to go to work. Here are the keys."

"We can take you home, Mom," offered Will.

I took a deep breath and said to Bailey, "Why don't you take the car to work and bring it this evening?"

"Really?" She smiled and glanced at the keys before saying, "Thanks." She looked at Abby and said, "I hope you feel better real soon. Bye." And she closed the door.

Soon after, the doctor came and released Abby. Will fetched the car, and the orderly helped Abby into a wheelchair and pushed her out to the curb. Will dropped me off at home, and I told them that Gary and I would buy supper and bring it to them when he got home.

It wasn't until I stood at the front door that I realized that I had given Bailey all my keys – including the house key. Fortunately, we always kept one hidden in the back yard, so I waved at Will, blew Abby a kiss, and walked around the house to find the key.

The house was quiet, and the yellow chiffon was still clamped under the sewing machine presser foot. I released it and smoothed out the wrinkles on the sewing table. On the shelf was a pattern for a baby quilt for which I hadn't yet even chosen fabric. So sad.

Gary would be home soon, and I knew what I wanted - and needed - to do until then. I pulled my Bible from the shelf, glanced at the calendar, and turned to the Psalm for the day, the 25th. It was mostly about asking forgiveness from sins and protection from enemies, but some of the verses were most comforting.

To You, O Lord, I lift up my soul. O my God, in You I trust.

Remember, O Lord, Your compassion and Your lovingkindnesses, for they have been from old.

Good and upright is the Lord.

Turn to me and be gracious to me, for I am lonely and afflicted.

I closed my Bible, and then I really prayed.

12

A week later, Daniel, as well as Abby and Will came for supper. Abby – and Will to a slighter degree – was, of course, still struggling with grief. We had encouraged them to come, hoping they could just to get out of the house. It started out as a quiet evening. Bailey had the night off and joined us on the deck where we ate Chinese food from little cardboard buckets and wished that summer would never end.

For dessert, Gary brought ice cream from the kitchen. As he passed the toppings around, he said out of the blue, "I've been thinking more about church, and, well . . . Bailey needs a church. And we need to find out what kind of a church she'd like and then brainstorm if such an animal exists."

I have to insert here, that although Bailey did not come with us to church again, every Sunday after her initial visit, something had happened to make us rethink our position on Bailey going with us at all.

One Sunday I was in the church kitchen again, arranging cookies, when one of the ladies asked, "Who was that girl you brought a couple weeks ago?"

"A friend of ours. She is staying with us right now."

"Oh." And the woman marched out of the kitchen and didn't come back until I was seated with Gary.

After a few weeks, it had leaked out that Bailey was from the Pregnancy Center, and although the words were: "Gee, you are such good people," the feeling we got was: "Better you than me."

I had not expected praise, but I guess I had expected encouragement, especially from women I had known for decades.

Gary continued. "If God is real, and the Bible is true, what kind of church would Jesus be the happiest in?"

Bailey looked uncomfortable and concentrated on her ice cream.

Everyone was silent for a while, busy with their spoons, until Abby said softly, "I think He'd like to have music."

"What kind?"

We all looked at Gary, and Will said, "You tell us."

Gary shrugged. "Would Jesus have listened to the music you young people listen to?"

"Of course," said Daniel.

Bailey snorted. "If Jesus is real, and the Bible is true," she said, parroting Gary. Then she sighed loudly and stirred her soupy ice cream, suddenly looking contrite. "Sorry," she said quietly, "I didn't mean to be snippy. I may not go to church, but I do know there are a lot of them in town."

Gary picked up her thought: "Yes, and can they all be right?"

"Or all be wrong?" Daniel added.

Bailey shook her head. "Why are there churches at all? What good are they? Like, what are they for?"

Silence enveloped us again. I didn't know the answer to the question, and I suspected that Gary didn't either, but I blurted out the standard answer: "To worship God."

"Why?" Bailey dropped that one syllable into the air and picked up her bowl to drink the remaining ice cream.

We all scraped our bowls, and I wished I hadn't said anything.

Finally, Will cleared his throat and said, "Can I invite you to our church this week? We do church kind of differently, and I think you might like it. They have begun the book of Acts, and this week they're teaching on how and why the church began."

Bailey shrugged. "They're all the same to me. Big building, colored glass, organs, choirs, preachers."

"Well, actually," Abby interrupted, " We don't even meet in a church building. We meet at a coffee shop. And we meet Sunday evening."

Gary's spoon clinked on his bowl.

Bailey spoke first: "A coffee shop might be good. I'll have to see if I can get off work."

Sunday evening, Gary and I arrived at the coffee shop before Abby and Will. As it turned out, Bailey couldn't – or didn't – get off work. She was vague about how hard she had tried to change her work schedule, and we did not press her.

We stood uncertainly outside the renovated, brick brewery building, watching people greet each other and wondering if we could possibly fit in. I felt over-dressed, even though I probably wasn't.

A young man in a white t-shirt and blue jeans approached us with his hand held out. "Is this your first time? I'm Eli."

We introduced ourselves, and he pulled a couple others in to meet us.

"Come on in. There's coffee inside, and you'll want to find a comfortable place to sit."

The décor was industrial: the ceiling and all the exposed pipes had been painted dark gray, and the LED lights cast sparkles on all the countertops, coffee flavor bottles and cutlery. The floors were slate, and the tables and chairs were interspersed with comfy couches and coffee tables. There were TV screens, like in a sports bar, and Christian music DVDs were showing on them.

Our new friend escorted us to the coffee bar and turned us over to one of the baristas, an elderly woman with a mop of curly white hair. While she fixed our tea, she connected us with a couple our age, who had also ordered tea. Morgan and Jan invited us to bring our drinks and follow them to the side room, where the service had not yet begun.

The industrial décor continued into this room, smaller than the coffee house area. Soft music played, and people milled around, greeting one another. A younger couple came up to introduce themselves as Morgan and Jan's son and fiancé. While they talked, Gary and I turned our attention to the screen at the front, where a series of announcements kept running a loop. There were several weekly Bible studies, youth activities, a kid's club, training classes for kid's club, and instructions on where the children would be meeting this evening. There were also opportunities to get involved in the community, complete with training and volunteer positions. Even the Pregnancy Center was mentioned. I hadn't known that Connie was looking for more volunteers.

The musicians began to arrive, picking up their instruments and getting that one last swallow of water before they began.

And then, there was Connie! "What are you guys doing here?"

"Will and Abby invited us. They go here. I thought you went to that church on Fourth and Main."

"We used to, but – " We were interrupted, as Will slipped onto the seat beside me.

"Sorry I'm late," he murmured. "Abby wasn't feeling up to coming."

"Is she all right?"

"Oh, yeah. She just couldn't face her friends yet."

I turned back to Connie and introduced her to Will.

The music began and cut us off, the words on the screen with colorful backgrounds. It was indeed contemporary. And loud! Was I already old enough to need earplugs?

After a few songs, a young man announced some upcoming meetings and then prayed before introducing Eli. There was no ritual, no pulpit, and Eli just held his Bible in his hands and taught out of the book of Acts. The passage from the Bible flashed up on the screen for us to read along. I couldn't remember the last time I had read anything from Acts. Had I ever? Yet the teaching that evening was all about how the very first church had begun only 50 days after Jesus had risen from the dead. Could it possibly be relevant for us?

After a long sermon, more music, and a question-and answer time back in the coffee house, we wandered out to the car.

I looked at my watch. "Do you realize that we were there over two hours?" I asked.

"I do," said Gary, "But it didn't seem that long, did it."

"No. What did you think?"

Gary unlocked the car and we both got in, but he didn't start the engine. He started talking to the windshield. "I think that our lives are about to change more than we thought. It would be a big change from what we're used to."

"I thought we were just looking for a church for Bailey. Are you thinking that we should switch churches?" The thought made my stomach feel strange.

"Well, I was struck by the fact that those young people all seemed to know exactly why they were doing church."

I agreed. "And they expressed it so I could understand their vision."

"And they had such an interest in reaching out to the community where there are real needs."

I sighed. "Yes. No one at Evergreen ever understood why I would waste my time at the Pregnancy Center. Some of them – well, you remember what they said." They had said that the girls needed self-discipline and morals and a good spanking; that they deserved the mess they were in, and I shouldn't be making their lives easier. It was one of the reasons I decided to volunteer.

"I do remember, Dorothy." He turned in his seat and looked at me.

I said what Gary was obviously thinking: "Why have we waited so long?"

He started the engine and backed out of the parking spot. "It won't be easy to leave. No one will understand, and there is no guarantee that Bailey will want to come with us. We have to do this because we believe it's the right move for us, not because we want to force her to follow."

"The music is so loud."

"We were right in front of the speakers. We can sit somewhere else."

"I liked the music, though."

"And the teacher was so good," he said, wonder in his voice. "I feel as if I have been on a starvation diet for my soul – and I didn't know it – and he fed me my first good meal in years."

"I had never even heard that section of the Bible before," I admitted.

"I had, but never so thoroughly and capably explained."

"We'd get to see Abby and Will every week."

"Yes, but we wouldn't want to stifle them. This is their church – their discovery – their vision. We can learn from them."

Gary drove a few minutes in silence, while my mind rushed through so many conflicting thoughts. I wondered how I would make new friend and how we could leave our old friends.

Gary chuckled. "Do you realize that they didn't take any offering? They didn't even mention money."

"You're right."

"Do you think you can make new friends?" he asked.

"Of course. I meet new people in my sewing business, and we get along all right."

"This will be different. You won't have automatic little jobs you can do on Sunday morning. You might have to find a new niche."

"The niches I fill on Sunday could be filled by anyone. Arranging cookies and planning baby showers are not exactly rocket science. I think, perhaps, the niche I really care about is already full anyway. In spite of the hiccups, I'm glad we asked Bailey to stay with us."

We were quiet for a bit longer as we pulled into the garage.

"I'm glad to hear you say that," said Gary. "It might be hard to tell people why we are leaving and going to a new church."

I don't even know why the thought crossed my mind, but it brought tears to my eyes. "What if we just left," I whispered, "and no one even noticed we were gone?"

"Don't worry. They'll notice when our check is no longer in the offering plate."

"So have we decided?"

"Let's try it for a month. We can still go to Evergreen, mornings, until we are sure.

· 13 ·

The following Sunday, it felt so odd to walk into Evergreen Church, knowing that we might be leaving in a few weeks. Many things suddenly seemed different – or even irrelevant. I found myself looking at all the rituals much as I had that first week when Bailey had gone with us. And how many of my "friends" actually knew me – knew anything important about me? Or Gary? Or my children? We usually chatted about the weather and about the upcoming city marathon, which would deplete attendance in a few weeks.

My daughter just had a miscarriage, I thought. *I am struggling to love an unlovable twenty-something, unwed mother. I'm up to my eyeballs in yellow chiffon, all of which must be sewn into beautiful dresses by next week. And what are you doing with your life? Where are you hurting? Can I help you?*

But I knew they did not want my help. They never opened up to me – the pastor's wife being the exception, that one sad evening – and they wanted the veneer of perfection to stay in place. They also wanted my veneer of perfection to stay in place. Had I given that impression? I thought about those who had left the church. Was that why they left? Had they found another church or given up entirely?

It made our decision easier as we realized how unnecessary we were and also that there seemed to be nothing there for us – not that it was all about us. Eli, the young pastor of Rocks and Mortar, invited us to a "beginner's" Bible study, where he was laying out the vision of the church from the Bible, beginning the book of Acts again, and promising to finish it in about eighteen months! We decided early on to invite Bailey and to do what we could to get her to change her work schedule.

And then she didn't come home one night. We waited until lunchtime the next day to talk with her. I had been frantically putting invisible zippers in all the lemon-yellow chiffon dresses, and Gary made grilled cheese sandwiches and heated a couple cans of tomato soup.

Bailey strolled into the kitchen, rubbing sleepy dust from her eyes, and said, "I love grilled cheese, but I can't stay."

"Work?" Gary asked, as he put three plates on the table.

She hesitated and then said, "Not really. I just – "

I patted the table. "Sit down and eat lunch. You must be hungry."

She sighed and dropped into the chair.

I decided to jump right in. "When you first moved into our basement, I really didn't know if it would work or not. I asked Abby that first day if she had any ideas about how we could make you feel comfortable and help you over this phase in your life. She told me that I needed to treat you like a daughter."

Bailey looked over her shoulder to see if the sandwiches were coming.

"Now, I know you have your own mother – "

Bailey snorted and rolled her eyes.

" – But I thought I could probably manage that, but it's more different than I thought."

Bailey said. "Don't stress out."

Gary spooned the soup into our bowls and put a plate of hot, gooey sandwiches in the middle of the table. He sat down and said a short prayer before we began to eat.

Gary picked up the conversation. "We have just started attending a Bible study at Will and Abby's church. By the way, the name of the church is Rocks and Mortar."

Bailey stopped mid-chew. "Really?"

"Really. We would like you to come with us. It's not like any church you – or we – have ever seen before. Very un-church-like."

"Mmmm. I probably can't get off work."

"We haven't told you when the Bible study is," I said.

She dunked her sandwich into the soup. "Okay," she said flatly.

Gary plunged in. "Do you enjoy working at the casino?"

She shrugged. "It's okay. I make really good tips."

"But do you like it? Is it your ambition to spend the rest of your life working as server at the casino?"

"I kinda don't think that'd be anybody's ambition, but it pays the bills."

"That's a good thing, but there are other jobs."

She made a face. "I'm not quitting my job." She snatched another sandwich from the plate and stood up. "Thanks for lunch," and she left the kitchen.

"That went well," said Gary with a grimace.

"I think she needs another reason besides church."

"Obviously."

A few days later, Daniel popped in, just in time for supper, and it just happened that Bailey had the night off as well.

Gary arrived home, while I was putting the casserole on the table, and he said, "I have to eat and run, as I have a client in 45 minutes."

Daniel held the chair for Bailey, and she looked up at him and smiled.

Gary caught my eye and winked as we bowed our heads for grace.

I didn't even hear the prayer. Why did he wink?

We ate quickly, and before I could say anything, Daniel suggested that he and Bailey could clean up the kitchen.

"Thank you," I said slowly. "The girls are coming for their final fittings tomorrow, and the wedding is on Sunday, so I really need to work."

From my sewing room, I could hear the two of them talking as the dishes clattered into the dishwasher, and I wondered suddenly if it was a really, really bad idea to have Bailey in our home. Then Daniel came in to say that they were going out to have coffee with some of his friends.

What could I say? "Have a nice time." This is a bad idea. A really, really bad idea.

I sewed, but my mind wasn't on the project. Instead, I was trying to understand why Daniel would encourage her. I found myself imagining conversations with him, trying to talk him out of being nice to her, pointing out her failings and lack of morals. I also was naming girls that I thought were much more deserving of him.

The sun went down, and Gary came home. I felt foolish talking to him about my imaginings, so I didn't. He settled down to watch a movie and fill out a real estate offer. Daniel brought Bailey back, and she hurried off to bed. Then he came in to say good night.

"Did you have a nice time?"

"Yup. I took her to the Christian coffee shop. There were a bunch of students there, and we watched music DVDs and talked about life. You'll never believe what I discovered about Bailey."

"What?"

"She would like to open a fitness studio. Especially now, she would like to train pregnant women how to stay fit safely."

"How in the world did that come out?"

"Well, people were getting to know one another, and that included saying what they would like to do when school is finished. She just blurted it out, complete with showing off her baby bump."

I smiled.

"One of the other girls – Kim, married to Tom White, remember him? Anyway, she is very pregnant and said she would hire Bailey on the spot. We all laughed."

"Then what happened?"

"Everyone continued talking and then one of the girls saw that Bailey was crying."

"Crying? Bailey?"

"She's not as hard as you think, Mom. She was just sitting there quietly, with tears dripping down her face. With a little prompting, we got her to tell everyone that she worked at the casino, and there was no way she could stop. Everyone started to brainstorm how she could change jobs. We came up with nothing concrete, but I think she felt understood. Before we left, Kim offered to pray with her, and she agreed." He hesitated. "Well, actually, she grumbled, 'Whatever!' but we prayed for her anyway."

"Amazing," I said. "Did Bailey tell you that your dad and I tried to talk to her about finding a new job?"

"Not a word."

"It was a train wreck."

"Sorry, Mom." He came in and kissed the top of my head. "Gotta go. Good night." At the door, he turned and added, "Well, maybe we can keep our ears open. None of us goes to fitness studios, but surely someone has an opening somewhere."

· 14 ·

I found a job opening on the day of the lemon-yellow chiffon wedding. The day dawned bright and cool. The bride's family had spiffed up their backyard, and the late summer flowers – gladiolas, dahlias, and roses – had all agreed to bloom at the same time. The bridesmaids had their dresses, and although I had not sewn the wedding dress, I had agreed to be there for little emergencies. One of the groomsmen carried my portable sewing machine into the house, and we found an unobtrusive corner for me to work.

I wandered around, listening for "Oh, dear, look what happened," and was able to calm a few frazzled nerves. During the reception dinner, the wedding planner, herself, actually asked me to mend the broken heel on her shoe. Fortunately, I had some glue in my bag of tricks, and she was back on her feet.

During dinner, two of the men at my table were talking, and one was bemoaning the fact that their receptionist had just quit. We had introduced ourselves at the beginning of the evening, so I didn't feel too weird asking, "Are you looking for a replacement?"

He looked surprised. "Well, yes, but it's only an entry-level job. I am the manager for The Gym."

"It's not for me." I tried to control my excitement. The Gym meant exercise classes, and a receptionist position would bring Bailey closer to that sort of job. "I know a young woman who would be very interested. Would you mind if I told her?"

He reached into his jacket pocket and produced a business card. "Not at all, but she would have to make it snappy. She can apply online."

"I'll tell her this evening, and she can get it to you by tomorrow."

When the dancing started, I excused myself and gathered up my things to go home. It had been a long day, and I was tired, but when I got home, I did not get to relax.

Gary had real estate papers spread out all over the dining room table so he could watch TV while he filled out forms. He glanced up and then kept writing. No "How was the wedding?" or "Glad you made it home." Daniel had been there, looking for me, and Gary informed me that he had gone back out for pizza. While he was gone, Bailey had returned from work unexpectedly early and had hurled herself onto the sofa, where she still lay when I got home.

I kicked off my shoes and kissed Gary. "So, what's Bailey doing home?" I asked quietly.

"I don't know. I didn't want to ask because I need to finish these forms."

"Well, you should have asked."

"Why don't you ask? She is probably lying there just waiting for one of us to ask. She's your friend."

I was still excited about telling Bailey about the job possibility, but it annoyed me that Gary seemed to think that he had nothing to do with Bailey. I really didn't want to hear her problems, so I got a glass of water and decided I would start the conversation with my good news.

Just then, Daniel came back with pizzas, and I had to postpone my good news until everyone had gotten their food. I wished I hadn't eaten at the wedding because the pizza smelled so good. Gary took his pizza back to the table to work. Bailey and Daniel went back into the living room and sat on the couch, so I followed them and settled into my wing chair.

Daniel put the TV on mute. "Were you at a wedding, all dressed up?" he asked me.

"Yes. The yellow chiffon is out of the house."

"I liked that color," Bailey mumbled through her pizza.

"I had forgotten that you had a wedding," Daniel said.

How to bring up the job at The Gym? Our last conversation with Bailey about quitting her casino job had gone badly, and Daniel's discovery of her dream job probably should remain his secret. I drank some water and gave up, asking Bailey what she wanted me to ask: "So Bailey, you're home early. Everything all right at work?"

She threw her plate onto the coffee table with a clatter. "No, everything is not okay at work!" she shouted. "They want to move me to reception in the hotel part of the casino. Same pay, less strenuous, they say. No tips, I say. I don't have a choice. They don't even ask me what I want. I think it's because they can hide my fat stomach behind the reception counter." Her voice turned mocking: "I'm not sexy enough to be a server anymore." And then she dropped her bomb: "Stupid baby. I wish *I* had miscarried."

The room went still. Daniel stopped chewing and swallowed hard. Gary quit writing. Bailey's eyes travelled around the room, daring any of us to challenge her. I set my glass on the end table and said very quietly, "Don't you *ever* say that to Abby and Will."

Daniel spoke, "And don't ever say that again to your baby. He - or she - can hear everything you say, you know." He reached for the remote and turned off the TV.

Bailey swore and jumped up, grabbing her pizza. I think she was planning to take it downstairs, but Gary stood up and ordered, "Bailey, you're not going anywhere. Sit down!" He came into the living room and lowered himself into the other wing chair.

Bailey sat.

Gary began: "I don't think you quite understand what your life here means." He stopped, almost unsure of himself. "I mean, what's going on here." He halted again.

"Dad," Daniel said, "Let me?" He turned and looked at Bailey. "You are angry about how you are being treated at work, but that is not your baby's fault, and it's certainly not our fault. So, yelling at us accomplishes nothing."

"Well, maybe I should just leave," Bailey retorted.

"No," I protested, the one word slipping out before I could stop it.

Daniel nodded. "No, we don't want you to leave. But I want you to understand the implications of what you just said: You're telling us that your happiness is dependent on the death of your baby. We have just experienced the death of a baby, and it's a sad, difficult time."

Bailey opened her mouth, but Daniel put up his hand. "I'm not finished. We want you to understand why you are in this house at all. When Mom told us she wanted to invite you to live with us, we thought she had gone squishy in the brain. But – and this is really important – she wasn't just thinking of you. She was thinking of the baby. She and Dad didn't take just one person into their home, they took two."

Bailey hadn't moved; she just looked at her lap, fiddling with a ring on her finger.

Daniel continued: "My parents have taught me to take care of the weak, and I'm going to be very blunt: your baby is completely helpless. You aren't. Whatever job you have – like it or not, whatever decisions you make – wise or foolish, whatever wishes you may have, those are all yours, and your baby is dragged along with you. Your baby has no choice in any of it. He – or she – is completely dependent on you. No matter why you are pregnant, or whether you want to be or not, the responsibility for caring for him – or her – is yours alone."

Daniel paused, and in that pause, Gary added: "But we didn't *want* you to be alone, so here you are. We want to share – as best we can – in the care and loving of your baby."

And I knew what to say next! "And that doesn't mean we care any less for you. As hard as you have tried to be prickly, you have grown on us, and we don't want you to leave."

Daniel spoke again, "My mother has volunteered for a while at the Pregnancy Center where you met her, but she has never brought any of the other young women home before. You're here because of your baby, but also because something in Mom made her choose you."

There was a long silence. Then Bailey sighed. "I'm sorry I said that. I don't wish my baby . . . dead. I couldn't do that, not after . . .." Her words trickled off, but then she asked, "Can he really hear everything I say?"

"Everything." Gary said, "You do need to think about what you say before you say it."

"I know. And I know that Abby and Will are sad about losing their baby. I wouldn't hurt them."

"It hurts us too," Gary told her. "Their baby was our grandchild."

Suddenly, tears popped from her eyes and her chin crumpled. "I'm sorry," she whispered.

I didn't know if she would take a hug, but she needed one badly. So, I got up from my chair and knelt on the rug, putting my arms around her. She sniffed and patted my back, but she pulled away and said, with a shaky chuckle, "I don't cry much."

I drew back on my heels and said, "Maybe you ought to."

"No," she stated emphatically. She looked around, and then said, trying to sound cheerful, "Well, this still doesn't solve my job problem. Everyone wants me to leave the casino. I want to leave the casino, but where can I go?"

Gary said, "Perhaps it's time we prayed about it. Together."

I hesitated and then said, "Well, we should, but I heard of a job while at the wedding. Perhaps we can pray for God to let us all know if it's the right one."

"Tell us," Daniel prompted.

So, I did.

Bailey was astounded. "You mean a job in a fitness place? Really?"

"If you apply quickly and if they take you," Daniel said.

"How do I do it?"

Daniel got his computer out of his backpack and guided Bailey through the application process. Gary returned to his real estate offer, and I tidied up the pizza mess.

At one point, Daniel told Bailey, "You need to tell them you're pregnant somewhere in this application, maybe a cover letter. They're not allowed to ask, but – "

"They won't take me," she whined. "I mean: look at me!"

He glanced up from the computer. "You look fine to me. If you don't tell them . . .." He broke off and stared at the blank TV for thirty seconds. "Whoa! I just had a great idea. But I'll ask my professor first." He wouldn't tell us what the idea was, but encouraged Bailey, "Just let them know you are expecting a baby in December, but also tell them your idea for a class for pregnant women."

When they hit "Send," all of us returned to the living room, and Gary prayed that God would give direction or provide a better job – soon.

In bed that night, after we had turned out the lights, Gary said, "Who was that young man tonight with all the wise words?"

We both broke into laughter. "Oh, I know what you mean: We are truly blessed."

· 15 ·

I wish I could say that things improved after that evening, but to remove the chip on Bailey's shoulder was going to take some major surgery. She had her moments when she would jump up from the table to pour one of us another cup of tea or ask how our day went, but most of the time she was still abrupt and surly, and her gloominess was usually laced with swear words that she tried to brush off with "Oh, I'm sorry, it just slipped out."

Daniel had asked one of his law professors if there was any way the casino should compensate Bailey for her lost tips. The professor turned the idea into a class assignment.

A few days after our conversation in the living room, Bailey banged into the house after work, calling, "Dorothy! Where are you?"

She found me on my knees cleaning the upstairs bathroom. "What is it?"

She was grinning and looking sheepish. "You'll never guess what!"

"What?" I asked, thinking perhaps I already knew.

"I had a job interview this afternoon."

"And?"

"I got the job! I couldn't believe it, but I got the job! Mr. Bauer – that's the person in H.R. – he said that he talked to my boss at the casino, and, like, the work I was doing in reception was good – considering that I just started – so if I, like, wanted the job, I could have it!"

"What did your boss at the casino think? Was that a problem at work?"

"Nope. I gave him two weeks' notice, and he said I could, like, go sooner if they needed me." She leaned against the doorjamb and frowned. "Actually, that sounds as if he wants me to go."

I shrugged. "Maybe he does, but you can't have it both ways."

She sighed. "All that work that Daniel's class has gone to. I was hoping that there would be some extra money." She pushed away from the door and went downstairs.

Thirty seconds later, she ran back up the stairs, gasping and wringing her hands. "Oh, Dorothy! There's a . . . a mouse in my room!"

"Did you see it?"

"Of course, I saw it! How else would I know? I went into my room and it ran – joop! – along the wall and disappeared under my bed." Her voice calmed, and she lowered her tone to say very seriously, "I'm not sleeping in there with a mouse."

I stood and dried my hands. "Can you show me where you saw him?"

She eyed me suspiciously. "How do you know it's a 'him'?"

I laughed. "I don't." I headed for the stairs. "Show me?"

She trailed behind me down the stairs. When I opened her door, I had to force it open.

"Here," she said helpfully, "Let me. There are a few things in the way."

The "few things" looked to me as if everything she owned was strewn about the room. The bed was unmade, several piles of clothes – dirty? clean? – were heaped in the center of the room. On her desk, surrounded by various containers of make-up, was a small pile of dirty dishes with uneaten food. No wonder the mouse had come: He had found paradise! A short wall of empty soda cans ran along the floor, the length of the bed. She was fortunate not to have ants too. The wastebasket overflowed with tissues and other unmentionable things. And the room smelled musty and unclean.

I turned around and just looked at her.

"I was going to clean my room," she protested.

"I'm sure the mouse loves it. He – or she – has probably been here for some time."

"I'm not sleeping in here with a mouse," she repeated.

"I'll take care of the mouse. I want this room clean before dinner."

"I have to go to work."

"When?"

She hung her head. "After supper."

I started to go upstairs and had second thoughts and looked back into the room. "Do you need a list of how to clean this room?"

Her shoulders sagged. "Maybe."

Cleaning our bathroom could wait; this was obviously much more urgent.

I gave her a few ideas of where to begin, but it became very clear that the poor child had never been taught anything about how to take care of her belongings. I had her collect the dirty clothes and put a small – small! – load in the washer.

While she was doing that, I texted Gary and asked him to bring a few cheap mousetraps home. "The kind that snap and kill the mouse instantly," I told him.

Back in Bailey's room, we tackled the clean clothes. No one had ever shown her how to fold her things and how to put them in drawers. She was still living out of her suitcases which were, of course, too small for all the things she had acquired since she had moved in with us. Some of her "clean" clothes had sprinkles of mouse droppings, so we added them to the dirty clothes pile.

We found containers for the make-up, and put them and all her hair things in the bathroom across the hall. I had been cleaning it (for which I now was very glad), but now I realized that I needed to teach her how to clean a bathroom as well.

Bailey took the dirty dishes upstairs and hauled the trash to the garage. When she came back down, she stopped to lean on the doorframe, frowning at her stomach.

"What's wrong?" I asked, suddenly afraid that I had made her work too hard.

"There's this regular movement that won't stop."

"Does it hurt?"

"No. Just blip . . . blip . . . blip."

I smiled. "Your baby has the hiccups."

"Hiccups?" She grinned. "That's cute."

While she folded clothes, I wiped every surface with a disinfectant. Finally, I vacuumed, moving all the furniture. Sure enough, that mouse ran from under the bed to under the dresser to avoid the noisy machine.

Bailey squealed and ran into the hallway. "I'm not sleeping in there with a mouse," she warned.

"That's fine. If we don't catch him – her – tonight, then you can sleep on the couch."

Gary brought home traps, and I set three in various spots in her room, baited with peanut butter. During supper we heard a loud snap, and the mouse was dead. We hoped it was the only mouse, but we didn't say that to Bailey.

Bailey started her new job the following week, with all of us taking turns driving her to and from work. It was a bother, and by the weekend, Daniel decided to loan her his car because he lived so near campus anyway. I wondered aloud if it was such a good idea.

Gary disagreed. "He's an adult, Dottie. What he does with his car is his business. Besides, you said she's a good driver, so it shouldn't be a problem."

As far as Daniel's class assignment went, there was no extra money because Bailey's contract with the casino didn't allow for any amount of severance pay. Daniel's class learned that just because an injustice seems to have occurred doesn't mean that the justice system can do anything about it.

It was October, and it was past time for me to make a break with the Pregnancy Center, so I took tea and cinnamon rolls over to the building on Friday to break the news to Connie.

"What's this?" she asked as I came in the door. "Is it Tuesday?"

"I wanted to catch you when you weren't too busy."

"Ahhh." She took her tea and added sugar and powdered creamer. "How have you been? Weddings?"

"One coming up the middle of December. Lots of forest green velvet."

"Sounds pretty. How's Bailey? I haven't seen her for a while. She is overdue for her ultrasound."

"You call her; I interfere enough."

She took a sticky bite of a cinnamon roll. "Maybe I should ask how you and Gary are doing with her."

"Well, that's what I need to talk to you about." I shrugged. "It's ups and downs. She finally found work at The Gym, so she was able to leave the casino, for which we are all grateful."

"Does she have a car now?"

"Daniel loaned her his. He doesn't need it very often."

"That's interesting."

"Interesting?"

"Just interesting." Connie took a sip of tea and then said, "So, what do you need to talk to me about?"

I sighed. "Gary thinks that with my sewing and getting accustomed to a new church and caring for – guiding – Bailey, I probably should bow out of my volunteer work here. At least for the time being."

"Okay. We'll figure things out. How do you feel about that?"

"I hate to let you down, but I think he's right. It seems that we careen from one minor crisis to another. Mostly, I'm having to teach her how to live. Things like how much laundry to put in the washer, how to clean a bathroom, how to clean her room." I paused and then decided to tell her: "And how to keep mice out of her room."

"Mice! You have been busy!"

"Yeah, well," I paused, realizing that I had probably said too much. "Please don't say anything to her about this. She knows I'm quitting, and she thinks Gary is a tyrant to suggest it, but I don't want her to know I told anyone how – how – how much she has to learn."

"You're probably very good for her."

"Mmm, I'm sure learning a lot about a world outside my own. But I can't leave her where she is."

"Well, we have a couple women interested in volunteering here, so I think we'll be okay without you."

"We still are very invested in what you are doing. Actually, I think we are more invested, now that we have really seen the depth of the need and the battles these women are fighting. I honestly don't know how Bailey could have survived alone. She had already made so many compromises." I paused, trying to think how to express what was in my heart. "I think . . . I think I should never talk about her to others, unless I could say whatever I'm saying, to her face."

"Probably a good decision."

"I mean, we really care about her and . . . .."

Connie reached over and patted my hand. "Just keep up the good work, and pray for her a lot."

"Pray for us!"

My cell phone rang. It was Bailey.

"Dorothy?"

"Yes?"

"Oh, Dorothy, the car is, like, gone! I – I locked it; I'm sure it did. But I just finished work and, like, I came out and it's gone. Oh, what am I going to tell Daniel?" she finished in a wail.

I didn't know. I guess my face must have registered panic or something because Connie whispered, "What's wrong?"

"Bailey, you need to call Daniel. But . . . .." I thought for a minute. "Are you sure it's not there. Sometimes I forget where I parked the car."

"I didn't forget," she snapped. "There are no cars in the parking lot except my manager's."

"Okay. Then go back into the building and tell your manager. He'll know what to do. I think you need to call the police."

"Daniel's going to be furious," she wailed.

Daniel? "Daniel will probably be mad, but he won't be furious."

There was a long pause and then she said quietly, "Oh yes he will be; he was, like, really angry at me that night we talked."

"That was different, and you know it. This is just a car." Just a car? What was I saying? I really didn't know what to do, and I hoped someone else would. "Call him. He's studying law; he'll know what to do."

"Well, okay," she said in a small voice.

I glanced at Connie. "God knows what He's doing," I told Bailey. "We'll pray about this."

Another long pause. "That would be nice," sincerity in her tone. Then she pulled herself together and asked, "Oh. And can you, like, pick me up? I got no ride home."

I looked at my watch. "I'll be there in about twenty minutes."

I hung up and looked at Connie. "How much more complicated can life get? We really needed that car."

"You need to pick her up."

"Yeah."

Connie and I prayed, and then I drove out to The Gym to pick up Bailey.

What if we never get that car back?

· 16 ·

The police found the car two weeks later.

But I'm getting ahead of myself.

Thanksgiving was imminent, and one afternoon, while hemming miles of forest green velvet, I found myself wondering about Bailey's mother. She had not mentioned her mother since the day after Bailey had been removed from her apartment. In fact, she never mentioned family at all, and I, blind fool, had never asked. Did she have siblings? And obviously, there was a father somewhere.

I decided to figure out a way to approach the subject when she got home from work that day. I practiced:

"So, do you have brothers or sisters?"

"Yes." Or *"No."* Or *"Duh!"*

Try again. *"Bailey, I realize I don't know much about you. Tell me about yourself."*

"Why would you care?" Or *"There's nothing to tell."* Or . . . maybe she would tell me a lot.

I acknowledged that Bailey might want to spend the holidays with her family, whoever they might be. A tiny piece of me – a piece of which I was ashamed – had a faint hope that she would have other plans for the holidays. Our family holidays were always so wonderful, and having her around would definitely change things. On the other hand, it might be nice to invite her family to our home so they could see where Bailey was living. I hoped they cared; they ought to care; I suspected that they didn't.

I stopped hemming and prayed that I would find the right words to dig deeper into Bailey's life. And that God would stop me, if the timing was off.

She arrived home just as I was grating cheese for the top of supper's casserole.

"How was your day?"

She peeled off her jacket and hung it over the back of a kitchen chair. "Long." She rubbed her hands over her very round belly. "Little Waldo, here, is wearing me out."

"You only have five more weeks. Can you take part of your maternity leave before the birth?"

"I can. I will." She washed her hands in the sink. "And, Dorothy, I've decided to find out the sex of the baby at my next appointment. Connie said I should come in for another ultrasound. I wanted the surprise, but it's not, like, practical. I gotta start buying baby things now."

"Of course. We need to find a crib and changing table and a dresser for the baby's things. I think there is room for those in your room. We could also have a baby shower for you."

She frowned and grabbed a few slivers of cheese. "Who'd come?"

"Well," I thought for a minute. "Abby and me and Connie. Maybe some of the girls you have met at the Bible study. Anyone from the casino?"

She shrugged. "Maybe one or two. Since I've been going to the Bible study, they don't want to be friends anymore." She helped scatter the rest of the mozzarella onto the casserole.

"I'm sorry. Do you have any family who might be interested? Your mother?"

Her head jerked up, and she looked as if I'd slapped her. "Why would you say that?" she demanded.

My hand stopped in midair, and I didn't know what to say.

Her voice was strained: "My mother would never come, and she sure would hate to find out she's gonna to be a grandmother."

"Oh, I can't believe that. Haven't you even told her?"

"Of course I haven't told her!"

"Then how do you know – "

"Because I know!" she shouted. "You know nothing!" She suddenly sank into the nearest chair and rested her head quietly in her hands. When she looked up, there were tears in her eyes, but it was also obvious that she was pulling herself together.

Maybe being speechless was a blessing. I sat down at the table.

She sighed.

"I'm sorry I brought it up," I whispered.

"You mean well," she assured me, "but sometimes you are so, like, so . . . .."

"Stupid?"

She cracked a tiny smile. "Yeah, well."

We sat in silence. I had already said too much, and I didn't know how to end the conversation.

Finally, she spoke, as if the words were wrung out of her "My mother wants to have young boyfriends. A grandchild would, like, really mess that up. She told me that. Many times."

"Oh, I'm so sorry. That must be hard for you."

She snorted in mild mockery. "Hard? I don't think you really understand, but thanks for trying."

"Well," I admitted, "I was going to ask you what you want to do for Thanksgiving, and if you – "

"If you don't want me here, I can leave." She started to stand up, but I patted her arm and she leaned back in the chair.

"No, no, that's not it at all," I explained. "I only wanted to say that if you usually go to your family, that would be fine, but you could invite your family here if you like. We'd . . . we'd like to meet them." Although I wasn't sure if that was a lie or not.

Bailey stopped me by grabbing my hand. Her voice was low and almost threatening. "My mother would not want to come," She paused and then spit out, "And I sure as hell wouldn't want her here!" She took a deep breath and tried to smile. "It's too – too – very peaceful here. You wouldn't want her here either. And my half-brother lives in Alaska. I haven't heard from him in ten years. He was smart and got as far away as possible. And you don't have to ask: I think my father's dead. He was an alcoholic." She stood up and laughed, but there was no humor. "So now you know why I'm, like, such a mess."

I didn't know what to say. She was a mess, but I didn't care. I realized that my heart was breaking for the hurts she had to endure. I held back my tears and stood up, moving in to hug her, but she held up her hands to shield herself. "And don't hug me. Please." She grabbed her jacket and fled down the stairs to her room.

I picked up the casserole, shoved it into the oven, and slammed the oven door. Dear God, why do you allow people to have children and then allow them to treat them so abominably? The tears popped from my eyes and splashed onto the counter. Well. We would have our family Thanksgiving and let Bailey know she was a part of this family.

17

Sometimes, it seemed as if our family was always having meaningful conversations over food. Perhaps that is because mealtime – or tea time - was a time when we were less busy and could focus on one another. Thanksgiving, of course, was the ultimate family mealtime. I was up early, peeling potatoes to boil and mash later in the day.

There had been a Thanksgiving about five years ago, when we had all admitted – rather sheepishly – that we didn't care for turkey anymore. After that, we had tried prime rib, barbecued ribs, pork roast, and even goose. This year, we were back to barbecued ribs, which was Gary's job. He would have to carry an umbrella on the deck, for the rain was torrential.

At 9 a.m., I turned on the television to have the Thanksgiving Day Parade running in the background. Bailey dragged up the stairs in her pajamas and found a cup of coffee before settling into a chair to watch the parade.

"I've never seen it," she said sadly.

"Well, I don't see much of it because I'm usually cooking, but I do enjoy the bands."

"Do you have a job for me?"

"As a matter of fact, yes. Gary found a recipe for cranberry barbecue sauce. Would you like to assemble that? Read the recipe all the way through before you start, and then just follow the steps. Ask me if you don't understand something."

She agreed, and I found all the ingredients, measuring cups, blender, and saucepan for her before I returned to peeling potatoes.

By 10am, the peaceful morning had been pleasantly interrupted by the arrival of Gary's parents (Nana and Pops), Abby and Will, and Daniel. Suddenly, the entry was filled with laughter, hugs, and flying coats.

We introduced everyone to Bailey, who dashed downstairs to get out of her pajamas. She took longer than expected, and the cranberries, which she had already set to cook, boiled over onto the glass-topped stove. Gary's mom had discovered it and moved the pan from the burner. "How did this happen?" she asked, just as Bailey returned to the kitchen, clad in stretchy yoga pants and a long tunic. Her baby bump was looking cute.

The burning cranberries and sugar on the stove smelled heavenly, and smoke swirled into the vent above the stove.

"I can't do anything right," Bailey moaned. She grabbed a few paper towels and applied them to the cranberry caramel, where they stuck in the smoking, gooey mess. "Ow! That's really hot!"

Gary's mom warned, "Don't touch it," and then asked me, "Do you want me to make the sauce?"

"No!" I said, probably faster than I should have. "Bailey's doing it, but if you would clean up the mess, that would really help."

Nana was a pro at cleaning up messes, but she kept looking over at Bailey to see if she needed direction. Now, I had told Gary's parents about Bailey before they came, but it was still difficult for his mom – outgoing and often pushy – to keep her opinions and helping ideas to herself.

By now, Abby was also in the kitchen, making her green bean casserole. I was able to catch Nana's eyes and beckon her into the hallway.

"Thank you so much for cleaning up the mess. I want Bailey to make the sauce, because she is learning how to cook, and I think she can do it. And, if it's the success that I think it will be, that will be good for her."

Nana grabbed me in a big hug. "You're such a good person!"

"Ugh! Don't say that! Let's just do what we can to help her enjoy her first Thanksgiving without stress."

We returned to the kitchen, where Abby was showing Bailey how to puree small batches of hot cranberries in the blender, so she would not explode them all over the kitchen.

"Have you tasted it yet?" I asked.

"Should I?"

"Of course!" exclaimed Nana. "Taste and adjust."

While they were tasting and adjusting, I went to the door to welcome my sister, Claire and her 12-year-old son, Ethan. Her husband, who was in the Air Force, had just been reassigned to London, and there had not been time for them to move the family yet. With Ethan's arrival, the men switched channels. Sportscasters opined, loudly, on all the merits and deficiencies of the various teams that would play football that day. While the guys watched the first game, and we put the finishing touches on the meal. When the game ended, Gary brought in the ribs.

Amidst much laughter and pushing, everyone moved to the table, carrying platters and bowls of goodness. Daniel seated his grandmother, and Gary pushed the chair in for Claire, while Ethan sat between her and Pops. Bailey seemed to be hovering in the kitchen doorway, uncertain, I thought, of where to sit. Will pulled out a chair for Abby and then sat beside her. Daniel sat down next to my chair at the end of the table, but before Gary could pull mine out for me, Bailey slid into it next to Daniel.

Nana looked across the table at me and raised her eyebrows. Pops, who was already seated, pulled out the chair beside him and I slipped into it. It didn't really much matter where we sat, but it was the beginning of things to come.

Gary prayed for the bountiful meal, and we started passing platters and bowls.

After a short time, Pops asked, "Who made this heavenly sauce! Was that you, Dottie?"

I shook my head. "Nope. Bailey did. It was a recipe we wanted to try."

"Props, Bailey!" exclaimed Pops.

Bailey's cheeks actually turned pink with pleasure, but she just nodded and kept eating.

"I agree with Pops," Gary said. "This is the best barbecue recipe yet. Thank you, Bailey. I couldn't stop tasting it, and I think I'm already full." He paused, "No, not really! Please pass the green beans."

Everyone talked and laughed and ate too much. A couple times, my eyes were drawn to the end of the table, where Bailey was filling Daniel's water glass, or he was putting more potatoes on her plate. What was going on?

"When we are finished eating," Gary announced, "We are going to go around the table and tell one another what we are thankful for. It's going to be like that game, where you have to remember what everyone else said, so I'm going first, so I won't have to remember anything."

"Oh, no," chided Nana, "You'll have to say them all when we're finished."

"Well, then," Gary said, "I think I had better start. I am thankful for this tableful of wonderful people. I love you all."

Ethan said, "I'm thankful for this tableful of wonderful people and for football. Can we go watch?"

"Not yet," Daniel told him. "We're recording the game so you won't miss anything. And I'm thankful for our new church. Oh. And the tableful of people – "

"Wonderful people!" Nana corrected.

"Wonderful people, and for football."

"My turn?" asked Bailey. "I'm thankful for the tableful of wonderful people – really." She paused and blinked. "And for football and for your new church, and for this friendly house."

Pops was next: "I'm thankful for this wonderful tableful of people and for football and for – what was next?"

Will prompted him. "For our new church."

"Yup. And for this very friendly house," He winked at Bailey. "And for the delicious dinner, which I hope includes dessert and coffee."

"Later," I said.

Claire raised her hand. "I'm thankful for our new home in Germany – although moving is a bit scary."

"And?" prodded Ethan.

"And for this tableful of wonderful people and for football and for your new church and for this friendly house."

"Are we next?" asked Abby. She looked at Will.

"We are thankful that we are expecting a baby again," Will said.

The table erupted into many congratulations and laughter, and I got up and hugged Abby and Will.

Ethan objected, "But they didn't do the rest of the thanks."

I hugged him too. "That's okay. We'll play the rest of the game later. Would you like dessert?"

"I want to watch the football game."

Daniel excused himself and he and Pops, Will and Gary went with Ethan into the living room. Soon, we could hear that steady crowd noise in the background, as we cleared off the table..

Abby came and put her arm around me. "Mom, you and Nana go put your feet up. Claire, Bailey, and I will put the food away and get dessert ready."

Nana and I did what we were told. Nana had brought her cross-stitching and was soon covered with tiny bits of colorful embroidery floss. I fell asleep in spite of the noise of the game. The next thing we knew, the girls invited us to come to the kitchen and get our dessert. They had arranged the pumpkin and apple pies buffet-style and there was about a gallon of real whipped cream. The men went for the coffee first, and pretty soon we were all back in our areas, enjoying the sweets.

I noticed that Claire, Abby, and Bailey were sitting at the table in the kitchen, talking earnestly. Occasionally, Abby or Claire would reach over and touch Bailey's arm. They were also laughing, which was a good sign.

Nana had noticed too. "I wonder what they've got up their sleeves?"

"I don't know, but it looks pretty serious. I'm so glad that Bailey can talk to others and that they also listen to her."

A cell phone rang and Daniel said, "It's mine." He talked for a moment and then got up from the floor and went into the hallway to get away from the football noise. When he was finished, he came back and said to me, "The police found my car."

18

Daniel's weekend was punctuated by more calls from the police. The car was "allegedly" used as a getaway vehicle in a bank robbery. There were many fingerprints all over the car, but of course Daniel's and Bailey's were most prominent. The police also found traces of gunpowder and meth in the car. They were holding the car as evidence until they caught the thieves.

"And my stereo equipment is all gone," Daniel lamented.

Unfortunately, because Daniel was a student with limited funds, and because the car was old, he didn't have comprehensive insurance to cover theft. My car, which often sat in the garage for days without being used, became transportation for Daniel to go to school and for Bailey to go to work. I just handed Daniel the fob and let them figure out their schedule.

After a few more days' work, Bailey announced that she was taking maternity leave, since the baby was due in two weeks. She didn't like being cooped up at our house, however, and one afternoon, I was the unwilling witness to an argument between her and Daniel.

I had been doing the final fittings for the forest green velvet bridesmaids' dresses, and the girls were coming and going throughout the whole day. It was just after the maid-of-honor left that Daniel popped in to bring our groceries.

Bailey hollered from the basement, "Daniel, don't leave!"

He waited at the top of the stairs.

There was bit of thumping, and then she slammed her door and came up the stairs, pulling herself up with the handrail.

"I need the car," she said.

"Um, so do I. Can I take you somewhere and drop you off?"

"Why can't I take *you* somewhere and drop *you* off?" she demanded.

"Because I have to go to a training session, and I don't know how long it will take."

With sudden sugar in her voice, she asked, "Well, can't you ask a friend to bring you home?"

"Can't you?" Daniel sighed, resigned. "Tell me where you need to go."

"It's none of your business," she snapped, glancing over to me. "I just need the car."

By now, I was getting interested in the conversation.

Daniel looked at his watch. "I'm leaving now. Tell me where you want to go, and I'll take you before my class starts."

She hesitated and then reached over and squeezed his arm. "Okay. I'll tell you in the car. Let's go."

Of course, I was very curious, but there was no way I could interfere in that discussion. They left, and I sat down at the sewing machine, trying to focus my mind on sewing.

Where could she be going that she wouldn't want me to know? Was she going to the casino? We hadn't met any of her friends, and I did often wonder when and if she saw them.

She returned just before supper.

Before she could escape to the basement, I noted, "I see you found a ride home."

"I did." She came into the kitchen and said, "Dorothy, I've been meaning to ask you something."

"Okay. Ask away."

"At Thanksgiving, I was talking to Abby and Claire, and they, like, thought it would be a good idea that I take childbirth classes. It's kind of late; they said that usually it's six weeks long, but I found one that crams everything into two weeks – which is, like, all the time I have left."

"That sounds like a good idea. Childbirth is definitely something you ought to learn about before you do it."

"Well, what I wanted to ask you was . . . .. Well, most everyone has someone to go through childbirth with them, sort of like a coach. A husband or a relative or a friend."

She paused, and I knew where she was going, and I wondered where I would get the courage to do it. The only childbirths I had ever experienced were my own and that was a long time ago.

Bailey continued, "I was wondering if . . . if you might be my coach? I know you have a wedding coming up. Would you have time to help me?" She rushed on. "They would train us both, so I will know what to do, and so that you will know how to help me." She sighed a shaky little sigh and said in a small voice, "I don't know who else to ask."

I took my own insecurity in hand and said, "I would be honored. Thank you for asking me. Yes. We will make it work." *Dear Lord, help me!*

"Thank you. What's for supper; I'm starved."

While we were cooking, I asked casually, "So, how was your afternoon?"

"Okay." She was now very good at making salads, but she paused and then amended, "Terrible. I went out with friends, just to, like, catch up – it has been a while. I thought we were going for ice cream – which we did – but then they wanted to do several Happy Hour stops. They got more and more soused, and

I was drinking soda water and apple juice. They were, like, really funny, but I wasn't, and pretty soon they weren't either."

"How did you get home?"

She grinned, "I took a taxi."

"Good for you!"

We would have begun the classes the following day, but the police called and wanted to interview Bailey.

"Why do they need to talk to me?" she demanded. "I'm the one someone stole the car from!"

"I really don't know," I admitted. "Do you want me to go with you?"

"Do you need to? Do I need a lawyer?"

"This isn't a TV mystery," I teased her. "They probably just want to know where the car was and if it was locked."

Daniel picked her up and took her to the police station. When they got back, Bailey was not happy.

"They asked me about all the people I know. and whether any of them had a key to the car or whether I told them where the car would be all day."

"They asked me all the same things," Daniel said. "You have to remember that they are looking for the person who robbed the bank. That person was driving my car."

"And they asked me about whether I took meth. Me!" She looked down at her very large belly. "I mean, look at me – as if I could rob a bank!"

Daniel chuckled. "Yes, Mom, you should have seen the poor detective who interviewed her. It was obvious from the start that they knew she had nothing to do with the robbery. The detective kept looking up from her notes as if she wished the day were over."

"Were you there?" I asked.

"No, but I could see them through the window of the office."

"Well," Bailey said, "I sure hope that's the end of it." She gasped and exclaimed, "Oh! We went out and bought stuff for the baby afterwards. You gotta see!"

We went out to the garage and brought in a disassembled crib, mattress, and a changing table. Daniel carried them downstairs, and we trailed after him to watch him reassemble the crib.

"Abby and Claire told me to go to the thrift stores, so we did."

"We went shopping," Daniel explained, "Because at the police station, Bailey had to give her birth date. It was yesterday!"

Bailey turned pink with pleasure. "So he said we needed to buy birthday presents. Aren't they great?"

"They are," I admitted. "Happy Birthday, dear! And I just realized that you need a car seat, as well. Gary and I will buy that for you."

"Really? I heard that it's not good to buy used ones."

"I've heard that too. It'll be our present for you." I went back upstairs, leaving Daniel to fiddle with the crib, but I remembered what I had been wanting to ask him, so I went back down.

Bailey was holding one end of the crib, while Daniel screwed the other end together.

"I need the car this Saturday for a wedding," I said. "Your dad is out of town, and I guess I'm doing this one by myself." I hesitated and then asked him, "Unless you're available? Do you want to come to the wedding? I can even pay you."

"Can't, Mom. I have a huge exam early next week, and I really can't spare any more time for anything."

"I'll go with you!" Bailey offered, and then looked as if the words coming out of her mouth had surprised her. "I mean, if you really need help," she finished lamely.

"Well, you won't be able to go into the groomsmen's dressing room, but if you think you'd like to come, there are always things to do." Actually, I could not think of anything, off the top of my head, that she could do, but I was so glad that she had offered.

Daniel patted the crib. "All done. Um, Mom, since the house will be empty on Saturday, could you pick me up early in the morning so I can study here? It'll be quieter than at my apartment, and there will be fewer temptations." He stopped and then grinned. "Except when I search for the pistachios."

Early Saturday morning – earlier than she had ever gotten up before, Bailey came up the stairs, despairing what she would wear.

"I have nothing that fits, and probably nothing appropriate anyway," she moaned.

I was gathering everything I needed for the wedding. "It's snowing too."

She glanced out the window. "Well, that could be romantic. I guess. What'm I gonna wear? I've got nothing!"

We went down and ransacked her closet, and that seemed to be true. Eventually, we found a gray, stretchy, sequined top that Connie had bought for her.

"Now, we just need a skirt."

"A skirt?"

"It's a wedding, and you are my assistant. I have a plain black skirt with an elastic waistband. I think we can fix it to fit you."

She followed me into my bedroom, but she was muttering the whole way. "A skirt? I don't do skirts. I'll look like a . . .." She stopped and laughed. "I almost said 'pregnant lady!' Oh, and by the way, I'm having a boy."

"Boys are wonderful!"

"I've been looking up names on the internet. But I'm not going to tell what I've decided."

"Good idea. Someone is bound to tell you about the person they hate with that name."

"Thought so." She hesitated and then continued. "But then I was looking up my name and Gary's and . . . and yours. Do you know that your name means 'Gift of God?'"

"I do." It always made me feel slightly unworthy when someone mentioned it.

"Well, you've been a gift to me."

"I'm glad." *No hugs*, I reminded myself.

She slipped into the skirt. Because she is taller than I am, with the waistband above the baby, the skirt swirled just at her knees. "Well, okay," she admitted, turning in front of the mirror. "This isn't too bad."

I looked at my watch. "Oh! I need to go pick up Daniel."

"I'll get him. Do you really want to drive in snow? You need a – a – what are they called that drive people around?"

"A chauffeur."

"Yeah. One of those. I'll get Daniel." She texted to let him know she was coming. "I wonder if he'll like how I look?"

I wonder.

19

We walked into the church and peeked into the sanctuary.

"Oh, my!" Bailey breathed. Actually, she didn't say 'oh, my;' she swore, but it was obvious she was dazzled by the beautiful decorations. "If I ever get married, it'll be at Christmastime."

"It's a great time to get married," I agreed, "because usually the venue is already decorated for the holidays, and that saves a lot of money."

"And the snowflakes outside the windows," she added, "And the dark green dresses against all the red and gold and lights!" She adjusted the velvet dresses she was carrying. "Where can I take these?"

"We need to find the wedding planner."

Eventually, we set up my 'headquarters' in a tiny room off the church office. Some of the bridal party had arrived, and they were finding their changing rooms, where we had hung the dresses.

"Now your job, Bailey, is to wander around and listen and watch for any little emergencies that I can solve: torn hems, broken zippers, lost buttons, broken heels, skinned knees. I'll be doing the same. Either find me, or bring them to me. Chat, be friendly, and feel free to ask if anyone needs anything. We can even run out to the store for snacks or socks if they forgot those."

"Socks?"

"Sometimes the groomsmen forget the right color socks."

She smiled, a look of relief on her face. "I can chat real good. This'll be fun!"

"You look very nice," I told her.

The smile was real and joyful. "See ya later!" and she was off to chat.

We were spared any huge emergencies, and several hours later, Bailey watched as I arranged the bride's dress and sent her down the aisle with her father. Then we went upstairs and slipped into the back row of the balcony.

The commitments the bride and groom made to each other were very natural and heartfelt. I was just beginning to enjoy myself, when the bride took off a ring from her pinky finger and showed it to her groom.

"My dad gave this to me when I turned twelve. It's a purity ring, and between him and me, we made a promise that I would keep myself for my one true love – you."

I felt Bailey stiffen beside me, but I didn't dare glance over at her. Her hands were in her lap, clenched with white knuckles.

The bride continued, "I give it now to you, as proof that you will always be the only man for me. Take it with my love."

Suddenly, Bailey leaned over and whispered, "I gotta go pee." She jumped up and bolted for the stairs.

I barely heard the rest of the ceremony. How could I have been so stupid? Bringing Bailey to a wedding like this one was a sure-fire way to inflict another wound on her. Why hadn't I seen that before it happened? I closed my eyes and tried to ask God how I was going to help her past this new hurt. Before the groom kissed his bride, I hurried downstairs to find the wedding planner.

"I was going to go to the reception, but I need to take my assistant home," I told her.

"That's fine. When is she due?"

"In about ten days."

"Well, you have both been wonderful. Thank her for us."

"Can I leave my sewing machine in the church office and pick it up on Monday?"

"I think so. Just stick your head in and let the secretary know."

I did that and then went to the ladies' room to find Bailey.

She was sitting on a chair in the powder room. When she heard me, she looked up from her lap and pushed away the tears.

"I can never do that!" she muttered sadly. "You know that? No one will ever have me." She paused and stifled a sob, "Well, no one like that man . . . or Daniel. I can never be good enough." Her voice began to rise in volume. "I've already ruined everything." She jumped to her feet. "I'm so angry! Why didn't anyone tell me this?"

"Let's go home, Bailey. The wedding is almost over, and we can go."

She picked up her little purse and threw the strap over her head, almost pushing me out of the way as she marched out the door. I followed but guided her through a back hallway to a parking lot exit. Snow had added a thin coating of ice to the parking lot.

"Careful," I said, "I don't want you falling."

I touched her, but she pulled away. "I'm fine!"

"Give me the keys," I said, holding out my hand.

"I can drive," she snapped.

"I don't want you to. It's my car."

"Fine!" She threw herself into the passenger seat and snapped her seatbelt around her very round belly. Something must have gone on inside her head because as I started the engine, she cast a look into the back seat and grumbled, "What about your sewing machine and things?"

"I'll get them Monday." We drove a few minutes in silence, and then I asked, "Would you like to stop somewhere and get tea, or would you just like to go home?"

"Home!" she stated bluntly.

We didn't speak again, until we turned into our street.

"Oh, damn! Daniel's home, isn't he?" she realized.

I had forgotten too. I drove past the house, a plan already forming in my head. Why did I feel so calm?

"Where are we going?" Bailey demanded.

"Rocks and Mortar. I need tea, and I don't want to talk with Daniel right now."

"Me, neither." She started to cry again.

I just drove.

After we parked at the coffee shop, I handed her a few tissues and then said, "Listen, Bailey, I am so sorry this happened. I never intended to have you hurt like this."

"You never do," she stated bluntly, "It just happens. I thought you wanted tea."

"Do you want to go in?"

She opened the door and got out, slamming the door behind her. I followed.

We ordered our hot drinks, and I led her to a table in the farthest corner, away from the TV's and other customers. I seated her facing the wall, so her voice wouldn't project into the room and no one could see her if she cried. We sipped our drinks in silence until Bailey finally spoke. "I'm not mad at you, Dorothy. I'm mad at . . . at the world. At my mother and father and all my friends. No one ever told me that I didn't have to . . . well, you know."

I nodded and decided that I needed to listen for a long time before I said anything.

"It's just so . . . so awful to think, like, I can never have what that girl has. There isn't a nice man in the whole world who would want me." She paused and looked at her stomach, "Or Bubba, here. I can never be good enough. I'm just so dirty and alone, and I've done, like, so many awful things. All the stuff we read about in the Bible study. You don't even know all the things I've done. I've done them all." She hesitated again. "Well, I've never murdered anyone. But right now, I'd gladly do that. I want to smash things and scream and swear." She looked around and hiccupped, laughing a bit hysterically. "They'd call the police, wouldn't they? We should have gone to the casino!"

"No one's going to call the police," I assured her calmly.

"What 'm I gonna do?" she wailed.

"About what?"

"My life? All I can see is working at The Gym for the rest of my life and trying to raise my little boy to be a better person than I am. But I don't even know how, because every time I try to change, something happens, or someone comes into my life to show me, like, I haven't changed a bit." She had been talking at the wall behind me, but now she shifted her eyes to look at me. "Oh, I'm so angry! Why did you take me there? All you did was show me how. . . how awful everything is! I think you did it on purpose to show me that Daniel would never want me." Her face crumpled up again as she began to sob.

"I'm sorry, but what does Daniel have to do with . . . all this?"

"I like Daniel," she wept.

"I like him too."

"Not like that; I thought he liked me, but now I know that he never will. I can never be good enough. Do you have another tissue?"

I did. I understood exactly what she was saying, and it disturbed me greatly, but for some reason my mind was able to focus in on her last statement. "Good enough for what?"

"To find a good man. Like Gary. But I've messed things up so much. And no one will want me, especially with a baby." She put her head in her hands and her shoulders shook with silent sobs. Perhaps some of those were for the baby.

I had hoped she would have wanted to be good enough for God. I knew that her happiness could not really rest on finding a good man, and if it did, it was a shaky foundation. I decided to say that.

I waited until she calmed a bit and handed her a napkin to mop her face. "Bailey, if your only desire in life is to have a good man to lean on, then you are choosing a very weak thing to lean on." She started to speak, but I held up my hand. "Let me finish. Joy and happiness do not come from having the right man. They come by having a right relationship with God. The young couple today were not hanging all their hopes on each other; they were trusting God – together – and that was where the joy and happiness for them will come from. Before you can find the right guy, you have to be the right woman, and that only happens if you are following God. And sometimes it doesn't even happen then. Life is uncertain. All that is certain is God."

She sniffed. "And why would God want me? He's – I mean – *really* good."

I smiled. "He is, but He loves you and – "

"I can't believe that! I'm not good enough."

"No. You're not. None of us are."

Bailey smirked. "Yeah, I remember you telling me about all your sins,"

"You don't have to put me down. There is no such thing as 'good enough' in God's sight. I don't know what you have been reading at Bible study, but you have already realized that you can't change yourself. Only God can change you."

"Big job!"

"Yes, it is, but God did the heavy lifting."

"How's that?"

"He realized that only He was big enough to change sinners into people who could love and please Him. The problem was that He is so holy that He cannot tolerate sin. He couldn't let those sins go unpunished, so He and Jesus decided that Jesus would become a man and would take the punishment for everyone's sins for them. And that's why it's called being saved from your sins. To be saved, we have to know what it is we are being saved from."

"Everyone's?" she asked in astonishment. "In the whole world? In all of history?"

"Yes."

"So, what's the catch? Why can't I change?"

"God won't change you unless you want Him to."

One side of her mouth tipped into a slight smile. "So, there *is* a catch," she said, with skepticism in her voice.

I was tired – amazed that God had given me what seemed to be the right things to say, but I was fizzling out. I could feel it. "What do you think?" I asked.

"I have to admit that I can't change."

That was pretty good. I nodded. "You have to give up the pride of assuming that you might *just* be able to change yourself."

I could tell she was thinking, so I added, "God loves and cares for humble people, but He hates sinful pride."

She straightened her shoulders and moved her neck as if it hurt. Her eyes wandered to the screen nearest us, on which a pretty girl was singing.

Our hearts are restless
Until they find rest in You.
Our hearts are restless
Until they find rest in You.
This is where my hope lies
This is where my soul sighs
I will always find my rest in You.
("Rest in You," by All Sons and Daughters, 2016,
Written by Leslie Jordan, Peter Leonard, Cara Fox)

Bailey sighed. "I think my heart is very restless."

I nodded. "Perhaps. But it has nothing to do with Daniel or with finding a good man. To find a godly man, you have to first become the woman God wants you to become."

She gathered our cups and napkins. "I think I understand that now; it's just me and God. Can you tell me how to do this?"

"You need to talk to God about it – just like you've been talking to me. You can use your own words. It's called prayer."

She blew air out of her mouth and announced, "Let's go home."

"Would you like to go buy a car seat first?"

"Let's!"

· 20 ·

As Christmas drew nearer, I did not ask Bailey if she had talked to God yet. I had told Gary about our conversation, and was able to express my wonder at being able to say the right things at the right time. We put the Christmas tree up, and we included Bailey in the evening of decorating. She seemed different – gentler, maybe – but I didn't know if I was seeing only what I wanted to see. The baby's space in Bailey's room was ready. I still had not revisited the idea of a baby shower. Perhaps after the birth would be a better time.

Then Bailey's due date came. She prowled around the house, grumbling and nibbling on carrot sticks and hot dogs. "*How* will I *know*?" she demanded, as she wandered into the living room after lunch.

I was working on a baby quilt. She had chosen the colors and pattern, and it would hang on the wall near the baby's crib. "Oh, you'll know!" I assured her. "Maybe you ought to go reread the material from the childbirth classes, and we could do another practice session."

"I'm tired of practicing," she pouted. "I just want to get this over with!" She put her hand to her back and flexed it as best she could, to emphasize how miserable she was.

I returned to sewing, and she lowered herself onto the couch and pulled out her cell phone to do whatever young people do on their cell phones.

The next morning, she arrived at the breakfast table with plans for the day. "I want to go for a walk," she demanded. "The book said that walking can encourage the baby to come."

"Good idea, but let's go to the mall. The sidewalks are icy."

"But then I have to wait until 10. I want to go now!" Was she stamping her foot?

"I'm not finished with breakfast. What would you like?"

She eased onto the kitchen chair and snapped, "You know what I like!"

Gary raised his eyebrows. I remembered reading that expectant mothers can get pretty grumpy right before the baby comes. "Was I like this?" I asked him.

He chuckled. "Probably. Time has erased unpleasant memories."

"I'm not being unpleasant!" Bailey complained unpleasantly.

I stood. "Hard-boiled egg and jelly toast, right?"

"Ugh! Egg sounds awful! Don't we have any hot dogs?"

"Why don't you take her to The Warehouse?" Gary suggested.

"Because I hate the Christmas crush," I reminded him.

Bailey perked up. "Ooooh! I want to go to The Warehouse. They have really big hot dogs."

Gary grinned and waved his hand, "The pregnant lady wants to go to The Warehouse," he said matter-of-factly.

I grinned a fake grin back. "Fine, but you're driving."

"Why me?" he asked.

"Because it's icy, and I don't want to drive, and Bailey won't fit behind the steering wheel!"

Bailey punched my arm. "I'll get my coat."

Gary dropped us off at the front door, where there were no carts available. That was not a problem, however, because we headed straight for the hot dogs. The line was long, and Gary caught up with us just as we were ordering. "I'm having pizza," he informed us.

When Bailey had eaten half her hot dog, she said, "Okay, I'm full. Let's go home."

I wasn't going to let her boss us around. "Nope. You said you wanted to walk. Let's walk."

"But it's so boring here!"

"We'll buy a package of hot dogs."

Gary agreed to meet us by the books, and I decided to walk Bailey up and down every aisle. We finally found a cart, and Bailey guided us first to the baby clothes and then to the toys.

"What shall I buy?"

"He's not going to need anything for a while. Most babies are happy with a brightly colored measuring cup and a spoon."

"Really?" she squeaked. "You're not pulling my leg?"

"Really."

So, we went to find the measuring cups.

We piled hot dogs into the cart. and then Bailey insisted on buying a pair of jeans in her pre-pregnancy size. "I *am* going to be thin again!" she announced.

Since she was in a spending mood, I suggested more diapers and wipes, which she thought was a good idea. I had already gotten most of my Christmas shopping done, but when I saw a bright red, loose-fitting Christmas dress, I knew Bailey would love it. She would need something new to cheer her, once she discovered that she was not going to be instantly thin again. I would take it to the hospital and surprise her.

I steered her over to where Gary was still perusing the books.

"Why don't you get some little books for him?" I suggested to Bailey.

She barely noticed when I left. I told Gary what I was doing, and then I fetched the dress and went through the checkout, which seemed to take forever. After texting Gary, who didn't answer, I texted Bailey and told her I was ready to go.

I waited a long time for them, and by the time they were through the checkout, Bailey was craving the other half of her hot dog. She started to rummage through my boxes.

"Hey! There are presents in there. Get out."

"But I want my hot dog."

"I'll get it."

About ten minutes after getting settled in the car, she moaned and said, "I feel like I felt when I had appendicitis."

Gary snorted. "Probably indigestion from that healthy hot dog!"

I slapped his thigh.

"Don't make me laugh," she begged. "It hurts."

"Constant, or coming and going?" I asked.

"Coming and going," she said in a small voice. Then suddenly, she shouted, "Oh! Is the baby coming?"

"Could be. Let's get you home."

"But shouldn't I go to the hospital?"

"Not yet. They don't want you until the pains are regular and fairly close together."

"But what if we don't make it home?"

"We will."

We did.

The emotional roller-coaster continued into the night. As her labor contractions increased, she vacillated between swearing and then apologizing, feeling sorry for herself and then telling me how grateful she was that I was there. She even asked me to pray with her one time when things got really intense. "I think I'm dying!" she whimpered, "Do women die in childbirth?" Mostly, though, she was very brave – and funny, at times – and did everything she was told to do – first by me and then later by the hospital staff.

Peter Gary Austin was born at 4:37 the following morning. Both Bailey and I were completely wiped out, but she seemed pleased and took to nursing him right away. We left her in hospital to sleep. Gary chauffeured me home, where I collapsed into bed.

Later that morning, Gary woke me with a kiss and tea and breakfast in bed.

"Eggs Benedict? Whereever did you get these?"

"I ordered them from Daisy's Diner. You deserved something better than hot dogs." He opened the bedroom curtains. It was snowing again.

I arranged the pillows and took a sip of tea. "Oh, dear, we have to go out in this to bring Bailey home. Before noon. Where's my watch? What time is it? It's after 11! I don't have time to eat."

"You do," Gary told me. "Daniel's going to bring her home."

It took my breath away. "Daniel?" I ran my fork through the hollandaise sauce and licked it off. "Oh, I – I don't know what to think."

"That reminds me: Daniel said I have to take my car out of the garage – " He paused to make 'air quotation marks', "So she doesn't have to walk on the snow and ice."

"Were those his exact words?"

He smiled sympathetically. "Exact. He came earlier this morning and put the car seat into your car and took it. I'll be back in a minute."

I picked at my breakfast, but soon realized I was really hungry. I had eaten through half of it before he returned to the bedroom.

"Gary, do you think Daniel has fallen for her?"

"No, I don't." He got his plate of eggs from the dresser and sat down on the chair beside the bed. "Do you remember when he said that women like Bailey needed good men to care for them properly? Or something like that."

"I do," I answered suspiciously. "Is that what he's doing?"

"I think he has decided to woo her."

"That shouldn't be hard," I said, too unkindly, "She's crazy about him. But fortunately, she doesn't think she's good enough for him."

"Fortunately? Honey, you're becoming a snob."

"And she – as far as I know – hasn't gotten things right between her and God. She can't possibly be the woman we have asked God to give to Daniel. Surely he wouldn't go for a girl who doesn't love the Lord. "

"No, but he also wouldn't lead her on. Honestly, Dottie, we have no idea what is going on between them – or between her and God, for that matter. Daniel's a man; he'll figure it out."

We finished breakfast and I got into the shower. My thoughts ran into corners I would not tell Gary or anyone else. Ultimately, I didn't like the idea of Bailey as a daughter-in-law. I wanted him to have a sweet Christian girl from his Bible study. I knew my thoughts were skewed and ugly. After all, Jesus died for all the sins and washed us white as snow. He could do that for

Bailey, but that wouldn't change the facts that this baby was not ours.

I dried off and dressed, trying to banish the thoughts from my mind. Although I wasn't hungry, I figured Daniel and Bailey would be, so I fixed a simple lunch for them.

They arrived in the early afternoon, Daniel carrying the baby carrier in one hand and supporting Bailey into the house with the other. She was wearing the red dress, and she looked beautiful. Daniel freed little Peter from his carrier straps, and Bailey lifted him out. Their looks of tenderness that poured onto the tiny baby, brought tears to my eyes.

She turned to me. "Do you want to hold him?" she asked me.

"Yes. Let me sit down." I did and then I held out my arms.

She set the tiny bundle into them. "Isn't he beautiful?"

"He is. Absolutely."

"This is your Aunty Dorothy," she told him and then looked at me hopefully. "Granny Dorothy? What do you like?"

I shrugged. "He will probably have his own name for me."

While they ate lunch, Gary and I took turns holding the baby. Then Bailey said to Daniel, "I think I need to take him downstairs." She retrieved Peter from Gary and spoke softly to the little boy: "Time for you to see where we live."

Daniel fetched her backpack from the car, and Gary carried the baby carrier down to Bailey's room. When Daniel came back upstairs, he muttered, "That baby needs a father," and then he seemed to pull himself together and asked, "Can one of you take me home? I really need to study."

21

That baby needs a father! But did the father have to be our Daniel? This thought niggled at the back of my mind all through the rest of the Christmas season. I even tried to pray it away, but every prayer ended in imagining all that could go wrong in such a relationship. The book of Hosea in the Bible kept coming back to me. The wonderful, faithful Hosea married the girl with a dodgy past, and even when she betrayed him, he still loved her because God told him to. It couldn't have been a happy life for him, and I wanted a happy life for my son. Sometimes I ended up crying, and hoping no one noticed. The worst of it was that I knew that the whole situation was of my making. I still cared about Bailey, but I felt like everything was out of control, and no one else seemed to notice.

The week of Christmas, everyone else seemed happy. Abby was blooming in her pregnancy. She was past the scary time, and she and Will were decorating a baby room. Abby chose colors and pattern for a quilt, and I decided to work on it right after the holidays and before the wedding orders started coming in.

Gary's real estate business was slow, but he enjoyed the extra time at home to work on projects in the garage. He was building Abby and Will a crib.

Although it was winter break, Daniel was immersed in reading textbooks for his last semester. "I probably won't see much of you this semester until I finish my papers," he warned us, "Then I have to study for the BAR exam." Bailey seemed to get the lion's share of his free time, and he was often at our house, holding Peter or running errands for Bailey. Sometimes I would find him with a sleeping baby on one arm and holding a textbook in the other hand, while Bailey napped.

As for Bailey, she nursed Peter, fussed over him when he cried, changed his diapers gladly, and caught naps during his. She ate whatever we put in front of her and drank quarts of juice and water. She was impatient to begin jogging again, but willing to go for walks in the mall.

Christmas day, we got up early and had a breakfast that Gary and Daniel cooked for us. Then we opened presents. Abby and Will were having their Christmas morning alone as a couple, which was the way it should be – setting up their own traditions. We saw them later after we all trooped over to Nana and Pops' house for more presents and Christmas dinner.

Nana and Pops lived in a small Craftsman house with a huge wrap-around porch and tiny rooms inside. Her kitchen was very old-fashioned, but the smells coming out of it were heavenly. The dining room table was decorated within an inch of its life with holly and candles and red placemats. They had a small tree on a table in the bay window of the living room, and there were presents for everyone under it. Pops' assignment was to keep the Christmas music playing in the background. Nana had provided Bailey with the pretty guest room so she and the baby could get away from the hubbub.

It was during one of those rest times before dinner, that Bailey emerged from the hallway looking pale and studying her cell phone. Some of us had been playing impromptu charades, and it took a moment for us to stop laughing and to register that Bailey was stressed.

She glanced around the room at us and dropped her arms to her sides. "I'm tired," she said flatly and turned and went back down the hallway.

We looked at one another, and I said, "Shall I go see what's up?"

"Somebody should," agreed Nana.

Daniel stood. "I'll go." He went, and the rest of us got up to go to the bathroom or to get something from the kitchen. He was back in two minutes. "Bailey wants to talk to you, Mom."

I found Bailey sitting on the bed with her cell phone still in her hand. She was frowning at the floor, and Peter was making little squeaking noises from the middle of the double bed.

I pulled up the rocking chair and sat down. "Daniel said you wanted to talk to me?"

She shook her head as if she could not believe it, and held up her cell phone. "My mother just called."

"Okay," I said cautiously.

"She wished me a Merry Christmas, and she wondered why I hadn't stopped by to wish her one."

"Oh." I paused, hoping my mental gears would get going. "Would you like to?"

"No!" she snapped and then added quietly, "I . . . I just don't know what to do." Her voice grew wistful. "I mean, maybe I should see her, and as you said a while ago, maybe she ought to know she is a grandma – although still I don't think she will be happy about that," she finished abruptly.

"You never can tell." I glanced over at Peter..

"He *is* beautiful, isn't he?" she said with a slight smile.

"I could go with you – Gary and I could both go with you." What was I saying?

She shook her head again. "I don't want to go there. It's . . . it's dirty and there's probably a boyfriend there. You had said once that we could invite her to us. Should I do that?"

"You could." A plan was whirling in my head. "We could invite her here, right now, for dinner. I mean, I'd clear it with Nana, of course, but I think she would agree."

"No!" she exclaimed, horror on her face, "This is too fast. I need to think about it."

"Did you tell her you have a baby?"

She looked sheepish. "No."

I chuckled, "Well, *that* will be a surprise. What *did* you tell her?"

"Merry Christmas, and maybe I'd see her today or tomorrow."

I leaned forward and removed the cell phone from her hand and took both of hers in mine. "Bailey, the people in this house love you, and we will all be here for you. If your mother is unpleasant, Pops can throw her out."

She started to giggle, but it ended in a sob. "But I don't know what she will say," she lamented, "She is not like all of you, and she knows so many things about me that I . . . that would make you all hate me. She can be so mean," she ended in a wail.

"I don't think there is anything she can tell us that would make us hate you. And if she is that mean, why would we want you to face her alone?"

Peter started to cry, and Bailey pulled away from me, saying, "He's hungry again."

"Okay. Tell me how you want to do this. Do you think you should see your mother?"

"Probably." The reluctance in her voice made me doubt her word. "But if I got it over with, then I wouldn't have to see her again, right?"

"That's true."

"Do you really think Nana and Pops wouldn't mind? She might ruin their beautiful Christmas dinner."

"Or it might be the nicest Christmas dinner she has ever had."

She snorted. "That wouldn't be hard."

"Shall I ask them? And you stay here and feed Peter. I'll be back and help you with the phone call."

"Okay. Thanks."

When I stood to go, she sprang from the bed and surprised me with an awkward hug!

Nana suggested that it might be easier on everyone, if we invited Bailey's mother for dessert later in the afternoon. Everyone agreed. When Bailey came from the bedroom, she handed Peter to me and called her mother, with all of us listening.

"Hallo, Mom. It's Bailey . . . Yes, Merry Christmas . . . Um, the people I'm staying with wanted to invite you for dessert later this afternoon . . . Well, they didn't say you could invite him, but . . .." She looked around at us helplessly, and Nana shrugged and nodded her head. "Sure. This way we can see each other today . . .." She was trying so hard to make it sound like a good thing. "Um . . . What? No, you don't have to dress up. We are all in jeans and . . . No, no presents. We are all done with that . . . Why do they? Um, they – they just like having people over for the holidays, I guess, and since you wanted to see me, they thought you'd like to come here . . .." Her shoulders sagged. "Of course,

I want to see you. Can you come? . . . about 4:30." She gave the address and said, "Okay, then, see you later." She clicked off her phone and looked sheepish. "I lied to her; I told her I wanted to see her."

Daniel reached over and took her phone.

"What are you doing?" she asked.

"Turning it off. That way she can't call back."

"But . . .."

"If she comes, she comes."

Pops was positively jovial. "Good job, Bailey! When do we eat, Mama?"

Everyone helped bring the food from the kitchen to the buffet at one side of the room, from which Nana would serve everyone. The roast was set at the head of the table before Pops for him to carve. But first, he asked God's blessing on everyone at the table and on the delicious dinner, and he asked especially for God to intervene when Bailey's mother came for dessert. It didn't help Bailey's appetite, however, and she didn't eat as much as the rest of us did.

I think 4:30 rolled around sooner than any of us wanted. The house was smelling like apple dumplings, and Pops had started up the Christmas music again. At about 4:15, Bailey started pacing, and I felt like doing so myself, but stayed firmly in my chair. The doorbell rang almost on the dot of 4:30, and Nana and Pops answered it, with Bailey hiding behind them.

"Merry Christmas!" exclaimed Nana.

"Am I at the right address? Does Bailey live here?"

"She doesn't live here, but she is here." Nana pulled Bailey into the doorway so her mother could see her and then said, "Come in. It's cold out there."

Pops pushed forward and put out his hand, "I'm Ken. Welcome to our home and merry Christmas. Let me take your coat. This is my wife, Twila, and here's your beautiful daughter."

Into the house came a short, plump woman with bleached hair, tied up in a ponytail with a red velvet ribbon. She was wearing tight yoga pants and a long bright green tunic, decorated with silver, sequin Christmas trees. She didn't look scary.

Bailey's mother shook hands with Nana and Pops, and then dragged Bailey into an embrace. "My goodness, you've put on a bit of weight." Bailey pushed away, frowning and looking as if she might hit the woman.

Nana prompted cheerfully, "And I didn't catch your name?"

"Oh, my goodness! Didn't Bailey tell you? I'm Josie. Oh, and Carl couldn't come. He had to visit his nephew and family."

"Please come in, Josie, and have a seat," Nana said. She introduced the rest of us and then said, "I'm just going to put the coffee on."

Josie chose the center of the couch like a queen on her throne, patting the spot next to her for Bailey to sit. Bailey shuffled to the couch and perched on the very edge.

"So how are you, Sweetie?"

"I'm fine," Bailey murmured. She jumped up and said, "I'll be right back."

Josie turned to Gary, and said, "It's right nice of you to give my Bailey a nice place to live. That last place she lived in was a wreck. I hope she's paying you enough. Young people can eat an awful lot. How much is her rent?"

Gary was saved from answering by Bailey's entrance into the living room with little Peter in her arms. "Mom, this is my baby, Peter."

The room went silent as we all waited for Josie's reaction. Bailey seated herself back on the couch, this time looking much more confident and a lot less like a thundercloud. "He was born two weeks ago."

"Well, knock me over with a feather! Why didn't you tell me? I must say, I'm floored." Josie was quiet for half a minute and then said, "A baby! Well, isn't he fine!" She leaned over to peer more closely at the sleeping baby. "Lemme hold him," she demanded holding out her arms.

Bailey pulled away. "No. He's sleeping."

"Well, I should know how to hold a sleeping baby!" She looked around the room for support. "Raised two of my own!" she quipped.

I finally spoke, "Bailey's a good mother and knows what Peter needs."

Gary cleared his throat and jumped in, "So, Josie, what do you do?"

She giggled and ran her finger over the sequins on her tunic. "I guess you could say I'm a housewife." She smiled at him and added, "I do volunteer at the food bank on Thursdays."

Bailey rolled her eyes.

Josie threw the question back to Gary, who said, "I'm a realtor."

"Ooh, there must be good money in that. Bailey, you ought to get into real estate. Lots more money than working at the casino."

Daniel spoke up. "She doesn't work at the casino. She is developing a fitness course at The Gym."

Josie shifted her attention to Daniel. "Does she, now? Well, it's good to hear that she's coming up in the world. And what do you do?"

"I'm a student," he stated bluntly.

Nana, who had been standing in the doorway to the dining room, announced, "Dessert is ready. Please come to the table."

We all got up and found our places, a bit more squished, having added Josie, who sat beside Bailey. Bailey still held Peter, and positioned him so that Bailey's shoulder was turned away from Josie. I thought she was using him as a shield between her and her mother.

"Oh, Nana," exclaimed Will, "You made my favorite: apple dumplings! I hope there's enough cream for everyone else."

The pastries, steaming hot from the oven, were sitting on a huge platter in the center of the table. Fortunately, Nana always made an extra one for Will to take home, so there were enough to go around. Pops served, and then we passed the jugs of thick cream.

"I have to watch my waistline," Josie tittered.

Abby warned, "Careful, they're very hot!"

Nana served coffee and tea. Most of us burned our tongues on the piping hot apples, but it was worth it.

"What's this in the middle?" asked Josie.

"Raisins, walnuts and cinnamon."

"Can't do walnuts," Josie announced, "They get caught in my bridgework." She spit several pieces of walnut onto her plate, and then looked up to say, "But it tastes mighty fine. I'll eat the apple and cream," but she left the delectable pie crust on her plate as well.

I was sitting on the other side of Bailey, at the end of the table with Nana. At one point, while we were eating, she looked over at me and asked, "So, Dorothy, wasn't it? What do you do?"

I finished chewing and swallowed. "I'm a seamstress."

"A seamstress. That means you sew things?"

"Yes."

"What kind of things?"

How could I know that I was about to stumble into a problem? "I sew mostly dresses for proms and for weddings."

Josie had just stuffed a large bite of the apple into her mouth, but her mouth dropped open anyway. Through the apple, she mumbled. "Imagine that!" She kept chewing and said, "You make wedding dresses! You can make me one! I'm getting married in February."

Daniel spoke up again, "You can't afford her."

His bluntness surprised me.

"Nonsense! I'm Bailey's mama; I'm sure there's a discount for Bailey's relatives."

Bailey pushed her chair back and stood up, looking into her mother's lap. Her voice was flat and emotionless. "You're marrying Carl."

Josie giggled again, "Who else? Of course, Carl. What did you think?"

Bailey turned to me and asked, "Would you hold Peter? I need to go . . . you know."

I gathered the sweet-smelling bundle into my arms, very aware that this was a pointed snub of her mother.

Josie also saw this and sniffed. "Well! Won't even let his own grandmother hold him!" Then she looked across the table at Pops and Will and whined, "You work so hard to raise them, and then they leave without saying thanks. She's got you bamboozled, I tell you. I could tell you a story or two – !"

Gary interrupted. "We don't need any stories, thank you. I think we all need to give Nana and Pops their house back. They've worked hard and deserve a quiet Christmas evening."

Will took the cue and helped Abby with her chair. "Thank you for the lovely day."

Everyone began to gather their things, while I held Peter and watched him breathe.

Will and Abby shook hands with Josie, hugged and kissed everyone else and told us they would see Bailey later. They left, and we turned to Josie. She moved reluctantly toward the door, although she kept looking down the hallway, I guess hoping that Bailey would come out of the bathroom. She did eventually.

Josie stood at the door, fastening her coat. "Where do you live, Bailey?" she asked.

Gary answered, "She lives with us."

"And where is that?"

"On the south side of the city."

"Well, I need to know, if I'm going to have my wedding dress made by Dorothy, here."

"Bye, Mom," Bailey said bluntly.

"Well, it's been real nice!" Josie tried to sound glad. "Nice to see your baby, and I hope we can do it again. G'Night, all."

Pops closed the door, and we all stood a moment in silent relief. Bailey started to cry, and Daniel led her back to the couch and sat down with her. I lowered myself into the rocking chair with Peter, and Gary helped Nana and Pops clear off the table. It was a few minutes before Bailey could speak. "You all were wonderful," she said through her tears. "Thank you. Where's Peter?"

I brought him to her and she snuggled her face into his belly. "I'm all the family you've got, Petey. But we've got good friends."

Just then, the doorbell rang.

Bailey shuddered.

"It's okay," Pops said, "It's only Will and Abby."

"What?" Bailey asked.

"This afternoon, after you called your mother, we all decided that when it was time for her to go, Will and Abby would be the first to leave. Christmas isn't over; we haven't had our late-night roast beef sandwiches yet!"

22

When we so blithely invited Josie for Christmas dessert, I don't think any of us realized the ramifications that we would have to live through in the next few weeks. The morning after Christmas day, Bailey did not come up to fix her usual breakfast of bagel and cream cheese with orange juice. I heard Peter cry for a little while, but then all was quiet. By 10, I decided to see what was up.

I tapped quietly on her door.

"Come in," I heard her say.

I opened the door. She was still in bed, propped up on pillows with Peter in her arms. Her eyes were red from crying.

"Are you all right?"

"Of course. I just decided to stay in bed. Is that a problem?"

"No. Are you hungry? I made waffles."

She sighed. "You heard my mother: I really need to lose weight."

I wanted to tell her that her mother was wrong, but I limited myself to: "You will. Nursing Peter and all your exercise will guarantee that."

She snorted. "Look at you: you didn't lose your weight."

I looked down at my less-than-in-shape body. "I didn't try very hard."

"Well, I'm going to."

I thought for a moment and then asked, "Would you like some fruit?"

"I'm fine," she said coldly. "When I get hungry, I'll come get something, okay?"

I know when I'm not wanted. "Okay," and I left.

When she finally did come up, it was after 2 in the afternoon. She mumbled "Hullo," boiled a couple eggs, and took an apple and a glass of milk and went back downstairs with them.

I made supper, but she did not come up to eat, and we went to bed without seeing her again.

"I wonder if her mother's visit caused this?" I asked Gary as we were getting ready for bed. "Maybe she misses her."

He chuckled. "I don't think so. Bailey was cold and hard toward her, and she deliberately gave you Peter to hold."

"What about 'Baby Blues?'"

"What about them? What are they?"

"Oh, I don't know; some women get depressed after a baby is born, and their hormones get all messed up, and they cry and start having trouble being a mother."

"She is a mother – and a good one."

"I know, but what if she needs a bit of counseling?"

Gary shrugged. "Call Connie. She'll know what to do, and if Bailey needs a counsellor, Connie'll probably know one." He headed toward the bathroom to brush his teeth. "On second thought, it's only been one day. Give her a chance to recover from seeing her mother."

But she didn't seem to recover. The next day, when she did come up, it was to fix herself a meagre lunch, just after I had finished mine.

"Dorothy, I need to talk to you about Peter, once I go back to work."

I had been rinsing the dishes, but I turned around to let her know she had my full attention. "Okay."

"How'm I going to continue to give him breast milk when I'm at work all day?"

"I suppose you'll need a breast pump."

"Weird." She dropped onto one of the kitchen chairs.

"Maybe, but plenty of working mothers use them, and then your daycare workers can feed Peter your milk."

"That's another thing: I really don't want to give him to just any daycare worker."

I had a sneaking suspicion that I knew where this conversation was headed, but I refused to take the bait. "Well, you have time to interview some and choose the best one. Maybe The Gym has daycare in the building. Have you asked?"

She heaved a huge sigh. "No. I only have eight more weeks of maternity leave." Her face crumpled, and she began to cry. How many times in the past three days had this girl who never cries broken into tears. "I don't know how I can bear leaving him alone," she sobbed.

"You won't be leaving him alone," I said automatically. "People will take good care of him." But I was already thinking about eight more weeks of having her around all the time.

"But he won't know them," she wailed. "Oh, I wish someone who knew him could take care of him."

"Such as?"

"Oh, I don't know . . . Nana? She's cross-stitching a picture for Peter."

"She's too old to take care of a baby. There's a reason why young people have babies."

"And what's that?" She wiped away the tears with the back of her hands.

"Energy level, strength, stamina."

"Abby?" she asked hopefully.

"Bailey, she's expecting her own baby. Would you have wanted to care for someone else's baby while you were pregnant?"

"Of course not! But I had a job. Abby doesn't. I could pay her."

I was getting tired of the conversation. "Just call The Gym and see if they have daycare."

She wasn't listening. "Or you could watch him, then he'd be right at home, and I wouldn't have to even put him in the car."

"I'm not going to be your babysitter."

"But you're home all day! How much more work can it be? He's just a baby, and he sleeps all the time."

"For now, yes, but what about later?" I interrupted myself. "Why am I arguing with you? I'm not watching Peter while you are at work."

She jumped up and shoved the chair violently against the table. "I thought you were wanting to help me!" she shouted. "You're not making my life any easier. I may as well move out!" She stormed downstairs and slammed her door. A few minutes later I heard Peter begin to cry.

How could I have handled this differently? I didn't know. But it seemed like we were back at square one. It was going to be a long eight weeks.

I called Connie and told her what was going on.

"Baby blues," she told me, "Only last for a few days – maybe a week – usually starting a few days after the birth. They clear up on their own."

"But it's been two weeks since Peter was born."

"Well, give her a little time. She's probably exhausted. Most younger women have no idea how sleep-deprived they are. And if there is anything you can do to help her, that might alleviate the strain."

"Like what? She's already asked me to watch Peter when she goes back to work."

"Oh," Connie said slowly in that knowledgeable tone of voice. "What did you say?"

"I said no."

"That's good." She was quiet for a few seconds and then said, "Things like doing laundry for her – things that a mother would normally do."

It was my turn to be quiet. "Perhaps some of the women in her Bible study could do that. I'm afraid that if I start doing laundry for her, it would never end.

"Could you offer to rock him for a bit while she takes a nap?"

I laughed. "Yes, I could manage that."

"And Dorothy, if the baby blues linger, she could have Post-Partom Depression. Let me know, and I'll recommend a counselor."

A few afternoons later, I heard Peter crying and went down and rapped on her door.

"What!"

"May I come in?"

"Yeah."

I opened the door. The room smelled like sour milk. Bailey was propped up in bed again, and Peter was crying so loudly that we had to talk over him.

"I was wondering if you'd like me to take Peter for a little while so you could get a nap. I'm sure you must be tired with the middle-of-the-night feedings."

She shrugged. "A nap sounds great. But only if you want to."

"I do." I went to the crib and picked up the squalling baby in his blanket. "I'll just take a diaper and burp rag as well. When does he eat next?"

She shrugged again. "Whenever I feed him," she snapped, and then amended it in a softer voice, "Around five."

Peter was already calmer. "Have a good sleep." At the doorway, I turned and took Peter's tiny hand and waved it at Bailey. "Nighty-night, Mama."

She smiled. "You be a good boy for Granny Dorothy."

I closed the door and hoped she would really sleep.

By five, Peter was definitely restless and hungry. I took him downstairs and knocked on Bailey's door. No sound. I called her on her phone, and she picked up and muttered groggily, "'Lo?"

"It's Dorothy. Peter's ready to eat."

"'Kay."

I knocked on her door again, and she opened it and held out her arms for the bundle of baby. "Thanks," she said, "I really needed that nap."

"Glad I could help." I wanted to offer to do it every day, but I thought I needed to talk to Gary first. A commitment like that would be hard to break. "Supper at 6?

"Sounds good. I'll feed him and then shower."

I started to cut up broccoli for supper, and Gary came home. He clicked on the Christmas tree lights, and pulled the curtains in the living room. "What have you been doing all day?" he asked with a grin.

"Coping with Bailey," I told him quietly. "I talked to Connie, and she suggested that Bailey may just need a nap. So, I held Peter for a couple hours, while she slept."

"Did she sleep?"

I became aware of Peter crying downstairs. "I think so. But I think I need a small folding bed for him up here, and then I can do it more often, while still being able to sew." I threw the broccoli in a pan with water and put it on the stove.

Gary sighed. "Is this something else you should say 'no' to?"

"I don't think so. When we took her in, we knew there would be hidden demands. It really wasn't that hard to hold him. In fact, I like holding him, but I just need a safe place to put him down."

We were interrupted by Bailey running up the stairs with Peter, who was squalling lustily. "Dorothy! I don't have any milk! What am I going to do? He won't stop crying and I don't know what to do."

Calm. Be calm. "I'm pretty sure you have milk. Sometimes it just seems as if we don't."

She jiggled Peter, trying to get him to stop crying. "But he nurses and then – " She broke off and looked at Gary. "Excuse me, but do you have to listen in?" she snapped.

He shrugged and withdrew to his office.

She watched him go and then repeated darkly, "He nurses, but no milk comes and then he cries."

"Maybe he's had enough."

"He hasn't had any yet," she said in exasperation.

I thought for a moment and then suggested, "You haven't been eating very much. Have you been drinking enough liquids?"

"I don't want to get all bloated," she protested.

I reached out and took the baby from her. He was sweaty from crying, and his voice was almost louder than ours. "Your number one job right now is to feed Peter. It doesn't matter if you ever get your pre-pregnancy figure back or not; you need to take care of your body so you can nourish him. Do you have a pacifier?"

"A what?"

"That thing that babies suck on."

"Well, Duh!"

I opened my mouth to reprimand her, but she immediately said, "I'm sorry. That was mean."

I nodded. "I'll hold him and walk him, and I want you to drive to the pharmacy and ask the pharmacist to help you choose a formula for Peter. We will call the pediatrician in the morning."

She ran down, put on some clothes, got the pacifier, grabbed her billfold and my keys, and was out the door.

The broccoli had begun to burn, and it smelled awful.

Gary emerged from his banishment and turned off the stove, carefully removing the offending pan to the deck outside.

Peter was beside himself with hunger, and I didn't feel much better. Over the screaming baby, Gary asked, "Pizza?"

I blew him a kiss and touched the pacifier to Peter's lips. He sucked it for a few seconds, and then turning his head away, he started to scream again. *Dear Lord*, I thought, *please help this little one, and help his mother, and help us to know how to help her.* We were just going to have to tough this one out.

23

New Year's Eve has never been particularly important to our family. Sometimes we have attended parties, but only to support the people hosting them. Staying up until midnight is sheer torture, and we usually leave before the clock strikes twelve.

Bailey had been restless all day. She kept coming upstairs and standing in front of the open refrigerator door, and then she would leave without any food. Gary was watching a college football game, although most of them would be broadcast the next day, and at one point, he invited her to watch with him.

"Don't understand football," she muttered and went back downstairs.

Later, I suggested that she join us in the living room and put Peter in the little bed we now had off to one side. She agreed.

It took her a while to come back up with Peter, but when she did, she was wearing one of her pretty maternity dresses, now classily cinched at the waist with a belt. Peter was dressed in an outfit I had made him – little blue overalls with a floppy-eared doggie on the front pocket.

"Wow! You look nice."

"It's New Year's Eve," she said simply.

Gary shifted in his chair and announced, "I put on my best socks this morning."

Bailey chuckled and laid Peter in the bed, before plunking herself down next to him. Then she asked, "Okay, so what's a 'down'?"

Gary loved to expound eloquently on football, so I went to the kitchen and tried to put together a festive New Year's Eve supper. There wasn't much fun in the fridge, but I made biscuits and tuna salad and found a frozen peach pie in the freezer.

The game ended, and the movie, "The Great Race" came on. With commercials, it would last until midnight. Bailey rolled her eyes and said that she needed potato chips and a dip.

"Who's going to go get them?" I asked.

She was already on her feet. "I will," she said, looking at the door. "Can you watch him for a bit?"

"Anything for potato chips."

"He won't need to be fed for a while, but his formula is in the cupboard, and there are diapers downstairs. I think I'll pick up some more while I'm out."

"You sound as if you're going to Antarctica for the chips," Gary mumbled.

She grabbed her coat, purse, and my keys and headed down the hallway.

I called after her, "Drive carefully. Watch out for crazy drivers."

The door closed, and Gary said, "You didn't need to tell her that."

I sighed and went into the kitchen to check the pie. We sat down to our biscuits and tuna, and Peter slept on.

During a commercial, Gary asked, "So where are the chips?"

I looked at the clock. Bailey had been gone for forty-five minutes. "Heavy diapers?"

Several commercials later, I began to worry. "I hope something didn't happen."

"She'd call us, if it had."

He was right. I took the pie from the oven and set it out to cool before we cut it.

There was a knock on the door.

"Now, who can that be?"

Before Gary could go to see, Daniel had let himself in. "Happy New Year!"

We gave hugs all around.

"I brought chips and dip. I see you have our movie on."

Peter started to stir, and I picked him up.

"Where's Bailey?"

"She went out for chips and dip a while ago," Gary told him.

I decided I had better find the formula and make sure there was a clean nipple for him. I also went downstairs to fetch a diaper.

Her room was, as always, a mess. I found a diaper, his sleeper, and a burp cloth.

When I came back up, I asked, "Should I call her?" but I was afraid that Gary would think I was being overly concerned.

He was not overly concerned. He was poking at the pie. "Can we cut it now?"

I shrugged. "Fine with me. There's ice cream in the freezer. I want vanilla."

Daniel called from the living room, "I'll have vanilla too."

Peter was whimpering, so I prepared his bottle and then asked again, "Should I call Bailey?"

"Sure. It certainly does seem that she's taking a long time for chips and dip."

"How long has it been?" Daniel asked.

"Two hours."

I called, but the call went to voice mail. "Where *is* she?"

A food fight had erupted in the movie. "I had forgotten about this," I told them. "I hate food fights; such as waste."

Gary laughed. "It's probably not real food anyway."

"They're eating it," Daniel chided. "It can't be shaving cream."

Gary brought out our desserts and set mine on the end table. "Don't throw it at me," he quipped.

I chuckled, gathering Peter into my arms, and settled into my recliner to feed him. He latched onto the nipple and drained the bottle quickly. The movie droned on. I couldn't keep my mind on it because I was worrying about Bailey. Pray, I told myself. *Lord, please watch over Bailey, and bring her home safely. Protect her from crazy drivers and bad people.*

After I changed his diaper and put him into his sleeper, I sat on the floor with him for a while, letting him stretch and wiggle. My ice cream had melted, but the warm pie still tasted good. I tried her cell phone again. No answer.

It was time for Peter to go to bed, so I put him back in the little bed, and Daniel and Gary moved it into the hallway near our room, so the TV wouldn't bother him.

"Call her again," Gary suggested.

I did, but every time I did, the fear grew.

Suddenly, Daniel stood up and stretched. "I'm going to go look for her. She's in your car, right?"

"Well, yes, but where would you look?"

"I don't know, but I can't sit here, watching a silly movie." And he was gone.

The movie ended, and it was midnight. We could hear fireworks going off in the neighborhood, the big ones exploding over the river. We went out onto the deck to watch a few, but it was too cold to stay out long.

"Happy New Year," Gary said, and kissed me. We stood holding each other for a few minutes before we both shivered and returned indoors.

Peter was still sleeping, but I knew he would wake up for a feeding sometime during the night. We got ready for bed and decided to move the little bed into our room. I put a note on Bailey's door, telling her where Peter would be.

"How can I sleep?" I moaned. "What if she needs us?"

"If there had been an accident, the police would have informed us."

I disagreed. "We aren't her family. No one would think to tell us."

"Dottie, there is nothing we can do. She probably went to a party."

That hit me like a punch in the stomach. "She wouldn't."

"I don't know. She's been jumpy all day. Maybe she was hiding something from us. She was awfully eager to go get chips."

"I'll kill her!" I said matter-of-factly.

Gary grinned. "If it will help you sleep."

"I don't know. I think 'mad' makes me even less sleepy than 'worried.'"

The baby sighed and snuffled, and we turned off the light.

At about 3 a.m., I woke out of a sound sleep, wondering why a baby was crying. Gradually, I came around and took him into the living room to change him and fix him another bottle. Once he was fed and back in his bed, I tiptoed down the hallway to look in the garage. My car was there.

Relief fought with anger. I sat in my chair for a while, asking God for wisdom for the morning. A dozen ways of approaching Bailey played through my mind, but I had no idea which was the right one. Finally, I went back to bed, but I slept fitfully and dreamed odd snippets of searching for something and never finding it.

Peter woke us both at seven.

"Bailey's home safely," I whispered to Gary. "The car's in the garage."

"I'll kill her!" he exclaimed, and we both laughed.

I got up and dressed and left Peter in his bed to wake up while I went to the kitchen to fix him a bottle. Gary joined me at the stove shortly after that. I was glad he was there when Bailey came running up the stairs.

"Where's Peter? He's gone!" she cried frantically.

"He's in our bedroom," I said.

"You had no right! He's my son, and no one can just take him from me." She rushed into our bedroom and came out with a groggy baby. "Poor little boy," she cooed, suddenly calm and sweet. "You're my sweet baby, and no one – " She stopped and glared at us and said more firmly, "No one is going to take you away from me."

What was going on?

Gary spoke. "If you will recall, you left him with us for the night without even asking if you might."

"That's what he said you'd say – that I would be a terrible mother and that I didn't deserve him, and that someone – you – would take him away and say that I'm just a whore and could never be a good mother." She buried her face in Peter's blanket and started to cry.

Gary looked at me and raised his eyebrows.

"Do you want Peter's bottle?" I asked, holding it out to her.

She snatched it and held it up to the light, tears running down her face.

"Bailey," asked Gary, "What's this all about?"

"It's none of your business!" she sobbed.

"It most certainly is. Where were you last night?"

"I went to a party, but I'll never do it again," she promised earnestly. "No one – "

"No one is going to take Peter away from you," Gary assured her. "Who said they would?"

She sniffed. "It doesn't matter. It's not going to happen. I'll never go back there, and I'll never see them again. And I will keep him with me all the time."

Peter had started to cry, probably sensing the tension in the air.

I sighed and realized that I wasn't going to be able to vent my own frustration at this time. "Give him his milk. We will help you keep him. That's why you are here. Just . . .." Something had to be said. "Just ask us, the next time you want us to watch him."

"I did, and you said no."

"I said I wouldn't watch him once you go back to work."

"It's the same thing."

Gary broke in. "No, it's not. And if we say 'no,' it means 'no.'"

"Look," I added, "We would be glad to babysit now and then, if we know where you are going and approximately when you are getting home."

"I'm never going anywhere ever again. I have to keep him safe."

True to her word, she stayed close to home for the next two weeks, only going out to buy what she needed. At those times, she left him with me, "Because if I take him out, they might get him."

24

I suppose two weeks with no break can take its toll on almost anyone. Bailey even hesitated to let us hold Peter, determined that she be the most important person in his life. As the two weeks progressed, Peter became fussier, and Bailey's temper was always on a hair trigger.

Then one night, she pounded on our bedroom door a bit after midnight. I could hear Peter crying, so I jumped up and opened the door. Before I could ask what was going on, she thrust Peter into my arms.

"Take him! I can't stand his crying one more minute!" She turned and headed back down the hallway.

"Wait a minute! Where are you going?" I demanded, as I adjusted Peter. His face was red, and he was squirming and screaming, and I suspected that he must have colic.

She turned and shouted, "To sleep. Oh. And change him. He stinks," before rushing down the stairs and slamming her door.

Colic. It had been a long time since I had had a baby, and I could not even remember if mine had had colic.

Gary turned on the light, for who could sleep with the noise! "What's going on?"

I jiggled Peter and brought him to the bed. "That's what I want to know. I think Peter has colic."

He picked up the alarm clock and peered at it. "So, what's with Bailey?"

"I don't know, but we can't talk until the baby is quieter. I'm going to change him. Could you find 'colic' on a reputable website, so I can know what to do?"

"Maybe he's hungry," Gary suggested, probably because he didn't want to get out of bed.

"Maybe." I had some of his things in the living room, so I cleaned him up and swaddled him in a clean towel. "I hope he won't be too warm."

"I'm freezing," my husband groaned.

I was too, and laid the baby on the bed, so I could put on my robe. "Pat him or rub his tummy, and I'll get him a bottle."

While the water was heating, I went down and knocked on Bailey's door.

"I'm sleeping!" she barked.

I opened the door and peered into the darkness. "Bailey, what's wrong?"

"I can't stand his noise. I want to sleep. He makes me so angry that I could . . .."

"You could . . .?"

"I was afraid I would hurt him. I wanted to shake him." Her voice was suddenly despairing. "And I'm so sick of changing him." She turned on the bedside lamp. "Please can you take him? I haven't slept for a week."

I sighed. "Yes, I'll take him tonight."

"Thank you."

"Is he hungry?"

"Maybe. I don't know. I just want to sleep. You figure it out."

"Okay, but we need to call the pediatrician in the morning."

"Fine. Whatever. Good night." And she snapped off the light. "And don't leave him alone."

Things were quieter in the bedroom when I dragged the portable bed into our room. Gary had loosened the towel and was rubbing Peter's tummy.

"You're a genius!" I said.

Peter was indeed hungry. He guzzled his milk and after I burped him, I laid him in the little bed. He hiccupped a bit and sobbed, but he seemed calmer.

"I talked briefly to Bailey just now."

"And?"

"His crying was getting on her nerves, I guess. She was afraid she would injure him."

"So, is he here for the night?"

"Yup. If he wakes up again, I'll take him to the living room. I know you have an early meeting tomorrow."

He turned out the light. "Does helping Bailey have an expiration date?"

I puffed up my pillow. "I don't know. I hope so."

I did get up in the night to feed Peter again, and we eventually fell asleep in my recliner. I woke up to the smell of bacon and syrup. Daniel was in the kitchen with Gary, and they were trying really hard to be quiet, shushing each other, while banging drawers and dropping things on the floor. I put the sleeping baby back in his bed in our bedroom and then returned to the kitchen.

"Good morning, you two."

"Breakfast's almost ready," Daniel announced. "It snowed last night!"

"Really!" I opened the blinds to the deck. Sure enough, about two inches of snow covered every surface and made the evergreen trees look like Christmas trees. "I wonder why we can never get snow at Christmastime?"

"I came to shovel," Daniel said, "But Dad had already done it."

"Wow! In your pajamas and robe? You must have been up early."

"I didn't really sleep much," Gary admitted. "And I cancelled the meeting this morning."

"Slippery roads?"

"No, I'm just not feeling great. Probably a lack of sleep. I thought the fresh air would do me good, but maybe I just need breakfast." He flexed his shoulders. "I think I strained my back shoveling."

"Tea's ready." Daniel handed us each a mug. "Where's Bailey?"

Gary and I looked at each other, and he said, "We're letting her sleep in. Peter has kept her up nights lately."

We were about halfway through breakfast when Bailey staggered into the kitchen and flopped into the chair across from Daniel.

"I'm starved!" She reached for a waffle.

"Peter is still sleeping," I told her, confident that a good mother would want to know.

She doused her waffle in syrup and murmured, "That's nice to hear. When he cries, I'll give him a bottle." She stuffed her mouth with waffle.

Daniel looked at Gary and me, baffled. "Did you get some good sleep?" he asked her.

She nodded and continued to chew.

Daniel took another long drink of tea and said, "I've got to get to class. Thanks for breakfast." He kissed my cheek, hugged Gary's shoulder, and patted Bailey on the back. "See ya."

"Bye," she managed to say as the door closed.

We finished breakfast in silence, while I tried to think how we could start a profitable conversation on the responsibilities of parenting. I supposed Gary must have been thinking the same because he had rested his head on his hands and was staring into his mug of tea. His uneaten egg yoke had congealed in a puddle of syrup.

Finally, I broke the silence. "Peter was pretty hungry when you brought him to me last night. I fed him and Gary rubbed his tummy, and he fell back to sleep. He woke up at four and finished off another bottle. I had thought that he had colic, but I think he's just growing and needs more milk."

As if he heard us, Peter began to cry from the bedroom.

Bailey raised her eyes slowly from her plate, and looked at me with eyes brimming with tears. "Dorothy," she whispered, "I don't think I can do this."

I reached out to touch her hand, but she snatched it away and put both hands in her lap. "You can," I told her. "We are here to help you."

Gary looked up from his tea, "But you can't just go dumping him on us without warning. Dorothy needs her sleep as well. You're young, and God gave *you* this child."

Bailey blinked in surprise, and the tears squirted onto her robe. "I didn't dump him on you!"

"Yes, you did!" Gary jumped up from the table. "I'm going back to bed." He turned to me. "If you want to continue this, it's all yours." He refilled his mug and tromped down the hallway. "Someone, get the baby out of the bedroom!" he shouted.

Something was very wrong.

Bailey sat as if glued to the chair.

"Bailey, go get Peter; I'll get the bed."

Slowly, she stood and shuffled to the bedroom. I followed her in, just in time to see Gary try to get into bed and slide off onto the floor.

My heart fluttered with fear. "Gary, what's wrong?"

He was clutching his arm – his left arm – and moaning, "Dottie, help me."

"It's a heart attack," said the brisk, confident voice of Bailey behind me. "Call 911. Stay with him. I'll be right back."

I heard her running down the hallway. I knelt beside Gary and touched the emergency number on my cell phone with trembling hands. "Gary, can you hear me?"

"Yes," he whispered. His face was gray and covered with beads of sweat.

The man at emergency dispatch was kind and efficient. It was difficult to hear over Peter's wailing. The man repeated questions and helped me to answer them, and then he told me that help was on the way – to unlock the front door.

Bailey flew back into the room and knelt beside Gary, pushing a couple baby aspirin into his mouth. "Chew these and swallow."

I could hear the sirens. Bailey ran out to lead the paramedics into the bedroom. There was no more room for me, as they crowded around him with machines.

At one point, one of the EMTs asked, "Could you take the baby from the room?" Bailey swooped Peter up and left the bedroom. It was probably only minutes, but it seemed like an eternity before they put Gary on a gurney and wheeled him out to the living room, with me following. They told me where they were taking him, but I was having a hard time assimilating the information. I kept asking, and one of the men finally looked at Bailey.

"We'll be there as soon as we can get ready," she assured him. And then we watched them go down the clean, dry steps that Gary had shoveled an hour ago.

Bailey shut the front door and turned to me. She looked at the breakfast table and led me to my chair. "You sit down and finish your tea," she told me. "I will change Peter and get dressed. Then I'll help you get ready. We'll have to make a bottle for Peter, but after that, I'll take you to the hospital."

She poured more tea into my mug and smiled at me. "You stay here. Don't move. I'll be right back up. Gary's in good hands. It'll be okay."

I probably could not have walked anyway. I felt cold and my hands were still shaking. My teeth chattered against the mug, and I choked on the tea. What would I do without Gary? What would any of us do without Gary? I needed to call Daniel and Abby, but my phone was still on the floor in the bedroom. I truly didn't have the strength to go get it, so I put my head on the table and cried.

I heard Bailey coming back up the stairs and tried to wipe off my face with the sleeve of my robe. She pulled a tissue from the box on the counter and handed it to me. When I finished mopping my face, she said, "You need to get dressed. I'm making Peter a bottle, and you can sit in back and give it to him while I drive."

Her calm seemed to calm me, and I went to find something to wear.

"Make it comfortable. You're going to be there a while," she called after me.

Before we left, she seemed to have a checklist in her head. "Phone? Charger? Purse? Something to read?" She thought a moment and then said, "Gary's going to need his shaving stuff and toothbrush. He's already got his jammies and robe."

I fetched his shaving kit, and Bailey fastened Peter into his carrier, to which he objected loudly! Once in the car, I plugged his mouth with the bottle, and it was quiet again. With a contented baby in the back seat, the trip to the hospital was relatively short. I pulled my cell phone out and murmured, "I think I'd better call Daniel and Abby."

"Daniel, yes," Bailey agreed, "But why Abby? We don't want her to have another miscarriage. Once we know how things are, we can call Will and let him tell Abby."

"How did you get so smart?"

"I guess I react well under pressure." She glanced in the rearview mirror. "Some pressure."

We drove into the hospital parking garage, and my heart began to pound again. What would we find here?

Bailey pulled Peter's baby carrier out and handed me the bag of things we had collected for Gary and myself. She threw the diaper bag over her shoulder, picked up the carrier, and then she linked her free arm into mine. Together we walked into the chaos of the emergency waiting room.

25

The good news was that Gary was still alive. The bad news was that we couldn't see him until he was stabilized. We sat in a corner and watched people come and go. It was grim. I texted Daniel and told him where we were. He texted back "Later."

"He's probably in class," Bailey said. She was busy on her cell phone, and I wished that she wasn't there because all I wanted to do was to pray. Finally, I said, "I wish I had brought my Bible."

She didn't say anything but went on fiddling with her phone. After a few minutes, she leaned over and showed me her phone. "I found you a Bible app."

"A Bible what?"

"An app. An application. Look," and she showed me how I could read the Bible on my phone.

I handed her my phone, and while she put the app on it, I marveled that this was the same girl who had melted down in our kitchen - what - about an hour ago! She handed me my phone, and I settled back to read some Psalms.

Bailey had warmed a bottle in a microwave she found, and then asked if I'd feed Peter while she went to find us tea and something to eat. I wondered what was keeping Daniel, and I really wanted to call Abby, but I realized that Bailey's idea was better. I gave Peter his bottle, and he and I had a talk with God about how much we all needed Gary. I had just read in Psalm 18 about how David gave God reasons for his requests. I had no problem finding many God-glorifying reasons for Gary to stay alive a while longer. I poured out my heart, and dripped tears on Peter's blanket. Even while begging God for Him to give us Gary for a while longer, I felt so unworthy – considering that I rarely spoke to Him in my normal, day-to-day life.

"Mom?" Daniel came to me and wrapped his arms around me and Peter. Then he looked at Peter. "Where's Bailey?" he asked, looking around, obviously perturbed.

"She went to find us tea."

"Oh. Well, then, how's Dad?"

"They are stabilizing him. And he might need surgery." I told him the whole story of our morning, leaving out the clash with Bailey, since it didn't seem relevant anymore. In fact, in the telling, Bailey became the hero, who knew what to do. "I don't know what I would have done without her," I finished.

We both saw her across the busy waiting room, dodging small children and preoccupied adults, while balancing a tray of tea.

"Oh" she said, looking at the two cups of tea. "I didn't know you were here. You can have my tea." She handed me mine and then giggled. "I didn't know which pastry you'd like, so I got four."

"You drink the tea," Daniel told her. "I think you probably need it more than I do."

"We haven't called Abby yet, because Bailey thought it would be better to let Will tell her."

"I'll call Will." He went outside so he could hear better and came back a few minutes later. "Will was home, so I got Abby as well. They will be here soon."

Daniel sat beside Bailey for a while, and we ate all the donuts. Then Bailey turned to me, "I think I'll go home now. I don't want Peter to spend the entire day in his bucket. Can I take the car? Daniel said he'd bring you home."

I looked at Daniel for confirmation. "Of course. Thank you for all you did this morning. And for driving me. And for helping me on my phone." We stood, and she let me hug her. Actually, I think she was hugging me. I patted Peter, and Daniel walked out to the car with her, carrying "the bucket."

I could see the car through the windows, as they fastened Peter into his car seat. Then they stood talking for quite a while. At one point, Bailey bowed her head, and Daniel put his hand on her shoulder, almost in a comforting way.

When he came back, brushing snowflakes off his coat, he asked, "So what really happened this morning? Bailey seems to think that Dad's heart attack was all her fault, yet you made her sound all heroic."

I sighed. "She was pretty awful last night.," I admitted. "And this morning. You saw her at breakfast: selfish and sullen."

"Yeah, I was a bit puzzled about the coolness in the kitchen."

"But when Gary collapsed, she knew exactly what to do and how to help me. Perhaps the added stress didn't help your dad, but probably shoveling the snow, while angry, is what caused the heart attack. We really don't know. We haven't yet heard from the doctors."

When Daniel and I finally got to see Gary, the effect was shattering. He slept, attached to so many machines – a tube in his nose, an IV in his arm, wires attached to his chest, a clip on his index finger. The screens above the head of his bed flashed and scrolled. His color was good, but the nurse – her name was Gracie – said that was because of all the oxygen they were giving him.

Gracie explained a few things; it was all designed to put me at ease. "The doctor will be in shortly and tell you more."

But we actually waited quite a while, as there was a flurry of activity in the corridor. An orderly pulled the curtains around us, and someone else was brought in to the next bed. Then, Gracie came and escorted us back to the waiting room until the emergency was under control.

Will and Abby had arrived and were reading magazines.

"How's Dad?" Abby asked.

"He's doing very well," Gracie reassured her. "The doctor will probably come out and talk with you all."

After she left, we filled them in on everything that had happened and told them what to expect in the ICU. Eventually, Daniel and I went back to see Gary, and the doctor clarified what we could expect in the next few days. After he left, Daniel said, "Mom, you need to go home; get some food and some sleep."

"I agree," said Gracie, as she came through the door with meds for Gary. "Take your mama home. We'll take good care of Gary. In the morning, you'll get to meet Kevin; he'll be Gary's nurse during the day."

I stood reluctantly. I truly was exhausted and felt shaky and hungry and extremely sleepy. Daniel helped me with my coat, and we sent Abby and Will to sit with Gary for a bit. Daniel and I trudged through the hospital corridors and picked our way through the snow to the car, only saying inane things like: "I think that's the main floor button," or "Watch out for that patch of ice."

We drove home in silence. I was wondering what I could find to eat. There would be waffles still on the table from breakfast. That seemed like weeks ago. Waffles would do.

As we arrived at the house, we could see the soft glow of the Christmas tree lights through the closed curtains of the living room. Bailey met us at the door from the garage into the house.

"You'll never guess what happened!" she exclaimed with a grin.

Well, it had to be good news, at least.

She practically dragged me down the hallway to the kitchen. "Look!"

In the center of the table was a huge bouquet of flowers. The waffles and bacon had been cleaned up. On the counter were several aluminum baking pans. I ventured a peek into one: brownies.

"And look what else!" With a flourish, Bailey opened the refrigerator door to reveal several casseroles and a huge green salad.

"Where did they come from?" I asked.

"Your church! Connie had my phone number, and she called to say that several people were going to bring us supper. And they came! They cleaned up the kitchen and the bathroom, made your bed, vacuumed, and helped me with Peter."

"How did they know?" I was completely befuddled.

Daniel cleared his throat. "I told them. Actually, I just called the church office and asked them to send out a prayer chain about Dad," he explained. "I guess this is their response. Besides praying."

"It's wonderful," I said and then I started to sob. I had dripped tears all day, but suddenly all the unhappiness and exhaustion and fear of the unknown came pouring out. Daniel held me while my shoulders shook. Then Bailey was in the huddle with us, Daniel with his arms around us both.

I tried to get myself under control, but couldn't until Bailey raised her head and asked, perplexed, "But I thought this is what God does. Isn't it a miracle? Aren't you hungry?"

I started to laugh through the tears. "Yes! I'm starved. And I thought I would have to eat dried-up waffles."

26

The following morning, I waited until Bailey was up before I left for the hospital.

"I'm sorry to leave you without a car, but if you want anything, I can stop at the store on the way home."

"We'll be fine," Bailey told me.

Gary was not fine; he was still in the ICU. I arrived in time to see the doctor when he made his rounds. Now, it seemed, Gary just needed round-the-clock monitoring until he was well enough to be moved to a room. "Maybe tomorrow," the doctor said.

It was rather annoying not to have any hand-sewing to do. The prom and wedding seasons had not yet begun in earnest, and I didn't even have the fabric for the one wedding dress order I did have. Gary slept, and I wrote a thank-you note to the church and read books until I fell asleep in the chair.

Daniel brought me lunch and sat with us for a while. I knew Gary was in good hands and decided to go shopping for everything I would need for the wedding dress. Once inside the shop, however, I couldn't think clearly and left the store empty-handed.

When I got home, Bailey was washing dishes, and Peter was sleeping in his little bed behind the couch.

"How was your day?" I asked her.

"Boring. I watched TV too much."

"Thanks for cleaning the place up."

She smiled and shrugged.

We warmed up leftovers in the microwave and ate in the kitchen.

"I'm not going to Bible study tonight," I told her. "I'm just too wrung-out. But you are welcome to take the car. I'll watch Peter for you, if you like."

She thought about it for a minute and then said, "I don't want to go to Bible study either. Let's see if Daniel wants to come over and watch a movie. I could go pick him up."

"I think he has a ride to Bible study with a friend. I wouldn't want to take that from him."

"But that takes him from us," she pouted. "I think he ought to come here."

"I think he ought to go to Bible study, so I'm not going to ask him," I stated.

Without another word, she left the table, fetched Peter from his bed, and stormed downstairs. I didn't see her for the rest of the evening, but I was too tired to deal with it or even to care.

The following day, they moved Gary into a semi-private room. He was able to talk a little, but it exhausted him. He was still hooked up to numerous gadgets.

The highlight of the day was when Eli, the young pastor of Rocks and Mortar, came to visit us in Gary's room. He brought a beautiful bouquet of freesia and a huge get-well card, signed by everyone in the Bible study. I was glad to see Daniel's name on it.

"They all miss you both, and they sent me to pray with you," which he did. I wished I could pray as he did, with such humility and confidence, knowing just what to say.

When he was finished, I told Gary I wanted to walk with Eli to his car.

"Please thank the group for all the meals," I told Eli. "It's really been a help and encouragement."

"You're part of the family."

"I still don't feel like it. Yet."

"If you stick with us, you will. It usually takes about a year to begin to feel like you really belong."

We got to the main entrance, and he said, "You don't have to come all the way to the car with me."

"Well, since you want us to be family, I – I had something I wanted to ask you."

He stopped and turned toward me. "Ask away!"

"This is going to sound really stupid, but I really want to know how to pray. Like you do. And I want to want to pray."

"Ah-ha." He shoved his hands into his coat pockets. "I don't think I can give you a quick answer right before I go to my car. Let me think about it. Let's get Gary back home first. And you keep trying to pray. The Holy Spirit will make your words acceptable to God."

I was disappointed, although it was silly to expect a five-minute solution to my doubts. I nodded. "Thank you for coming."

He patted me on the shoulder and went out into the blustery afternoon.

There wasn't much conversation with Gary. He was so tired that he would fall asleep while I was talking with him. Finally, he murmured, "I feel bad zonking out on you, but I really want to sleep. Go home and rest, and I'll see you tomorrow."

When I got home, I was greeted by Peter's cries, and dirty dishes waited forlornly in the sink.

Bailey jumped up from the couch and snatched Peter from his little bed. "You're early!" she accused. "I was just going to clean up. I'm just so tired. It's a lot of work caring for a baby."

"It is," I agreed. "Let's fix some supper. You get the dishes in the dishwasher."

"I can't," she stated bluntly. "I need to feed Peter."

She was beginning to annoy me. "Then feed him," I said evenly, wishing to snap at her.

I cleared a space on one counter while she heated water for Peter's bottle. How could one girl make such a big mess? There were not many leftovers, but I didn't care; it was food I didn't need to cook.

Then the doorbell rang.

How sweet it was to see Connie's face! "I've brought you supper. Did Bailey tell you?"

"No. She didn't have time, I guess." I could smell the delicious aroma and led Connie into the kitchen. "Please excuse the mess. Bailey also didn't have time to wash the dishes."

"Let me help you," Connie offered.

As nice as that would have been, I decided against it: "No, I think I had better save them for her. What did you make us?"

"Chicken and dumplings."

As it wasn't really suppertime yet, I brewed Connie a cup of coffee, and made myself a cup of tea, while Connie cleared off the table. I dug out some of the brownies.

"How are you coping?" she asked after we sat down.

Before I could answer, Bailey called from downstairs, "Dorothy, come quick! I can't handle this!"

I rolled my eyes at Connie and said, "Come and see."

As usual, Bailey's room looked like a tornado had struck. What wasn't usual, was that she was holding Peter at arms-length over his changing table. He was dressed only in his little white onesie, but it wasn't white; The bottom half was the color of newborn baby poop – mustard yellow.

"What am I going to do?" she howled. "This makes me want to puke!"

"Put him on the changing table and take his clothing off," I told her.

She shook her head, as she laid him on the table. "I can't stand to touch him."

Connie went to the changing table. "You can do this. Your hands will wash."

"I'll puke," she warned.

"If you do, you'll have to clean that up too," Connie announced cheerfully.

Bailey glared, but she began to peel the onesie from Peter's body. "Now what?"

"Take off his diaper and then give him a bath."

"A bath? I don't know how to give him a bath!"

Connie and I exchanged glances, but she asked, "He's a month old. Haven't you given him a bath yet?"

"Well, duh!"

"Bailey, that's enough!" I snapped. "Bring him into the bathroom, and we'll show you how to bathe a baby."

On the way to the bathroom, Peter urinated all over Bailey's shirt and the floor.

"Gross!"

"You'll wash."

Connie filled the sink and laid a bath towel in the water. While she washed Peter, she explained what she was doing and not doing: "Don't let the baby's head go down into the water and don't get water in his ears."

When the little boy was sweet and clean, I wrapped him in another towel. "You need to wash off the changing table. Then you can get him dressed."

"Why did he do that?" Bailey asked.

Connie answered, "My guess is that you didn't change his diaper enough today."

"Probably," she murmured.

But this was not to be our worst crisis. On Thursday, it snowed again. Daniel called in the morning to offer to drive me to the hospital. "I got my car back yesterday, and I know how you hate to drive in snow." I accepted gladly.

Gary was feeling much better, and I was given the assignment to walk with him down the hallway and back, making sure that he held onto the hand rails. When he returned to his bed, he was winded.

Kevin, the nurse, checked all his vitals, and everything was fine. "You're just very out of shape," he said. "The doctor will probably prescribe some exercise for you."

"Yay," Gary remarked dully.

"What do you do all day long?"

"Work on my computer."

"It exercises your fingers," he joked, wiggling his fingers in the air.

Once we had him settled in bed again, I asked, "So what have they been feeding you?"

He grimaced. "For breakfast, I had a hard-boiled egg and whole grain toast with fake butter, no jam, a cup of tea and an apple."

"Sounds healthy."

"Yeah. No bacon, sausage, pancakes or waffles."

"I wonder for how long?"

"A dietician is coming in tomorrow morning, so please be here, so you can help me remember things and ask the right questions. I suspect that pizza is going to be on the 'no-no' list."

"We'll learn. The church has been bringing us some amazing meals, every other day."

"I'm so glad. How're things going with Bailey?"

I didn't want to worry him. "So-so. Connie brought supper last night, and we discovered that Bailey didn't know how to give Peter a bath."

He shook his head. "These kids spend so much time on social media, and you would think that *they* would think to learn things. Surely there are websites that teach a person how to take care of a baby."

"I'll mention it to her."

We watched TV together for a while, and then I went to the cafeteria to get my lunch. When I returned, Abby and Will were visiting with Gary. I ate my lunch and listened to them chat. A colleague from the realty office came in, and Will and Abby left. I read my book while Gary and Ron talked, but after he left, Gary took a nap. I tried to pray for a while, but my mind kept wandering.

Then Bailey called. "Dorothy, can you come pick me up?" I could detect the panic in her voice.

"No." I slipped out into the hallway. "I don't have a car. Daniel was going to take me home when he got off work."

Her swear words moved through my phone without any hinderances.

"What's going on? Where are you?"

"Um, on the corner of Grandview and Maple."

I tried to figure out why she needed me to pick her up. "Where's my car?"

"Um, it has a flat, and it's cold, and it's snowing, and I can't walk home with Peter."

I was glad she realized that at least. "Of course not."

"I could call Daniel."

"He doesn't get off work until 4:30."

More swear words. Then: "We'll freeze to death!"

"Aren't you in the car?"

"Yes."

"Well, start the engine."

"Is it okay? I mean, I, like, slid into the curb, and the engine died."

I sighed. "Start the engine and turn on the heat." I heard her do it. "Okay?"

"Okay."

"I'll call Daniel and then either he or I will call you back."

"Okay. I'm really sorry."

"It wasn't your fault." Was it?

"Well . . .."

I called Daniel, and he said that business was slow because of the storm, so he would come get me now, and then we would go rescue Bailey. I asked Kevin to let Gary know, and then I went to the main entrance to wait.

Once I was in the car, Daniel asked, "So what's with Bailey and cars?"

"I don't know. She's a really good driver. Flat tires just happen."

"That's not what she told me. She said something about a stupid doctor and a stop sign and another car."

"Oh."

"I already called the auto club. I'll stay with the car until they come to change the flat, and you and Bailey can take my car home."

When we pulled up behind my car, Bailey jumped out and immediately began to apologize. The tire was definitely flat. We all stood in the falling snow, trying to figure out how it happened. But all she could do was to keep talking about the stupid doctor and the other car.

Finally, Daniel interrupted to tell her that we were trading cars. She started to wrestle Peter's car seat from the back.

"Wait a minute," Daniel said. "It's going to be practically impossible to get the car seat into the back seat of my car, since I only have two doors."

"I can't take him in the car without the seat," she protested. "It's, like, illegal."

He looked at his watch. "The auto club will be here within the hour. Why don't Peter and I hang out together, and you ladies take my car and go home and throw supper in the oven?"

For once, Bailey was speechless, frozen in a look of utter disbelief. "Oven," she whispered.

Daniel tried to jolly her out of her obvious shock. "It'll be okay. Really. Do you have a bottle for him?"

She nodded, but the look hadn't gone away.

Daniel turned to me and gave me his keys. "Drive slowly, and I'll see you in about an hour."

I had to smile at his fatherly care.

"So, where's the bottle?" he asked Bailey.

"Bottle?" Moving like a sleep-walker, she fumbled in the back seat and handed Daniel the diaper bag, in which, we assumed, the bottle resided. Without a word, she pulled her little purse from the front seat, handed Daniel the fob, and got into the passenger's seat of Daniel's car.

We were only a couple miles from home.

Suddenly, Bailey burst out, "Dorothy, I'm so sorry I messed everything up. But Peter wouldn't stop crying and I didn't know what to do, and so I -"

"You can apologize when we get home. Right now, I need to think about driving."

Out of the corner of my eye, I saw her snap her mouth shut, but she still looked very worried.

"Peter's going to be fine with Daniel," I assured her. "They will be home before we even get supper reheated."

"I'm not worried about Peter. I'm – "

"Shh. It can wait."

I parked the car in front of the house, but opened the garage door so we could go in that way. Before I had even turned off the engine, Bailey was out of her seatbelt and running toward the garage door. I got out, and the loud screeching of a – of a smoke detector – filled the air. Oh, no, what did she do now?

27

The house was filled with smoke. Bailey was already in the kitchen and had yanked open the oven door. Smoke rolled out, but fortunately, no fire. She glanced around – probably looking for pot holders – and grabbed the tea towel on the counter.

"Bailey, stop!" I shouted above the squeal of the smoke detector. I pushed her away from the oven and turned on the ventilation fan. Both of us were coughing. There was a cookie sheet in the oven and on it, tiny blackened lumps of what I presumed had been cookies. I turned the oven off, took the tea towel from Bailey, and started to wave the smoke away.

"Open the glass slider," I told her, "And then open the front door." She did it without a word. As the smoke began to clear, the alarm started hiccupping, chirped a few times, and finally quit. Blessed quietness! I went back to the oven with pot holders and removed the charred cookies.

"I'm sorry, Dorothy," Bailey sighed.

I sighed too and shook my head. What could I say?

"It's been a horrible day, but it wasn't all my fault," she protested.

I really didn't want to hear about her horrible day, but she was not to be stopped.

"I wanted to make cookies, so I put Peter in his little bed, but he cried and cried, and when I looked at him, his face was, like, all red, and he kept raising his legs and kicking them. I didn't know what to do."

She was following me from room to room as I opened windows.

"So, I fed him, but then he screamed even more. I changed his diaper, but there was, like, nothing in it, and I had such a hard time putting another back on because he was kicking so hard."

The fresh, snowy cold blew through the house, and soon, it was relatively smoke-free.

She grabbed my arm to stop me from walking away. "I wanted to slap his legs to make him stop kicking, but I know that a tiny baby can't help it, and that only a terrible mother would do that." Suddenly, she sobbed. "But why would I want to do it at all? I *am* a terrible mother."

"I'm glad you didn't slap him. Of course, he can't help it." I turned her towards me and looked into her eyes. "I lost count of how many times I wanted to shake my kids until their teeth rattled." A crooked smile touched her lips. "But I didn't do it."

"But you're a *good* mother," she said.

I'm just a blessed mother, but this was *her* time to clear *her* conscience. We walked back through the house, closing windows. "Well, Peter wasn't crying when I saw him in the car, so what did you do?"

We were interrupted by Daniel's entrance into the house with Peter in the baby carrier. "Are you all right?" he asked. "What's going on? Why are all the doors open?"

He set the carrier on the couch, and Bailey unbuckled the straps, wincing as she lifted him out. Before we could answer, he had spied the lumps of coal on the cookie sheet. "Wow! Charcoal cookies! What happened?"

I asked Daniel to close the slider in the kitchen. "Peter wasn't feeling well, and Bailey didn't know what to do, so . . .." I looked at Bailey, who was glaring at Daniel.

She sighed again and dropped onto the couch with Peter. "So, I decided to take him to Urgent Care." She looked at me. "That's when I forgot that I had cookies in the oven. We had a really long wait; there were a lot of people there, and a couple people were, like, serious enough that the rest of us had to wait, like, even longer. And Peter was screaming the whole time, and people were looking at me as if they wished I'd leave." She looked at Peter, now nestled contentedly in her lap. "I wish we *had* left."

The house was beginning to warm up, and we unzipped our coats. Bailey freed Peter from his snowsuit, using only one hand.

"So, what was wrong with him?" Daniel asked, sitting on the couch next to her.

She closed her eyes, as if deciding to take really nasty medicine. "The nurse asked me questions, and we had to shout over Peter's crying. Then we waited probably ten minutes longer until the doctor came in. He picked up Peter, jiggled him, and Peter spit up all over his shirt."

Daniel chuckled.

"Peter stopped screaming, and the doctor – he handed Peter back to me and said, 'I have a lot of really sick people in the waiting room; I don't have time to be burping babies.'"

"Ooh." I could feel her embarrassment.

"When I went out to pay, the lady at the desk glared at me and said there was no charge. Then she tore up my papers and threw them in the wastebasket."

"Not nice," Daniel agreed.

"I was so mad, that I wasn't careful, and I slipped and fell down in the parking lot. Peter was in his carrier, and he's okay, but I think I did something to my hand." She lifted it for us to see.

"You're moving it, so it's probably not broken," Daniel observed.

"But I'm not going to Urgent Care," she warned us.

"Of course not," I agreed.

"So, what happened to Mom's car?" Daniel asked.

I thought we already knew the answer to that question, but Bailey knew otherwise. "Well, it was snowing pretty hard, and the traffic was heavy, so I decided to take some back streets, but I, like, missed the sign at a four-way stop. Another car was already moving into the intersection, and I might have been going too fast, and it was so slippery that I couldn't stop, so I, like, swerved to miss the car – I could only use one hand – and hit the curb. That's why I had a flat tire," she stated with a finality that seemed to legitimatize her whole day.

"Two flat tires," Daniel corrected.

"Two?" Her disappointment popped her balloon of confidence.

Daniel, obviously annoyed at her, turned to me. "Mom, we will need to take the car in to the shop soon because the tires you are driving on don't match the others. I can probably do it tomorrow."

As if on cue, my phone rang. "It's your dad." I headed down the hallway to our bedroom. "Hi."

"I get to come home tomorrow!" he announced.

I thought of the car. "That's great," I said cheerfully. "What time shall I pick you up?"

"They will release me after 11, before lunch. But if you could come early to help me, maybe at 8? Then you can hear all the doctor's instructions and help me remember."

Before I could say anything, he added, "Oh. And please bring me some clothes. How are you?"

"Fine."

"The nurse said you had to leave early. No problems?"

"Nothing I can't handle." *Liar!* I told myself.

"You're wonderful! Oh. They just brought in my tasteless supper. Do you have time to talk?"

"Not really. Daniel and Bailey are here, and I think I'd better get us some supper too."

"Okay. I'll see you tomorrow. Love you."

"Love you, too."

I returned to the living room to figure out how we were going to do that with only one car.

Daniel solved it. "No problem, Mom. I'll take your car to the shop, and you take my car to pick up Dad. And if Bailey doesn't have a car, she can't get into trouble." He grinned at her, and she rolled her eyes and punched him in the arm.

A man's voice from the front door startled us all. "Hello? Is anybody home?" He peeked around the corner into the living room. "Is everything all right?" He was carrying an aluminum casserole pan on which sat a pie. "I come, bearing gifts. Shall I close the door?"

Daniel turned and jumped from the couch. "Evan! Yes, please close the door and come in," He introduced everyone and then said, "We had a smoke alarm incident."

"I remember seeing you at church," I said, not wanting for Daniel to tell Bailey's story. "Don't you have two little girls?"

"I do. They're at home with Sarah. She made this for you, but I'm the deliveryman."

I thanked him, and Daniel took Evan into the kitchen to set our dinner on the counter. They talked quietly for a short time and then came back into the living room.

"It's been a crazy day," I told him, "And I didn't know what we were going to eat tonight."

"Well, I hope you like it. We didn't have any info on allergies or preferences, so it's pretty simple."

Daniel led Evan to where Bailey was still sitting on the couch and took Peter from her arms. "Show him your hand. He's a nurse."

After a few questions and a bit of prodding and poking, he said, "It's a sprain. It needs rest, ice, compression, and elevation. That's R.I.C.E., so you can remember. And be careful how you lift Peter."

"Thank you," she said in a small voice. "I really didn't want to go to Urgent Care."

"Nobody does," he agreed.

· 28 ·

Gary was home.

"What do you mean: I can't have butter?" Gary sat with his knife poised over his baked potato. It was his first night home, and I wanted things to be nice for Gary, but the doctor had been adamant about diet changes.

"You heard the doctor," I told him, probably more forcefully than necessary. "He said that your arteries are so clogged with cholesterol that you'd need a plumber's snake to clean them out."

"He didn't say that," Gary protested.

"He implied it."

"That's a horrible thought."

"I made a dressing with olive oil and herbs."

"No sour cream?"

I shook my head.

"Just let me die."

"That's not even funny."

He set his knife on his plate. "You're right; I'm sorry."

"I'll have some," Bailey offered helpfully. She drizzled it over her half of a baked potato.

"It's potato salad," Gary protested. "I don't even like potato salad."

"You don't like mayonnaise potato salad. Have you even tried this?"

His shoulders sagged. "The doc said I couldn't eat anything tasty."

I shrugged. "Well, then. Eat your potato dry. Or don't eat it at all. Your choice."

Bailey had taken a small piece of chicken breast. "This is really good."

"I know, but I didn't make it. It's left over from last night. Maybe it's time I finally learn to cook. I did bake the potatoes."

If only praying could be learned like cooking can. I struggled through a couple days, anticipating Gary's needs, thankfully eating what others brought us, and trying to make time to pray. As usual, my mind wandered, and I ended up apologizing to God for not giving Him my full attention.

Bailey drooped around the house, and she spent more time upstairs because she needed help with Peter while her hand was healing.

"Dorothy!" She flounced into the living room, where I had laid out the lace on a large table. She thrust Peter's bottle at me, and some of the baby formula splashed onto my work surface. "I can't put the lid on Peter's bottle."

Another time: "Dorothy! I can't change his diaper because he keeps wiggling, and my wrist hurts."

And: "Dorothy! Can you buckle Peter into his seat? I need to go shopping."

I didn't ask her how she was going to drive and manage Peter in the store. I'm a wimp.

The next couple days, she joined us in the evenings, sitting on the couch while Peter kicked his little legs on the carpet. We watched TV, and I continued with the wedding dress. Gary had begun to pick up his real estate work again, mostly touching base with those who had jumped in to help during his hospital stay. We didn't talk much, except when Daniel had time to pop in.

One evening, he brought me a bag of pistachios.

Bailey jumped up from the couch and said to him, "Let's make cookies!"

"Actually, I came to take you to the Bible study," Daniel said.

A pout formed on her face. "I'd rather bake cookies."

"Well, it's your choice. I'm going to Bible study. Do you want to come?"

She hesitated and then looked at me. "Could you watch Peter?"

I was ready to say 'yes,' simply because I wanted her to go to Bible study, but Daniel spoke before I could. "We'll take Peter. Get your and his things. I don't want to be late."

"But it'll be past his bedtime," she whined.

"He's a baby. He can sleep in his seat or in my arms. He's going."

She was not speedy, but eventually they were on their way. When I heard his car start up, I asked Gary, "Why is he doing this?"

Gary stood up and stretched. "I don't know. But I told you I thought he was wooing her."

I didn't like hearing that. "But she's not a believer."

"Well, he's doing what is best for her. I think he has decided to be her Hosea."

The thought made me sick. "Hosea had a terrible life."

"Not from God's point of view. Hosea did what God asked of him."

"But so heart-breaking."

"True. But it's his life, and you and I are just old married folk, who are used to life being what we want it to be."

I went to him and wrapped my arms around him. "And we almost lost that."

"I know. I did a lot of thinking as I lay on that incredibly uncomfortable bed in the hospital." He led me to the couch, and we cuddled while he continued. "I think we need to dust off the list of our expectations that we gave Bailey when she first arrived. She hasn't been living up to her side of things. Second, I'd like to start reading through the Psalms at breakfast."

"She won't get up."

"You're probably right, although it's for you and me, not so much for her, but I guess we can do it at whichever meal she shows up at."

I had been wanting to ask him this question for a while: "How much longer do you think Bailey should live here?"

"Hard question. We never put an end date to it. Do you want her to leave?"

"No!" I was surprised at how quickly I knew that.

"How much longer is her maternity leave?"

"Until mid-February."

"Wow! That's a long time to be idle. She needs a project."

We sat for a bit in silence, and then he kissed me and stood up. "I'll have to think about that for a while." He went back to his real estate papers, and I went back to the wedding dress.

When Daniel and Bailey returned from the Bible study, Gary was wandering around the kitchen, banging cupboard doors and peering into the refrigerator.

"What are you looking for, Dad?" Daniel asked.

"Food. Something that won't violate Dr. Tempe's orders."

Bailey spoke up. "You need water. Usually when we are hungry at night, it's because our body really needs water."

"Yum!" Gary laughed.

A bit on the defensive, Bailey added softly, "Well, you're used to eating something in the evening. You have to develop, like, a new habit."

Gary got a glass of water and turned off the light in the kitchen. "And that's not the only habit I'm supposed to develop. The doc also said that I need to start exercising. I guess a walk around the kitchen is a start."

Bailey turned to Daniel. "Could you carry Peter and the seat downstairs for me?"

Gary returned to his papers, and about fifteen minutes later Daniel and Bailey came back upstairs.

Bailey said, "Peter conked right out. He was really good at Bible study, and all the girls wanted to hold him."

I suddenly had visions of everyone thinking that Peter was Daniel's son, and I concentrated on my sewing.

Daniel spoke up, "Dad, Bailey had, what I think might be, a good idea."

"Okay."

She took a deep breath and said, "I'm a trained physical fitness trainer. I could help you start exercising. Your doctor could even, like, write you orders, and I would know what he was talking about and could help you follow them."

Gary wrinkled his brows. "I could join The Gym."

"I work at The Gym," she insisted, "And by the middle of February, I need to get back in shape after Peter's birth. We could do this, like, together. I know how. Let me do my job."

"I'll think about it," Gary said.

After Bailey had gone to bed and Daniel had left, Gary asked, "So what do you think about Bailey being my trainer?"

"Well, we wanted her to have a project."

He laughed. "Guess I didn't know it would be me."

"I'm not wild about you and her jogging around town together."

"You could join us."

I made a face at him.

"She's young enough to be my daughter. No one's going to talk. In fact, everyone who knows us would understand right away."

And so, we began some new things, hoping they would become good habits. Now, if only I could find a prayer trainer.

29

I didn't pray about it, but Eli called one afternoon and asked if he could come over for a few minutes. When I let him in, he handed me a pretty journal and a fancy pen.

"Have you ever kept a journal or diary?" he asked.

"Only in high school."

"Well, this is a prayer journal. Keeping our mind on task while we pray is one of the biggest challenges of praying. With a journal, you write your prayers. You can write long sentences or only phrases and lists. The benefit is two-fold: it keeps you focused, and you will also have a record of prayers answered." He stopped and corrected himself, "Three-fold: You also won't be forgetting to pray about things."

"I never thought of it," I admitted, flipping through the beautiful blank pages. "Thank you."

"On Sunday, I want to introduce you to Treva. You have probably already met the white-haired lady who makes your coffee at our coffee shop. She is a prayer warrior, and she said she would be willing to talk with you about what prayer has done in her life."

"A prayer trainer!"

"I guess so." He looked around. "Is Gary here?"

"No. He's out walking. The doctors said he needs more exercise."

"Okay. Well, tell him 'hi' from me. I have to run, but I didn't want to leave you hanging about the prayer."

I took the journal into the living room and set it on my sewing table. While I pinned and marked fabric, I kept glancing at the book. How could I have been a believer so long and not have known what to write in a prayer journal?

When Gary and Bailey returned, they were talking quite earnestly, but they stopped as soon as they closed the front door.

"How was your walk?" I asked.

"Fine!" Bailey quipped. She grabbed the baby monitor and galloped down the stairs to shower and change.

"Boring," Gary admitted. "I just can't get excited about going for a walk."

"You sounded as if you were having a good discussion when you came in."

He shrugged. "We talk. Rather: *she* talks. But she doesn't say anything earth-shaking, and I'm hesitant to engage her in something meaningful. It's all about health tips for me or Peter's learning how to eat rice cereal and wondering what she's going to do when it's time for her to return to work."

I didn't say anything.

"Which brings me to that question: What *is* she going to do with Peter?"

"I don't know, but Connie doesn't think I should automatically become the nanny."

"I agree, but what options does she have?"

"Daycare. I suggested she find out if The Gym has daycare. After all, mothers come to exercise. Maybe they have a childcare center."

"Mmm." He showered and changed and came back to the living room, where I had been cutting strips of fabric for Abby's baby's quilt. "I've been thinking."

"Okay."

"Well, wondering: Can you help me come up with something to talk to her about, while we walk?"

"Oof. I'm not a great one to ask. You know me: I just let the conversation go where it goes."

"Would it be out of line for me to ask for clarification for some of her past outbursts?"

"I guess that would depend on how much she trusts you."

As counsellors, we had no idea how inept we were. Gary went on that walk the next day and talked with Bailey about her outbursts, but it backfired on us. Bailey returned from the walk a good ten minutes before Gary. She charged into the house, slammed the front door and raced downstairs, banging her bedroom door as well.

When Gary came in, he looked embarrassed and confused. "Where's Bailey?"

"She crashed through the house about ten minutes ago."

"I probably need to apologize to her. I think I really made a mess of things."

"Why? What happened?"

"Well, I asked Bailey about the New Year's party. And it seems she trusted me to tell me. She had been shopping with Peter New Year's Eve afternoon and had run into a few old friends at the grocery store. They asked her if she wanted to come to the party, and she said she'd think about it. They admired the baby, assuming she was babysitting."

"Oh dear."

"She told them at once that Peter was hers. And they laughed at her. They told her how sorry they were because obviously she couldn't come to the party. Angered by that challenge, she determined to show them that she could do anything she wanted. So, she came up with the excuse to us to go get chips and dip."

"But why didn't she ask us to babysit?"

"Because you had said you wouldn't watch Peter when she went back to work." Gary looked around the kitchen. "I'm hungry; aren't you going to make supper?"

I had been sewing all day and had forgotten to eat lunch. "We're still eating leftovers. I'll heat them up."

We moved into the kitchen, and while I put food in microwave dishes, he continued. "She arrived at the party, and everything was as it always had been. People were already drinking heavily, and they pressed her to drink as well. She stayed and drank too, and danced and some of them began to pair off. She admitted to me that it didn't seem as much fun as it used to be."

"Well, that's good."

"Her old boyfriend – What was his name?"

"Which one?"

"I don't know." He thought for a half a minute and then said, "Anyway, the old boyfriend asked her where her baby was and told the group what a terrible mother she must be. He told her that for the kid's sake – that was a quote, Bailey said – 'for the kid's sake,' she should give the kid up to someone who could raise him properly."

"Oh, how mean!"

"And then he told her that the state always takes children away from parents like her. And that the state would give Peter to the babysitter – assuming that she hadn't left the baby alone in the car."

"Poor Bailey."

"His parting shot was that she should have had an abortion."

"It's no wonder she was so upset the next few days."

"Well, while we were talking, we were walking up Baxter Street and all of a sudden, Bailey started to run. I couldn't keep up with her and called for her to stop. She didn't turn around or anything; she just kept running."

The microwave beeped, and I scooped leftover chicken and dumplings onto our plates. We had only taken a couple bites when there was a huge thud somewhere in the house.

"What was that?" I asked.

"It sounded as if a large bird flew against the window."

And then we heard a wailing cry, and we knew it was Bailey. Even though we were upstairs, we could hear Bailey crying in her room: great, sobs – keening, I think the old novels used to call it – expressing terrible sorrow. Intermittently, there was another crash. Eventually, Peter began to cry.

And then he stopped.

Gary looked at me across his steaming chicken. "I think we had better see what's going on."

We both hurried down the stairs, just as another thud shook the walls. Bailey continued to sob, but quieter.

I knocked on her door, my heart pounding, not knowing what we might find inside. "Bailey, it's me." I twisted the knob, but the door was locked. "Open the door, Sweetie."

Suddenly, all was still.

"Bailey, if you don't unlock the door, we're going to unlock it from out here," Gary told her.

There was a click at the door. I tried the knob and it turned. Bailey was sitting on the floor, pulling Peter onto her lap. Her face was wet with tears, as she pressed her damp cheek against his head. She looked up at me and whispered, "Dorothy, how can I live with myself?"

I still was not sure that Peter was all right, so I went to her and knelt beside her. "What's happened?"

She held up her bright-eyed son, who blinked and pursed his mouth. "Look at him. Isn't he beautiful?"

Relief poured through me. "He is," I agreed.

Suddenly, she raised her voice in a howl, "How could I have killed my baby?"

"You didn't," I assured her. "You – "

"What do you know?" she cried. "My mother told me to. She said that a baby would ruin my life – that everything I ever wanted to do and be would be destroyed by that – that – thing growing inside me." She crushed Peter to her breast and whispered, "That – that precious baby."

The light went on in my head. "Oh, Bailey, did she make you have an abortion?"

She looked at me and nodded. "How could she!' she shouted. "What right did she have? I hate her!" Her voice grew suddenly deep and calm again. "I hate her." She paused and then warned, "And don't tell me you understand. You have no idea the hell I have lived through, like, all these years. And my own mother." She shuddered.

I turned toward Gary, who still stood in the doorway, tears in his eyes.

Then Bailey suddenly started talking again, and this time, we could barely make out her words through the sobs that seemed to tear from her soul. "And now you'll hate me too, and Daniel, and someday – Peter will – will know, and – and he will h –

hate me. Oh, how can I ever forgive myself?" she finished in a whisper.

In that moment, there was a lot that I knew. I knew she had been greatly hurt by the realization that she had, indeed, been coerced into letting others kill her baby. I knew that she needed counseling, but I also knew that Gary and I were in over our heads. Most importantly, however, I knew that Jesus Christ had died for the sins of everyone in the whole world, and that He offered forgiveness to anyone who would ask. This was the time.

I made myself more comfortable on the floor and beckoned Gary to join us. When he was settled, I said, "You are absolutely right: I have no idea how you feel. I feel so sad for you, and I can imagine that the words you are saying are completely inadequate to express the anger and sadness and hurt and hate you feel. But we don't judge you and we certainly don't hate you. I'm so sorry you have had to live with this pain for so long."

She nodded and sighed.

"I can only tell you that there is a solution to your unhappiness. But first you have to know that the person you need forgiveness from is not yourself or anyone else. God is the one who created life, and He is the One you have wronged."

"Great!" She snuffled and wiped her nose on her sweater. "Now God hates me!"

I was glad to see her attitude returning.

Gary knew exactly where I was going. "He doesn't hate you; He loves you, but your sin stands in the way of you seeing that love. All of us are born into the world with a sin problem. Sin separates us from him, and there is nothing we can do about it. It was Adam and Eve's fault, but we won't go there now."

Her voice lowered in pitch as she grumbled, "This isn't very good news and doesn't make me feel better." She laid Peter on the floor and flexed her legs.

"You're right," Gary said, "It's bad news. And sin – whether it's lying or stealing or ending the life of a baby – is still sin, and He makes no distinction. If we stay separated from Him, we will never be able to be with Him, and that means that when we die, we will go to hell, because we can't go to heaven where He lives.

"More bad news," she volunteered.

"Yes, but there is good news, too. Do you remember the verse that says that God loved the world?"

"Yeah. That famous one."

"Well, God does love you."

"Why would he love me?" she grumbled.

"I don't know why God loves us; He just does, and He wanted to find a way to tell you He loves you, and He wants to get rid of the separation."

"Did He?"

"He did. At least He did what He could on His end. The verse says, 'God loved the world so much that He gave his only Son, so that those who believed on Him should not die, but have everlasting life.' He asked His Son, Jesus, to come to earth and to pay for our sins with His own life."

"How could Jesus do that? What about His own sins?"

"Actually, He had no sins, which is why He could die for ours."

"That doesn't make sense. Why would He do that?"

A thought had just popped into my head. "It's like in the movies, where the good guy gives his life to save someone else – or a whole village. He's usually motivated by love."

"Or," Gary interjected, "He's just a really good person. God's super good, and He also loves every human being."

Bailey mopped her nose again. "So why didn't God die? Why did Jesus have to?"

Gary's shoulders sagged. "Too complicated. The important part is that if you want God's forgiveness, it has to be by accepting Jesus' death on the cross for your sins. God's done His part; Jesus did his part. Your part is taking His love and acceptance as a gift."

"That's it?" she asked. "What about the Ten Commandments?"

"What about them?"

"Don't I have to be really good, like, like Dorothy?"

"Nobody can ever be good enough to please God." He looked at me. "Not even Dorothy. So, God had to make it so that anyone could ask for forgiveness, without doing good things. It's a gift. You have to accept it."

Bailey didn't like that. "But that's so wrong! I thought the whole point of God and religion and the church and Christianity was so that people could be good."

"How good does a person have to be?"

"Huh?"

"How many good things should we have to do to deserve heaven?" Gary challenged.

"For that matter," I added, "How many sins are we allowed?"

"But I have to do something." Bailey sighed again. "I'm going to have to think about this." She looked at Peter and rubbed his tummy. Her knuckles were bleeding and one of her fingernails was torn. "Abortion is really, really bad," she said with a quiver once more in her voice. "I don't see how God could ever forgive that."

I took her injured hand gently in mine – the same one she had sprained. "What did you do?"

Tears spilled over again and she whispered, "I was so angry, and I wanted to . . . to . . . ." She glanced up at the wall beside the door, where it was obvious she had slammed her fist.

Gary said, "Bailey, you can't pay for your sin by damaging yourself."

"But it makes me feel better," she protested in a small voice.

He gave her a skeptical look. "Really?"

"Yes. No. I don't know."

"Only God can take away the guilt and pain and the hate."

She lifted her hand and looked at it. "It really hurts." I think she meant more than just her hand.

Gary picked up Peter and wrapped him in his blanket. I helped Bailey to her feet, and we all went upstairs to wash and bandage her hand, which fortunately was not broken, so we didn't have to go to Urgent Care.

30

Each weekday morning, I pulled out the Prayer Journal and wrote a letter to God. I wrote about the previous day and also about my hopes for the coming day. I prayed for Abby and Will - that they would soon have a baby. And I asked God for the perfect woman for Daniel. I had met with Twila, as Pastor Eli had suggested, and she told me to read my Bible and then pray things I read into my prayers for myself and for others.

One of the things that weighed on my heart the most was that I really wanted Bailey to get some counseling, but I didn't want to be the one to suggest it.

At Bible study the following week, Bailey talked with Eli and was relieved when he assured her that every tiny - even unborn - baby goes to heaven.

"He even showed me in the Old Testament where David and Bathsheba's baby died soon after childbirth." Bailey's eyes were bright with hope. "David said that he knew that he would see the child in the future when David died."

Daniel, acting on impulse, invited Eli to come that week to the house and hold a short memorial service for Bailey's aborted baby. Bailey didn't know the sex of the baby, but she decided to name her Gabriella "because it's an angel's name." Although it had seemed like a good idea, Bailey sobbed the whole afternoon, and none of us was able to console her.

I was pretty emotional, myself. Gary finally decided that there was never going to be a good time to give her our present. We had ordered a heart-shaped paving stone, engraved with Gabriella's name and a picture of Jesus with the children. We gave it to her, and she held it to her chest and bowed her head over it, tears running down her face and dripping onto the stone. When she could breathe, she whispered, "She would have been four years old. I don't know how to live with this. It will be with me forever and will never let me forget."

I didn't know what to say, and I was spared saying much when I heard Peter waking up. "I'll get him," I murmured. I squeezed her arm and went downstairs. After I had changed Peter, put him in a clean outfit, and brought him upstairs to fix his bottle, I found Gary alone in the kitchen making tea. Bailey, Eli, and Daniel were nowhere to be seen.

"They went for a walk," Gary clarified.

I mixed the formula and took Peter into the living room to feed him. Gary brought in our tea. "I sure wish I knew how to help her," I sighed.

"We cannot understand what she is feeling. Admitting that we can't help her is probably just honesty. We have to go by faith that if she would turn to God, He would help her."

"It does sound awfully trite, doesn't it? I mean, I look at my life, and I have problems, but they are not big ones, although they seem big to me. Yet, I know people with smaller problems who don't know God, and they think their problems are just huge. Is it all just relative?" I paused to catch my breath and lifted Peter to my shoulder. "I mean, people say: 'Just think how bad things could be if we didn't have God!'"

"You're definitely off-topic," Gary informed me with a smile. "Bailey."

"We can hope that Eli can give her something we haven't been able to give her."

Peter belched, and I told him he was a good boy. I laid him on the carpet at my feet and took a sip of tea.

While we were sitting for an hour, cozy in the living room, Bailey, Daniel and Eli had been walking in a drizzling March rain. We finally heard them coming up the walkway, and then they dripped into the house, chilled to the bone, but all of them smiling.

"Tea!" Bailey begged, shivering.

Daniel ducked into the guest bathroom and grabbed three towels, which he distributed to Bailey and Eli.

I turned on the electric kettle, while they were drying off, and Bailey went downstairs to change. Once everyone had a mug of hot tea in their hand, Bailey exclaimed, "Come sit down; I've got to tell you." Then she looked at Eli, and asked more quietly. "Or can I?"

He gestured toward her and said, "It's your story to tell."

She took another sip of tea and then laughed. "I – I . . .." She turned her head toward Daniel, as if looking for support.

"Just tell them!" he encouraged her.

"All right; I asked God to forgive my sins."

"You did?" I reacted.

"He does that, you know," she clarified. "Because Jesus died for my sins."

Gary grinned. "He did. Tell us about it."

She rubbed her damp hair and said, "Well, I have known for some time that having an abortion was, like, really bad. But I kept telling myself that it was all my mother's fault." She paused and then added. "It *was* her fault, you know. But it – Gabriella – was my baby, and I could have said no to the abortion. I hardly ever did what my mother told me to do anyway."

Peter had begun to fuss, and Bailey set down her tea and picked him up from his blanket on the floor. "I knew that God can forgive sins." She nodded at me. "Dorothy had told me that a lot. A lot! But her sins were not nearly so bad as mine, and I really thought God couldn't – or wouldn't – forgive an abortion. The – the weight of my shame was, like, so heavy this afternoon, and for the first time, I really thought about Gabriella being a real person and I – I let someone kill her." Bailey's chin crumpled and tears dribbled down her cheeks again. She laughed through the tears and said, "I really wasn't going to cry again." She gulped some tea and continued. "When we went for a walk, Eli told me that Jesus had died for all the sins in the whole world. All of them!" she exclaimed, looking at Gary and me in wonder, as if we needed to grasp this, as if we hadn't already told her this before.

We nodded, and she jiggled Peter a bit before saying, "Well, I guess I can make this shorter. Ya know, it's . . . it's really hard to let go of your sin." Her excitement glowed from her eyes. "I mean, you have to, like, be humble and admit that you really were the one at fault. And we can't save ourselves. And we can't do anything to please God. But Dorothy already told me that too. And . . ." She glanced around the room at each of us. "I told God about my sins and asked Him to forgive them. I believe that Jesus died for my sin, and I want to try to do better from now on."

Eli spoke up, "With His help."

"With His help," she agreed. "And I sure do need help 'cause I'm not a good person."

Eli turned to us. "Bailey has agreed to go to counseling concerning the abortion. I think it will help her let go of some of the pain."

"Oh, that's a good idea," Gary said, giving me a sidelong glance.

I just smiled.

· 31 ·

All of us – including Bailey – were thankful when she finally went back to work. The Gym did have childcare, and Bailey had relaxed about allowing 'strangers' to care for Peter. Daniel watched Peter on the evenings when she had counseling, and they still took the baby to every Bible study, for which I was also thankful. I mean, I was thankful that she was going to counseling and Bible study, but the fact that Daniel seemed to be involved in all this was not a comfortable thought. I wanted to talk to him about Bailey, but I didn't know what I would say.

Nana's birthday fell around Easter that year, and, as usual, we planned a miniature golf outing with dinner afterwards at her restaurant of choice. She loved to have the staff make a fuss over her and embarrass her with their silly birthday songs. Peter had weathered the miniature golf tournament, swaddled to Bailey's chest with some ingenious wrappings. He got a bit cranky at the restaurant though, and Bailey slid into a corner and gave him his bottle. The rest of us were eating and laughing, when Daniel switched places with Abby so he could sit by me.

"Would you mind taking Peter home and putting him to bed? I want to take Bailey to a movie."

What could I say? "Sure. Um, what time will she get back?"

"Around 10:30, I should think. Is it okay with you?"

"This time, yes. Let's talk about it another time."

"Thanks, Mom."

"Sure." But I really wanted to ask him 'why?'

A few days later, I was struggling to smooth out several yards of electric blue taffeta on my sewing table. Bailey arrived home with a sleeping baby and took him downstairs to finish his nap. When she came back up, she helped me arrange the folded fabric.

"That's a pretty wild bridesmaid's dress," she noted.

I laughed. "I guess it would be, but it's actually a prom dress."

She shuddered. "Proms!" she snorted. "A horrible tradition!"

"You've said that before. How's that?"

"The girl buys a way-too-expensive dress, and the boy spends way too much money on flowers and dinner, and then he expects to be paid back with . . .." She stopped and shrugged one shoulder. "Well, you know."

I knew what she was getting at, but I said, "Not everyone does that."

"Don't they?"

"It depends on the boy and the girl."

She laughed, but it was a mocking laugh – no humor, just bitterness. "Well, we know what kind of girl I am. Or at least the guy did. That was the night I got pregnant for the first time."

I sighed.

"I didn't even like him that much, and afterwards I hated him. I think I hate him even more, now that I know more."

"I can imagine," I murmured. "Have you told your counsellor this story?"

"I have."

We both fiddled and straightened and re-straightened the fabric. I sure didn't know what to say, and I think she was embarrassed to have dumped it on me. Finally, I said, "I'm sorry that happened to you. You deserve to be treated better. Every boy should be taught to treat women with respect and care."

She chuckled. "You sure don't sound very modern."

I opened my mouth to respond, but she rushed on, "But that's okay. I want to teach that to Peter. Daniel's that way. He treats all the women at Bible study the same as he treats you."

I smiled, but realized that in teaching him to respect women, I had made him a magnet for women like Bailey who had never been treated well. I wanted Bailey to heal, but I didn't want that healing to include falling in love with Daniel. She was not a mother's dream daughter-in-law.

Bailey gave the fabric one more twitch and abruptly ended the conversation by saying, "Shall I make supper? What would you like?"

The talk with Daniel was far from satisfying.

It was one of those cool, drippy April days, better for sitting in front of a fire than wrestling with yards of fabric. I heard Daniel let himself into the house, and he came into the living room, bearing a huge bouquet of miniature carnations.

"What's the occasion?" I asked.

He looked a bit chagrined and admitted, "Well, I had something I wanted to talk to you about, and I thought I'd butter you up."

"Really."

"I think we need hot chocolate and pistachios first."

I put the flowers in water and then went to hunt for the pistachios in my desk. When I returned to the kitchen, Daniel was warming milk on the stove. I already had a suspicion what he wanted to talk about. I felt unprepared and wished Gary was home to run interference.

While we measured and mixed, I asked him about his day.

"Well, until I pass the BAR, I get to do all the research at the law firm. I'm pretty low on the totem pole and just get a weekly salary."

"Is it interesting?"

"Sometimes." He grinned and looked up from stirring the chocolate. "But I can't tell you about it or I'd have to kill you. They are going to pay me for studying for the BAR, if I complete it in their allotted time."

"Well, that's good."

We poured hot chocolate into our cups, added marshmallows and sat at the kitchen table, shelling pistachios.

Finally, Daniel ventured, "I suppose you can guess what I want to talk about."

I nodded. "Bailey."

"I know this will seem weird to you, but I am becoming very fond of her." He put up his hand to stop me from saying anything. "It's definitely not been love at first sight. I've felt sorry for her ever since I met her and learned a little about her, but even before you decided to invite her to live with you guys, I just wondered what it would be like for a man to love a girl like her, as Jesus loved the Church."

"Feeling sorry for someone is not a very flattering way to begin a relationship," I warned.

He sighed. "I know, and that's why I did nothing. But then, you invited her to live with you guys, and she was suddenly around all the time."

So, it was my fault. I broke my fingernail on a pistachio shell, and Daniel fetched the nail clippers from the junk drawer. The interruption was a relief, as he returned to the table and showed me how to open the nuts using another shell instead of my fingernails. I trimmed my thumbnail, and he reached out his hand for the clippings, which he threw in the garbage. I really didn't know what to say, so I kept quiet, as his strong hands made a pile of shelled pistachios in front of me. Then he seemed to remember the topic and started talking again. "Of course, I had no intention of getting into a relationship with a girl who was not a believer, so it was easy to just be a part of our family, caring for her."

"She needs a lot of care."

"She does," he agreed.

"But you started dating before she became a Christian," I protested.

"You're right. She's impulsive and has a quirky sense of humor. She's a great mother, and you have helped her so much."

"I've tried."

"I found those things very attractive. She came to all the Bible studies and eventually to church, and I saw that God was pulling her towards Himself, and she was responding."

"I think all I saw was the problems."

He placed his hand over mine and said gently, "That's what you do. And your gift is to try to solve them. But there were many problems, and I wanted to do what you were doing – help her change the course of her life."

And now Bailey was going to change the course of all our lives. I didn't want that for Daniel. I wanted a nice Christian girl from a nice Christian family, and I felt so ugly and cruel thinking that way. Oh, how I wished Gary were here! He would know what to say. I blinked to keep tears from coming and finally was able to say, "What's next?"

He pulled his hand away from mine, swirled the last of his cocoa, and gulped it down. Mine had grown cold and formed a gooey skin on top. "I'm going to ask her to marry me. Little Peter needs a father, and he needs one now. I don't see any advantages for either of them in waiting any longer."

"What about advantages for you?" I insisted.

"You mean: to give it more thought? I've already spent too much time thinking about this, talking to Eli . . .."

"Have you talked to Dad yet?"

He took a deep breath. "I did."

"And?"

"He doesn't want me to jump into something I might regret later."

Relief. "I couldn't agree more. Girls often grow up to be like their mothers."

His eyes narrowed, and he said, "Do you honestly think Bailey wants to be like her mother?"

"No. Of course not. But . . .." I stopped. What I wanted to say was that most girls can't help it, but that sounded so harsh.

He pushed back from the table, and frustration marched across his face. "Mom, I know this is hard on you, but she has changed so much, and she's going to counseling and Bible study and has friends at church who are also spending time with her. You need to give her a chance and *some* credit for the changes she *has* made."

I pulled myself together. If this was his choice, I certainly would support him. "I can assure you that your father and I . . .."

He held up his hand to stop me. "Mom, I know that if I marry her – if she will have me . . .."

I interrupted, annoyed that any girl wouldn't want him. "Why, on earth wouldn't she have you?"

"It is her choice," he reminded me with a shrug. He stood up and gathered the pistachio shells. "What I was going to say is: If I marry her, I have no doubt that you and Dad would be good in-laws for her and would grow to love her as a daughter."

I nodded. "We would." And I remembered what Abby had said last year: that loving Bailey as a daughter would be enough. Was I doing that? Had I done enough? Or was I still in the pitying stage, trying to give her a better life but not really loving her?

Daniel tossed the shells in the trash and looked at his phone. "I gotta run," he apologized, "I hope you're not too shaken by this."

"No. I sort of suspected this was coming." I stood up and sighed, dumping my gooey, cold chocolate into the sink. "I hope the rest of your day goes well."

He hugged me and left.

· 32 ·

I needed to talk to someone, and Gary was busy at work, so I drove to the Pregnancy Center, hoping Connie would have time for me.

"You already know this," she said, peering at me over her coffee. "We can't control whom our children fall in love with."

"But I don't even think he has fallen in love with her," I protested. "I think he's choosing out of pity or compassion or . . .."

"Is that a bad thing? Think of it: You have a son who is so full of compassion that he would choose a hard life for himself just to make someone else's life easier."

"But I want him to have a happy life. I have a happy life."

She laughed. "I don't think you mean that. You want him to have a joyful life, but your 'happy' is so event-oriented. Look at Jesus: He went to the cross because of the joy set before Him."

"Daniel is hardly Jesus."

"Of course not. But sacrifice has its own rewards."

"This is an awfully big sacrifice. I mean, marriage is the second most important choice anyone ever makes."

She laid her hand on my wrist. "Dorothy, you can't make this decision for him, and if you fight him, you will just risk losing your relationship with him." She stood up and looked around. "Are you here to work?"

I finished my tea. "I guess so."

"I need to wash woodwork. The painters are coming tomorrow."

Connie found us rubber gloves and buckets, old toothbrushes and rags. We worked for a while in silence, but my brain was trying to find the perfect argument.

Connie spoke first. "Will you have time to make curtains for us?"

I looked at the old, faded yellow drapes. "What do you want?"

"I was thinking of sheers across the windows, so people can't see in, but we can see out and have light. Then something feminine. The walls are going to be pale blue."

"I'll bring you some samples to choose from. Maybe a soft plaid."

We worked a while longer, and then I said, "When I had the idea to ask Bailey to live with us, I had no idea how many pitfalls there would be. Did you?"

"I knew it wouldn't be easy for you, but serving others is never easy. This Pregnancy Center takes a lot of juggling and soothing of feelings and just plain hard work. And people are not easy to live with. And the young women who come here are often searching for an easy solution to what they know is going to be a lifelong commitment. We pray and do our best, but sometimes it seems it's not enough." She squeezed out her rag and asked, "Are you sorry you did it?"

Was I? "I guess not, but Daniel wanting to marry her had not been on my list of things we would have to work out." I scrubbed for a minute and then said, "Did I tell you we met her mother at Christmas?"

"No. How did that happen?"

I told her a bit about it and then summed it up: "Her mother was so unkind and selfish. I'm just afraid that Bailey will be like her someday, and I don't want that for Daniel."

"Who says she has to be like her mother?"

"Well, girls often grown up to be like their mother."

"Is Abby like you?"

"Um." I had never thought of this. "Abby's funny; I'm hardly ever funny. She's a great cook, and I'm not. She never wanted to learn to sew, but she is heavily involved in Will's bookstore. I would be useless in Gary's real estate stuff. I'm neat – too neat – and Abby, well . . . she's not. Maybe we aren't that alike."

"Nice list, but those are things that don't really matter."

"What do you mean?"

"I mean: What is Abby really like? She is a kind and loving wife. She will be a great mother. She loves God and she loves her husband and her church, and she is generous and hospitable. She is just like you."

"So, girls *do* grow up to be like their mothers!" I insisted.

"What is the difference between Abby's relationship with you and Bailey's relationship with her mother?"

I considered for a minute. "Well, for Abby and me, we respect one another and love one another and we're – I guess we're friends." A light bulb went on in my head. "Bailey doesn't respect her mother at all. She doesn't want to be around her, and she doesn't want her mother to influence Peter – so much so, that she made a point of giving me the baby when she had to leave the room."

"What makes you different from Bailey's mother?"

I frowned.

"And it's not her taste in clothes."

"I suppose it's how I talk to and about people. Maybe how I treat people."

"But why do you act that way?"

"It sounds so trite, but it's because I am a believer in Jesus Christ, and it's how I think He wants me to live. I'm just so used to it, I guess I don't think about it."

"Have you changed over the years, as you have walked with Christ?"

"I have," I admitted, but clung to one last argument that might prove my point. "But what if Bailey doesn't want to change?"

"Is she a believer?"

"Yes, she says so."

"Then the Holy Spirit will be working on her life, apart from you, or even Daniel."

Connie dropped her rag into the bucket. "Dorothy, you can't control the world. On the bright side, though, Bailey loves you and Gary, and she admires you a lot. And you have been such a model and mentor and teacher for her. Maybe she will grow up to be like you."

I laughed. 'Oh, dear! An inflexible, insecure control-freak."

"You're too hard on yourself," she chided, pushing herself to her feet. "Even if you are those things, they are not *you*." Pulling off her gloves, she looked toward the office. "I just heard someone come into the waiting room. I'll be back. Keep working."

I scrubbed woodwork and carried on conversations in my head, as I struggled to put down my desire to prevent Bailey from loving Daniel. I got nowhere in my head, but finished the woodwork and stood up, unkinking my back. Maybe I needed to join Gary for his walks.

After peeling off the gloves and dumping the dirty water, I went back through the office and waved good-bye to Connie, who was still talking with two women: one quite young, and the other looked like her mother.

Supper. Prom dresses. I needed to focus.

And I needed to pray. *Lord, please calm my heart and guide Daniel. And give me the grace to accept his decision.* The prayer made me cry, and I felt sick.

That evening, over baked fish and Tater Tots, Gary asked, "So did Daniel talk to you about Bailey?"

I filled him in on our conversation, which just brought me back to feeling protective and frustrated. "I was glad that he said you and I are on the same page and don't want him to regret his decision."

Gary nodded. "The hard thing is letting him make the decision. He's wise beyond his years, and right now, he's into caring for those who are weaker than he is."

"Why do you say that?"

"Well, look at his job: he's doing *pro bono* work, and I can't imagine him becoming one of those lawyers who is only in it for the money. I think he really wants to help people, and Bailey is number one on his list right now."

"If only he would listen to advice."

"Whose advice?"

I was surprised he'd have to ask. "Ours', of course."

"I think that's what he's doing. Maybe we haven't added anything new to his decision.

Finally, I said what I had been thinking all day. "This is all my fault."

He laughed. "My darling Dottie, of course it is! If you hadn't responded to the prompting of God that day to reach out to a young woman in a really difficult position, none of this would have happened."

Tears burned my eyes.

"Do you regret it?" he continued. "I don't." He took my fork and laid it on the table, and grabbed both of my hands. "Most of the awful things we imagined never happened. She didn't steal from us or murder us in our beds. She has, in fact, been a blessing in many ways. All of us – Daniel, and Abby and Will – have seen her grow and change. What probably touched Daniel's heart was seeing how much Bailey cared for you."

"For me? I don't understand."

"Yes, while you were so busy teaching her and caring for her, she was taking care of you. She drove you places, sat in hospital rooms with you, ran errands, and trusted you with her baby." He paused, fiddling with my wedding ring. "Honestly, Dottie, I like Bailey. Oh, she's a work in progress, but she is making progress. If Daniel decides to marry her, I know it won't be hard to accept her as a daughter because we love Daniel so much. But even if Bailey married someone else, I don't think our relationship with her would end. Your example of wife and mother have been a part of her change, and she looks up to you. I wonder if she hasn't been given to us."

"I like her too," I admitted. "She has more spunk than I have, and I really admire that. She thinks on her feet. I wish I could do that. I guess I'm a work in progress too."

He laughed again. "You have spunk; it's just quiet spunk." He paused. "You were the one who marched right into that clinic and pulled Bailey out. Quietly."

I shivered. "I was so scared."

"But you did it."

"And I'm glad I did. Another abortion would have shattered her."

Gary pushed my plate toward me. "Eat!"

I took a couple bites before he looked up with a twinkle in his eyes. "So. After we marry Bailey off to the greatest catch in the state, shall we do this again?"

33

Gary could joke about it, and I could laugh, but I still was not really happy with the prospect of Bailey as a daughter-in-law. I still hoped Daniel would change his mind, yet I couldn't forget what Connie had said about the Holy Spirit. *Dear Lord, could Your Holy Spirit really change her and make her someone who would be a good wife for Daniel?*

Someone like Frances, who came to our house to order her wedding dress the following week. I had met her at church one Sunday, during fellowship time. Bailey had dragged her over to me and announced, "This is Frances – we call her Frankie. She's getting married this summer, and still doesn't have a wedding dress. I told her that you make, like, bee-u-tiful wedding dresses."

Frankie was holding little Peter, and she hitched him onto her hip, pushing her curly, red hair from her face with her free hand. "I'm not sure if I could afford to have one made, though," she admitted quietly.

I glanced at Bailey - who obviously knew I could solve this problem immediately - and then looked at Frankie. Who wouldn't want to make a dress for this lovely girl, with her fiery locks and creamy skin, sprinkled liberally with freckles! "Well, I can certainly work within your budget."

Bailey shoved Frankie's shoulder and said triumphantly, "See, I told you it would work!"

We set up a time for her to come to the house, and the two young women walked off, chatting and laughing. Bailey had a friend – a nice friend!

On the day Frankie was scheduled to come to the house, Bailey got up early to bake cookies. I was working hard to finish a last-minute flower girl dress, so I was glad to have her so involved. The whole house smelled like cinnamon sticks, when Bailey welcomed her friend.

"I made snicker doodles," she announced at the door. "Please come in. You're going to choose a dress, and while you're doing that, I'm going to make tea."

I had pulled out my patterns, the magazines, and brides' journals, and Frankie and I sat at the dining room table to look through them. She would perk up at the sight of a dress and then, after a few pages, she would drop her head into her hands and murmur, "Oh, I don't know."

"What do you want? Have you been to a wedding and seen a dress that you really liked - or hated. We certainly can rule out certain styles."

She smiled and said, "No off-the-shoulder or strapless, please. I'd like something simple, but elegant." She stopped and bit her lip. "No, not elegant, just pretty." She sighed.

We flipped through a couple more magazines with little success. Finally, I had to ask, "Would it help for you to have your mother here? Or a friend – maybe your maid-of-honor?"

Frankie turned and looked into the kitchen, where it was obvious that Bailey had been listening.

Bailey snorted. "Don't look at me. I know nothing about weddings!"

Frankie sighed again. "My family lives in Idaho."

"I see." But I didn't. How was I going to help her choose a dress when she had no one to help her, and she obviously didn't know what she wanted. So, I asked, "How did you end up so far from Idaho?"

"I came here to go to university and then I found a job." She paused, uncertain if she should speak further.

I pressed on: "How did you meet your fiancé? What's his name?"

"Ben. I met him at work, and we just hit it off." She wasn't big on communicating.

"What does he do?"

"He's a nurse, and I'm a physical therapist, so we . . .." Her voice trailed off, uncertain and apologetic.

It may have seemed abrupt to her, but I announced, "I think it's time for tea. Are you ready, Bailey?"

"Ready! But you don't need to bring the mags."

"Okay, but . . .." I let my voice trail off, as I saw Bailey waving her cell phone at me.

Once at the table, Bailey plunked her cell phone down in front of of me. "This is what you need."

I looked at her phone, and there were photos of bridal gowns. "Okay," I said again, "but you girls are going to have to show me how to do this on my computer."

I brought my computer, and Bailey poured tea. Frankie found a website with lots of wedding dresses and began scrolling through them.

"So," I said when we had settled, "tell me about Ben."

"Ben," Frankie said, as if unsure where to start. "He's really good with patients and can make them laugh, even in the midst of their fears and pain. He makes me laugh, too, although I wish I was able to be funny for him."

"I know that feeling."

"He wants to be a missionary." She looked at me, as if expecting disapproval.

"Does he?"

She took a deep breath, and suddenly the words tumbled from her. "That's the problem. There's a hospital in the jungles of Zambia – you can only get there by little airplanes – and they really need another nurse. And they could use a physical therapist; they've never had one before. Ben's been there, and he loved the work they're doing among the people. There's even a school to teach some of the people nursing, and I could teach physical therapy. We've been working extra hours to earn enough money to support ourselves for a while. And we want to get married soon, so we can go – only . . .." She snapped her mouth shut.

"Please," I pushed the plate of cookies toward her. "Only?" I prodded.

Her shoulders sagged. "Only Ben's parents hate me." She stirred more sugar into her tea and then revised her comment. "Well, they don't hate me, but they don't like me. They think I'm dragging him off to Africa, and that he needs to stay here and become head of nursing at the hospital. But he already wanted to be a missionary before I ever met him." She paused, pushing the cookies around the plate, as if they were checkers. "They also don't like it that my parents are potato farmers."

"They've said that?" I asked in surprise.

"To him, yes, but I know because of how they treat me. I'm not good enough for him." She stopped again, and I risked a glance at Bailey, who was scrutinizing her plate.

Frankie admitted, "I'm too quiet, and they want someone who's more forceful and on their side."

"What do *your* parents think?"

"They love Ben, but it's been hard on us both. They're so far away, and Ben's parents live here, so we get more disapproval than encouragement. They told him that I will ruin his life."

I heard that thought echo in my head, but this was Frankie's story. I was aware that Bailey had stopped eating and now was watching us intently.

Frankie chomped off half her cookie, chewed it, and swallowed hard. "How can being a missionary be a bad thing?" she asked through tears. "Why would I ruin his life? I love him and want to help him follow his dream. I want to be worthy of him. Why do they want to alienate him? I don't want him to have to choose between me and them, but he's already said that he will choose me."

"That's a hard choice, especially if he's had a good relationship with them." Was I listening to myself? Bailey hadn't moved, and I didn't dare look at her. My heart was pounding in my ears.

Frankie put her head in her hands and whispered, "I just don't understand why they can't leave us alone to live our lives as we think God wants us to."

I took a deep breath and dared to ask the big question: "How should they be reacting?"

"I think they need to trust his judgment. They raised him; now they need to just . . . just trust him." She sobbed and cleared her throat. "I wish Ben had parents like you and Gary," she finished in a tiny voice.

Bailey suddenly jumped up from the table, knocking over her chair. "Sorry!" She righted it and said gruffly, "I think I hear Peter. See ya later." She dashed down the stairs.

Frankie's heartbreak had already broken through my own attitude towards Bailey. I don't know how long I sat there in silence, hearing in my mind all the unkind things I had said and thought about Bailey – all the manipulative arguments I had imagined using to change Daniel's mind.

Finally, Frankie's voice penetrated my guilt. "Dorothy?"

I collected my thoughts. "Sorry. I was just thinking. I guess we will have to pray about this." I pulled my computer toward us and said, "Now, let's find you a pretty dress."

After Frankie left, I felt so guilty. I wanted to find a way to make amends for being so unsupportive to Daniel. I also knew that the conversation had undoubtedly hurt Bailey, but I had no idea what I could say to correct that. I went downstairs, but Bailey and Peter weren't there, so I assumed they had gone for a walk.

Later, after tidying the kitchen, I sat on the edge of our bed and stared out the window, wondering how to change how I felt. I knew there was a verse somewhere in the New Testament about people becoming new creatures, with the past gone. I hunted around in my Bible for a while, and couldn't find it. Then I remembered the Bible app Bailey had shown me in the hospital.

There it was: 2 Corinthians 5:17: "If any man is in Christ, he is a new creature; old things have passed away; behold, all things have become new." I opened my prayer notebook.

Bailey: a new creation of God. Could I see that? I realized that I was still looking at the old Bailey. This new Bailey had the Holy Spirit living in her, and He had given her gifts and talents to use for God. Her past was behind her – forgiven and buried in the deepest sea. And she now had the power to become a woman of God. She was no longer just the girl who had had an abortion and who had come to us for help.

Dear Lord, please show Bailey somehow how blessed she is. I am so sorry I have been so fixed on Daniel's happiness that I missed how much Bailey means to this family. Let her discover this verse and live it. And change the way I view her, so that I can see her through the lens of the new creature she is – the one Jesus died for and forgave of her sins. Forgive me for my blindness, for not seeing her as You see her. Show me how to love her and guide her, so she can truly put the past behind her and live for You. Heal the hurts that have been inflicted on her, and help her become the woman she wants to become.

I lay down on the bed and cried until my head ached.

Life must go on. Even if we make horrible blunders, the family still needs to eat, groceries still need to be bought, and wedding dresses still need to be sewn. I had a lot of time to think, as I ran my sewing machine, rehearsing what I ought to say to Bailey and Daniel. Then I drove to the grocery store and tried to think of something for supper.

34

"Bailey did *what*?" Gary's voice exploded through my speaker phone.

"She left. She's gone! I. . .." How could I explain to Gary? "I went to the grocery store, and when I got back, her things - well, most of them - are gone."

"Did something happen?"

"I . . .." My throat tightened, and I murmured, "Oh, Gary, I messed up so badly."

"What did you do?"

I tried to control my voice and finally blurted out, "Not over the phone. Can you come home?"

"Not now. I have a house-showing in fifteen minutes. I'll come home after that. Probably in a couple hours."

"Okay." I ended the call and pulled my prayer notebook toward me. As I read through what I had written for the past few months, I began to realize that all my prayers for Bailey were for her to change her life: turn around, learn how to be a mother, discover her potential, heal from previous hurts. I know they were all good things, but until today, I had never prayed for my own wisdom and attitude.

I remembered Daniel's comment before we had even invited Bailey to live with us: "You aren't going to be too good for her, are you?"

I really didn't want to be too good. I had thought that we were doing all right. We wanted Bailey to feel at home, and we tried not to interfere in her life, even though her life interfered with ours. We had seen change in her attitude towards us and towards God, and she seemed happy. But I was sure that somehow, my reluctance to have her become my daughter-in-law had communicated itself loudly.

Gary eventually came home, and I was able to tell him about the conversation with Frankie - and Bailey's reaction.

Ever practical, he said, "But we don't even know that's the reason why she's gone."

That stopped me short. What if she had left for another reason? No. I was certain. "You had to have been here, Gary," I insisted. "Frankie's situation was so similar. And Bailey didn't even finish her tea. She knocked over her chair, left her friend to me, and stomped downstairs."

"Did you call her?"

"I did; it went to voice mail."

"Did she take your car?"

I hadn't even thought to look, but she hadn't. "How could she take all her stuff and Peter without a car?" I wondered.

"Maybe she called a cab."

"Her mother?"

Gary shook his head.

"A friend from the casino?'

"She has no friends there anymore."

I was puzzled. "Work?" And then it hit me: "Connie! The Pregnancy Center! But why wouldn't Connie let me know?"

"You don't even know she's there," he reminded me.

"I'll call."

"You may not hear what you want to hear."

I dialed, and Connie picked up after the second ring. "Hi, Dorothy."

"Connie, did Bailey call you?"

"You *do* realize that I have to keep confidences."

My heart flopped. So Bailey had called her. "Is she there?"

"She's fine. Don't worry about her."

"But . . .."

"She's fine. I'm not going to tell you where she is."

"Oh, Connie, I have made such a mess of things."

"Perhaps. But I don't want to be your confessor."

I sighed. "Okay. Thank you."

"Bye."

Gary and I sat for a minute, listening to the wall clock tick. Finally, I had to ask, "How am I going to fix this?"

We had no answers, but neither of us realized how bad things were until Daniel burst into the house while I was cleaning up after supper.

"Are you hungry?" I asked. "We have left-overs."

"No," he said abruptly and then added, "Thanks." He ran his fingers through his hair and spun around toward the living room where Gary had just turned on the television.

Something was wrong. Maybe he already knew. I tossed the dish towel on the counter and followed him.

"She turned me down!" He moaned, bewildered.

Gary muted the TV.

I gulped, uncertain where to begin. "Daniel, I . . .."

He raced on, as if he had not heard me: "Bailey and I have talked about marriage, and she seemed so positive, and now she says no. I was so certain she wanted to be a part of our family. I don't understand. And then I find out that she's moved out! Why would she do that? And she wouldn't tell me why - just that she wasn't good enough for me. What would make her say that?"

He dropped onto the couch and hunched there, head bowed, hands clasped between his knees.

Gary and I exchanged glances and I took a big breath when he nodded.

My hands were shaking as I admitted, "Daniel, I think it was because of what happened this morning."

He turned his head slowly and grumbled, "So what happened this morning?"

I told him, trying always to keep to the facts and not embellish with what I thought.

When I was done, he still looked at me and finally asked, "So how was this a problem?"

"Well, I think that when she heard Frankie's story, she saw herself in the story and compared herself with Frankie and -" I turned to Gary for help because my throat closed up and I couldn't speak. Tears dribbled down my face.

Gary cleared his throat. "It is a possibility that she thought that if Frankie was considered not worthy of Ben, then Bailey would be worthy of no one."

Frustration filled Daniel's voice: "But why would she think that? We all love her!"

I sniffed. "We do, but . . .."

"But?"

This was so hard to say. Was I going to break my son's heart? Was I going to damage our glorious friendship? "I'm so sorry, Daniel," I whispered, "I didn't want you to marry her."

"Did you say tell her that?"

"No."

"But you told me it was okay!" he protested.

"I know. I know, but I think I communicated otherwise to Bailey."

"How did you communicate it? What did you *say* to her?" he demanded.

"I didn't *say* anything, but as I listened to Frankie's story, I realized that we raised you to be the man you are, and we - I - needed to trust your judgment. But I think that Bailey got stuck in Frankie's comment about Ben's parents thinking she would ruin Ben's life. That's when she knocked over her chair and ran downstairs."

Daniel sprang to his feet. "I think you're assuming too much! You don't know what Bailey was thinking! Give her the benefit of the doubt, for heaven's sake."

Gary stood as well, his voice calm. "You're right, son. We need to find her and talk to her and find out why she decided so suddenly to move out."

Daniel raised his hands as if to ward off an unwelcome intrusion. "I'll go find her. I think you guys had better keep your distance until I find out what she's really thinking." He marched to the front door and then came back. "I'll be in touch," and he was gone.

I turned to Gary. "I've shattered him."

He dropped back into his recliner. "He's not that fragile," he grumbled.

"How can you say that?" I protested. "You saw the look on his face! Oh, I have made such a mess of things."

"Dottie, you are not able to screw up the whole world. What's happened, has happened. You had no idea that Frankie was going to have that story to tell. You had no control over Bailey's reaction to hearing Frankie's story. And the fact that you kept your mouth shut about disagreeing with Daniel's choice for a wife, was a good thing. We both agreed that we would love whomever he married, right?"

"Right," I sighed.

"At this point, there is nothing we can do, so you finish in the kitchen, and I'll watch the rest of today's bicycle race."

So annoying! Yet what was I going to do but wallow in guilt that might or might not be deserved. I decided to bake cookies.

· 35 ·

I really needed to sew. The next wedding was in two weeks, and Frankie's was in September. While I sewed, Bailey was proving to herself that she was indeed worth fighting for.

She had run down the stairs to escape from me and Frankie, but she had not really heard Peter. Opening her bedroom door slowly, Bailey tiptoed into the room. Peter was breathing softly, his little pink lips pursed like a kiss, his long dark lashes resting against his chubby cheeks.

She sat on the floor next to her open Bible. Psalm 4, which she had thought so irrelevant this morning, seemed as if it was shining from the page: *"Answer me when I call, O God of my righteousness! You have relieved me in my distress; be gracious to me and hear my prayer."* She dropped her head onto her arms and started talking to God.

It was so stupid - *so* stupid! - for her to believe that she could be the heroine in a Cinderella story. Daniel would be foolish to risk marrying a girl who knew nothing about faithfulness and purity. He could have any of the girls at church, and most of them were virgins and loved God and came from wonderful families. Why should he be stuck with a ready-made family and a woman who knew nothing about how to make a marriage work?

Angrily, she scrubbed the tears away and got up from the floor. "I have to move out," she whispered. "I have to be able to make it on my own with God's help."

But where to go?

Quietly, she began to pile her things into a duffel bag. Peter stretched in his sleep and opened his eyes for just a moment. She slipped across the hall to the bathroom to fetch her toiletries. She could hear Dorothy and Frankie in the kitchen, still talking about wedding dresses, and she closed the bathroom door to shut them out. When Frankie left, Dorothy would probably come down, and Bailey didn't want to talk to her.

She roused Peter and tiptoed upstairs, letting herself out the garage door to go for a walk.

The fresh air cleared her head. Where to go? She couldn't call anyone at the church because they would want to know why she was moving out. And she didn't want to tell them. Dorothy and Gary had done so much for her; she didn't want to badmouth them. But she couldn't stay. Seeing Daniel so often would be torture.

She couldn't ask anyone at work for help because they would assume the worst. And besides, they also knew Dorothy and Daniel.

The casino? She had no friends there anymore - if they had ever been real friends.

Connie! Connie would help her. Although Connie knew Dorothy and attended the same church, her job at the Pregnancy Center required her to maintain confidences. Besides, she already knew about Daniel.

She walked back to the house and saw Frankie drive away.

Back in her room, she changed Peter's diaper and packed some more. Everything would not fit in her duffel bag and suitcase. It seemed a lifetime ago since she had dragged that suitcase up the walkway and thrown up her margarita on the front steps. So much had happened. So may joys and sorrows. She had learned to be useful, not just to survive.

"The Lord hears when I call to Him. Tremble, and do not sin; meditate in your heart upon your bed, and be still. Selah."

I wonder what 'Selah' means, she thought.

"Offer the sacrifices of righteousness, and trust in the Lord."

Can I trust Him? Do I trust Him enough that I can strike out on my own?

Peter began to fuss. She would have to feed him. She opened the door and listened. It seemed quiet in the kitchen. She ran up and fixed Peter's bottle and grabbed his baby food from the fridge.

"Dorothy?' She called softly.

No answer. No one was home.

While she fed Peter, she called Connie, who answered after the third ring. "Bailey? How's it going?" she asked with a cheerful lilt.

"Connie, are there any places I could move to? I need to get away from Dorothy and Gary for a while."

Connie's voice was suddenly tense with urgency. "Are you in danger?"

"No, no, I'm safe. I just need to learn to live on my own, and I don't want to talk to them about it right now."

"Are you sure?"

"I need some space and time to think."

"Well, the Salvation Army has tiny suites that might do for a while. I can call and ask them."

"Would you do that? I'm packing right now, and . . .." She hesitated, thinking about her options. Not very many. "Connie, could you come pick me up? I don't have a car."

"Is Dorothy there. It might be awkward . . .."

"She's not home. I don't know where she is or when she will be back."

Connie sighed. "I'll come now. Are you ready?"

"I will be. Thank you."

Why did she not feel panic, or unsure, or frustrated? Why was the way so obvious?

She fastened Peter into his carrier and hauled him upstairs to wait by the front door. Then she went back down and took apart the crib and carried all the pieces upstairs.

"Carseat base!" she exclaimed to the hallway. It was in Dorothy's car. Well, she would just have to make do.

Connie arrived, and they packed everything into the trunk of her car. The carrier had grooves for the seatbelt, so they figured out how to secure it.

Once they were all settled, Connie asked again, "Are you sure you want to do this?"

"Did you find me a place to stay?"

"I did." She started the engine, and they drove away from the house that had been Bailey's home for over a year. Unpredictably, Bailey felt tears coming, and she blinked to chase them away.

The Salvation Army apartments were meant for women in danger, so Connie had found her a small private room downtown at City Sanctuary.

""You'll have your own key, and there are bathrooms in every room. It's not meant for a long-term stay. People who are transitioning from life on the street to finding a job can stay until they can afford a place of their own."

Bailey knew where the City Sanctuary was, only a block from the casino. As they drove into the downtown area, Bailey felt her courage and assurance drain away. She no longer belonged here, but now she had returned to a place she didn't want Peter to even know existed. They passed the casino, where there was no parking, and she felt only revulsion. Then a sorrow passed over her - a longing she had never felt before - a feeling of missing and being missed and knowing that things would never again be as good and as carefree and as *safe*.

Inside the building, an elderly man greeted Connie at the front door with a hug and then turned to Bailey. "Well, well! Is this the little lady who needs a place to stay? And look at this fine boy. What's his name?"

"Peter," she mumbled, suddenly shy.

"Good name! Solid as a rock!" He started to chuckle. "Solid as a rock! Peter! Did you hear that Connie?"

"I heard it, Douglas. You're very clever. Now could you show us the room?"

While he went to fetch the key, Bailey shifted Peter to her other arm and took a deep breath. It smelled like coffee. The room was bright with large windows on two sides. Against the windows were tables and chairs, and a few people sat and talked quietly or worked jigsaw puzzles.

Douglas returned with two keys, pressed a duplicate into Bailey's hand, and led them up two flights of stairs and down a long hallway. "God must be smiling upon you, young lady. They just finished cleaning this room, and it's far enough away from the others that your little one won't be disturbed. See: There are storerooms on both sides of the hallway and you're at the end."

Inside, the room was hot, and Bailey knew at once that it was too small to set up the crib. Douglas opened the windows, told Bailey that supper was on the main floor between five and seven, and he showed her the paper of regulations and instructions.

He did a quick inventory of the room: "Microwave, bathroom, mini-fridge, table, chair, new mattress, dresser, lamp, yup, it's all here." Then he led them back downstairs to show her the dining room, and they went back to Connie's car.

Once they had hauled everything except the crib up the stairs to her room, they shoved the bed against the wall so Peter wouldn't fall out. "But you need to be careful, sleeping next to Peter," Connie warned.

Discouraged, Bailey murmured, "I probably won't sleep much anyway." She closed the window, wondering how she would sleep at all with the trucks and cars and motorcycles stopping and accelerating right under the window.

After Connie left, Bailey carried Peter down to the dining room, where supper was being served. She fixed Peter's bottle and nibbled at an unappetizing plateful of macaroni and cheese with hot dogs. She was in no mood to talk with anyone, so when a woman came to her table, she told her, "My son has to go to bed," and left.

Back in the room, she was greeted by the rumble of a freight train one block away, shaking the room. She opened the the window anyway because the heat felt as if it was squeezing her lungs.

Bailey's first night in the tiny room was punctuated by trains going past every hour. Traffic noises rose and fell, depending on the traffic lights, and people loitered on the sidewalk under her window and yelled at one another. The sun didn't set until after 9 o'clock. She couldn't get comfortable on the strange bed, and the sunset made it hard to sleep.

A bus drove by, spewing diesel fumes, and she suddenly realized that she needed to study a bus schedule for the next morning to go to work.

She rolled out of bed and turned on the lamp. While looking for her phone, she also found her Bible. She looked at her watch: 11:45; it was still the 4th. She opened her Bible and read Psalm 4 for the third time that day. How long ago it seemed since she had discovered it that morning! The final verse made her smile. "*In peace I will both lie down and sleep, for You alone, O Lord, make me to dwell in safety.*"

She climbed back into bed and pushed Peter over a bit. Goodness, but a hot, sweaty baby took up a lot of space if you let him! She closed her eyes and fell asleep.

For several days, peace and quiet hung over our house until my ears rang with the sounds of silence. It should have been easier to get my sewing done, but I kept listening for Bailey to pound up the stairs, moaning, "Have you seen my phone?" In the stillness of the day, sometimes I thought I heard Peter and wondered, Where are his diapers? How easily some things become habits!

I was folding laundry when Gary popped in just before lunch. He galumphed down the stairs and watched me for a minute.

"I think I need a cat!" I told Gary.

"Are you saying a cat can replace Bailey and Peter?" he scoffed.

I had to laugh. "Well, no, when you put it that way. But at least there would be something alive in the house."

"Are you done here?"

"Almost." I picked up a pile of his things. "Here. You can carry these up and," I gave him *that* look. "And put them away."

"If I can remember where they go." He trudged back up the stairs. When he got to the top, he turned and called down, "I brought lunch. And I have news."

Over deli sandwiches and chips, he told me the news.

"Bailey is fine and safe. Daniel found her."

"How did he do that?"

Gary chuckled. "Well, it wasn't that difficult. He just sat in his car in the parking lot of The Gym and waited until she got off work. He had a few of his law books, his computer, the 'hot spot' on his phone, and plenty of time to study. Eventually, she had to leave work, and so he was able to talk with her." He paused to take a gargantuan bite and started chewing.

"And?" I asked.

He finally swallowed. "I had coffee with Daniel this morning, and he told me."

"What did he tell you?"

"That he had found her and that she's safe."

Men can be so infuriating. "Was that all?"

He nodded. "That's all Daniel said about Bailey. After that, we talked about his exam, which is coming up soon."

"So we know nothing about their conversation or future plans or anything?"

"Nope. Nothing."

I sighed. "How am I going to make this right?"

"I honestly don't know. We need to pray for Bailey and Peter, and probably ask God to orchestrate a meeting in which we can all say what we need to say."

"I wish I knew what to say."

"I think when the time comes, you will. We all will." He stood and collected the bits on the table to throw away. "What are you doing this afternoon?"

"I have *got* to finish that wedding dress. The wedding is in a week, and I still have the maid-of-honor's dress as well."

"Well, I'll get out of your hair. Get on with it!" He left, and silence descended once more.

I had been sewing about an hour, when Abby interrupted with a text. "Could I come for tea?"

"Of course."

A few minutes later, she blew in with a hot blast of mid-June sunshine.

"Ahh!" She crooned. "Air conditioning! The heat is awful at our place!"

"You could spend the day here and go home later when it cools off."

She sighed and rubbed her very large abdomen. "I like our place. It's just . . . hot."

I fixed us some iced tea, and then we found her a relatively comfortable chair in the living room near the air conditioner. I thought maybe we should give them a window AC for the baby.

I savored my iced tea and then said, "I'm so glad you came over; the silence is driving me crazy."

"Where's Bailey?"

I hadn't realized she might not know what had happened. "Um. At work, I guess. She moved out about a week ago."

"Did something happen?"

I told her about the conversation with Frankie, and the resulting flight of Bailey and Peter from our house.

"Well surely, it can't be that bad."

"It's worse. Did you know Daniel wanted to marry her?"

"Yes, he told us. He also said she turned him down."

"I do think it was because of me. I . . . I really wasn't crazy about the idea. And I think she knew it."

"Oh, no, Mom. That couldn't be." She thought for a moment and then added, "Is that why she moved out?"

"We don't really know, but I think so."

Abby drank deeply from her glass and then wiggled a bit to find a more comfortable position. "Well, I know Daniel loves her, so he'll have to convince her. I'll see her on Saturday. Maybe I can find out what's happening."

"Why are you seeing her?"

"She asked me to babysit because he's teething, and he looks like he has a cold, and the daycare workers don't want him at daycare." Her statement hit me like a punch in the stomach. I didn't know what to say, so I drank some tea and tried to compose my face. It shouldn't matter to me whether or not Bailey asked me or Abby to babysit. Never mind that I had a wedding that day and wouldn't have been able to babysit anyway. When I could trust my voice again, I offered, "Oh, I hope he's not sick. And you be careful lifting him."

She laughed and reassured me. "It's only for a couple hours. Then Will comes home and can do the heavy lifting."

I pushed my hurt feelings down and realized that I wasn't going to get any more sewing done this afternoon. I would just have to sew into the night. "Would you like to call Will, and you can have supper with us?"

"That would be great!"

"I'll show you how far I have gotten on your baby's quilt."

She pushed herself out of the chair. "And I need to talk to you about baby clothes. I think it's time to tell you that we are having a girl."

· 37 ·

It had not been a good week. I worked on the dresses, but my mind wandered into all sorts of possible conversations with Daniel. And Bailey. And I saw neither of them. And I made mistakes and had to rip out seams and redo the hem of the maid-of-honor's gown. A couple of times, I even considered calling Daniel, but the time was so short before the wedding, and I still had so much to do. I knew there would not be time to talk things out.

Gary was no help. Real estate always moves fastest in the summer, and he was into his busiest season. Saturday morning, he dashed off before breakfast, and I hauled everything out to the car by myself and drove to the church, keeping my mind on driving.

The usual, congenial chaos enveloped me, and I had little time to think of anything except how to make this wedding as trouble-free as possible. The biggest crisis came when the flower girl threw up. A search was on to find another little girl approximately the same size. The sash, pulled tightly, made the dress fit just fine.

It wasn't until I had arranged the bride's dress, given her nervous father a pat on the shoulder, and pushed them down the center aisle that I thought once more of how much I had tampered with Daniel's plans. My gaze was drawn to the groom, his eyes shining with love for his bride, and my own eyes filled with tears. *Dear God, please help me make this right.*

I slipped into a chair at the back and looked at my watch - three more long hours. I heard the gentle swoosh of the door opening behind me as a latecomer slipped into the chair beside me.

"Hello," he whispered.

It was Daniel! He leaned in toward my ear. "Abby's in labor. She wants you to come."

I pulled my purse from the floor and stood up. Daniel followed me. Once outside, he clarified, "Your phone was turned off for the wedding. We called Dad, and he knew where you were, and Bailey called me and told me to go get you, and she took Abby to the hospital because Will was farther away."

I turned on my phone, and it buzzed with several messages:

Abby: "Mom, where are you? My water broke and I need you."

Will: "Please bring Abby to the hospital, I'm thirty minutes away."

Bailey: "Dorothy, turn on your phone!"

"Busy afternoon," I said. We had to collect my sewing machine and inform the wedding planner that I was leaving.

"Your car or mine?" I asked.

"Yours. Bailey has been using my wheels, so I asked a friend to drop me off here." He paused to let me lead the way to the car. "I'm driving."

Relieved, I settled into the passenger's seat. The relief quickly turned awkward when I realized that now I had my opportunity to talk with him, but I didn't know how to begin.

I tried, "How was Abby?"

"I don't know; I didn't see her. I was at the library when Bailey called." He chuckled. "I assume she is doing all right: Bailey took charge."

"I'll text Will and tell him I'm praying."

We lapsed into silence while he waited to turn left onto a very busy road. I turned over possible things to say, glad that we loved each other, and hoping I had not caused too wide a gulf between us. Once on the main road, I said, "I'm so glad you found Bailey. I was worried about her."

He glanced my way quickly. "I knew you would be." He took a deep breath and said, "She's waiting at the hospital until we get there."

"Well, I hope we make it before they take Abby into the delivery room."

"We're almost there. I just hope there's no train at the crossing."

There was, and because of traffic, there was no way around it. The freight cars lumbered past us at a snail's pace, and then stopped and reversed. Daniel turned off the engine. "Okay, we can talk. You do realize that this whole thing isn't between you and Bailey; it's between you and me. I want Bailey to know that."

I zipped my mouth and waited.

"I know your strengths - how you have compassion for people, and even in your sewing, you go above and beyond what anyone else expects or would do. You're the one who risked arrest by marching into the abortion clinic and rescuing a stranger."

"Yeah, well, I didn't know what I was doing."

"You cared." He paused and then qualified, "But you're also a bit of a snob, because you want to do things for them, but sometimes you don't understand their world, and you are unintentionally unkind. Eventually, you see this, and then you feel terrible until you can figure out how to fix it. I know you want to fix things with Bailey, but you have to trust me to fix this one without your help."

"Of course," I murmured.

"I think you and I talked once about pity being a bad foundation for a relationship. I know Bailey recognizes that when we met her, she was a mess. You saw that before I did, and you knew that she needed help and grace." He watched the train for a few seconds and then he asked, "How did you know?"

"I . . .." How *did* I know? Back then, she was hard and impolite and profane. Neither her physical appearance nor her personality was attractive. "I don't know for sure. There was just something that pulled my heart to her. I met lots of girls at the Pregnancy Center, but I wanted to give her love that she had never had - and that was even before I met her mother. It was probably God's prompting."

"Well, you were listening," he continued, "As I got to know her, I realized that she hated her life. I watched her change and learn. And much that she learned, she learned from you."

I thought about dirty diapers and mice and cranberry barbecue sauce. I remembered the talk at the coffee shop after that fateful wedding. I saw her again, when Gary had his heart attack, loving, caring, and calm. "I wonder who learned from whom," I murmured, and the tears came once more.

We were quiet for a bit as the train stopped reversing and slowly began to move forward again.

I really am a snob, and I still did not see how Bailey could be convinced that I did want her to marry Daniel after all.

Daniel sighed. "I want to be a father to Peter, and I think he likes me that way. Bailey has been living at City Sanctuary . . .."

I gasped.

" . . . For the past two weeks. It's safe, but crowded, and Peter doesn't even have his crib. We have to change that."

"Their room's waiting."

"Of course, but I mean a permanent change. No one has ever thought she would live in your basement for the rest of her life."

"No, your father and I have talked about that. But the house is so empty without her. Our lives . . .." My voice cracked. "Our lives would be empty without her."

"She needs to hear that. She has imbedded herself into our family and church. She has gained the trust and friendship of a lot of people. If she walks away, it will devastate not just me, but you and Dad, people in the church."

I could imagine.

"Mom, you need to realize that you need Bailey. You're always doing all the helping, but one of the things I loved about her was how she jumped in to drive you places, help at a wedding, or make you a cup of tea. I'm not sure you saw that."

"I usually did," I protested, "And I appreciated her help, but perhaps I didn't communicate gratitude." The thoughts in my head tumbled out. "Daniel, I want you to marry her. Your dad and I love her and would miss her terribly if we never saw her again. I am so sorry that I communicated a . . . a disdain for her. I have wanted what was best for her, and in my opinion you are the best there is."

My phone buzzed with a new text. "Will says that Abby's going into the delivery room. Wow! That was fast. I hope everything is all right."

The last engine finally chugged past the crossing, and the gates went up. Traffic began to crawl across the tracks. A few minutes later Daniel turned into the hospital parking lot. "We sure do spend a lot of time here! I'll text Bailey and find out where she is."

Daniel and I wandered around hospital corridors until we finally found one of the small maternity waiting rooms. Peter was sitting on Bailey's lap, and she was bouncing him to "Trot, Little Pony."

She looked up, suddenly uncertain of me. "I'm . . . I'm so glad you came," she said and then laughed. "Well, Abby will be, like, *really* glad you came."

"Is she all right?"

"I think so. They wouldn't tell me anyway. I'm not family; I'm nobody."

"You're *not* nobody," I insisted. "You belong to us."

She turned her eyes toward Daniel, but said nothing.

He sighed. "We've got time. Let's talk." He moved the diaper bag to the floor and lifted Peter from her arms. "Sit down, Mom, and keep him busy." The sweet, sweaty baby was pushed onto my lap, and Daniel settled into a chair at right angles to Bailey, leaning forward, his elbows on his knees.

"Do you want me to leave?" I asked.

"No, please stay." He turned back to her. "Now, Bailey."

"Yes," she squeaked.

"Mom told me about the conversation with Frankie and of her lament that her folks don't like her choice of . . . of . . ."

"Ben," she murmured.

"Of Ben. Yes. And shortly afterwards, you called Connie and ran away to hide in the City Sanctuary. Mom's guess is that you decided that you couldn't marry me because you think Mom doesn't want it. Is that right?"

She studied her lap, and the auburn twist of hair on the top of her head wobbled and then fell down around her face. "I'm not good enough for you," she admitted in despairing tones.

"You could have any girl in the college and career group at church. They're all better than I am. And your mom knows that."

Daniel shook his head. "If Mom doesn't like the girl I decide to marry, then I will work that out with Mom. That's not your problem."

"But . . .."

He shushed her. "Don't talk. Listen.

She pressed her lips together.

"You can't fix things between me and Mom. I know her a lot better than you do, so if there is an issue, I will deal with it. Okay?"

She nodded, looking up at him with heart-breaking adoration.

Tears welled up in my eyes. I needed a distraction or I would start sobbing. Fortunately, Peter provided that distraction by shrieking and arching his back. I moved us to the floor and spread his blanket for him to sit on. Somewhere were toys, and I dug through the diaper bag looking for them. And his nose was running.

Daniel had been watching me for a moment, when the hallway door opened. A man and a woman looked around the room, finally focusing on Peter on the floor. The man said to the woman, "Not here; there's a baby," and shut the door again.

Bailey snorted and started to laugh. "It's, like, a maternity floor. What did they expect?"

We all giggled about that for a good minute before Daniel reined himself in and said to us both, "I've got to stay on target." He grabbed Bailey's hands and said, "Bailey, I love you for who you are. There was a time when I pitied you, and prayed for you. I watched you battle yourself, until you realized that only

God could save you from yourself. Somewhere along the line, I stopped pitying you and began to respect you. I was drawn to your spunk and determination to make Peter's life different from yours. And I found your willingness to learn very . . . um, poignant."

"That's a big word," she stated bluntly. "What's it mean?"

Daniel chuckled. "Um . . . It means that you snuck into my heart and wound yourself all around it, until I couldn't get away."

A sob burst from her, and I gulped to silence my own.

"If you want to talk about where you came from and where you are going, we can do that, but later. Right now, I want you to know that I love you, as you are, *right now*. And I want to marry you. Still. If you refused me before because of what you thought Mom or Dad were thinking, that's no longer on the table. This is now between you and me." He lifted her hands and kissed them. "I have a question for you: Do you love me? As I am? Who I am?"

She raised her tear streaked face toward him and whispered, "I do love you. I think I have loved you from the moment you held my chair for me that first day in your kitchen."

"Wow . . .. Really? Well, then." He stood up and fished around in his pocket and then knelt beside her. "Bailey Austin, will you marry me?" He glanced over at the baby, who was chewing on his giraffe. "Would you and Peter - I adore Peter, by the way - would the two of you like to marry me and become Bailey and Peter MacGregor?"

"I would like that very much," she said firmly.

He slipped the ring onto her finger. "You've made me very happy." He sat down and took both her hands again. "As much as I would like to kiss you now, I'm saving our first kiss for our wedding day, if that's all right."

"Oh, wow," she breathed again.

He stood and offered me a hand so I could get up off the floor. Then he picked up Peter. "But until then, I'll give Peter lots of kisses!" and he did, until the little boy was giggling. Bailey stood and joined them - their little family-to-be.

Suddenly, the room seemed silent, and I sure didn't want to break the spell, but Daniel turned to me and said, "Mom, don't you have something you'd like to say to Bailey?"

And I knew what to say! "Bailey, I said earlier that you belong to us, and I meant that. While you were gone, I missed you so much, it hurt. You have, indeed, woven your way into our lives, and I think you were created to be a part of our family. I want you to be my son's wife because you are strong and helpful and supportive, and funny. And because he loves you. We all love you, and I'm going to hug you. You're going to have to get used to hugs."

She came willingly to my arms. I had heard once, from a counsellor friend, that you should hug someone until the other person wants to stop. That makes a good hug.

Bailey's shoulders shook with sobs, and then she pushed back and took a deep breath. "I have wanted to call you Mom," she whispered hesitantly, "Ever since the day you rescued me from that clinic. You have been a mom to me, like, teaching me all the things I needed to know about life. Things like cleaning a bathroom, how a washing machine works, and how to love your husband and children." She grabbed a tissue from a nearby end table and mopped her face. "Gosh, I wish I could stop crying." She laughed through her tears and drew another shaky breath. "I was so afraid that I would disappoint you as Daniel's wife. That's why I left. I thought I had to live with the consequences of my . . . my sins alone. But I missed all of you so much." She pushed her hair out of her eyes. "Can I, like, call you Mom?"

"Oh, sweetie, I hope you will," I had trouble controlling my own voice. "And I definitely choose you to be my second daughter." I took a deep breath. "And you need to know that I have been praying for you since Daniel was born. Praying that God would give him the woman who would be perfect for him and who would do him good all the days of her life."

"Really? How can that be me?"

"Really. You are the answer to my prayer and a gift from God to our family. I want to be your biggest fan, a listening ear, and . . ." I looked over at Peter. ". . . and your favorite babysitter."

She gave me another hug, but the nurse interrupted by bursting through the door and announcing, "You may go in now to see Abby and little Anita." She looked at Peter in Daniel's arms. "Your baby, of course, will have to stay out here with Grandma," she told him.

Daniel looked very pleased. "You go first, Grandma. We'll go when you get back. And don't spill the beans. We want to tell Abby and Will ourselves."

I laughed and grabbed a tissue to catch my own tears. Then I trotted down the corridor after the nurse.

I mean, how many women become Grandma twice on the same day?

Epilogue

Initially, Bailey didn't want her mother to come to the wedding or even to know about it. When Gary and I brought it up over lunch, she grimaced and slammed her fork down on the table.

"She will ruin everything!" she moaned. "You don't know her. She'll want everything her way, start bossing everyone, and she'll tell anyone who will listen all the bad things I did in my life, even though she's done them too."

Taken aback, we were both silent for a moment. Then Gary raised his eyebrows and smiled a fake, toothy smile. "No. She won't," he growled.

I turned to him, amused, but from the look on his face, I knew he meant it. "She won't, "I assured her. "Gary will make sure of it."

Gary patted Bailey's hand and gave her fork back. "Besides," he said, his voice returning to normal, "Your mother needs the Lord Jesus too. What a great opportunity for her to hear of Him from Eli at your wedding."

She sighed. "I just don't know if I can stand it."

Gary chuckled. "You can. And I'll stick to her like glue. Don't give it another thought." He chewed for a minute and then said, "We'll ask Nana and Pops to help as well. She may try to control things, but we won't let her. And she probably won't even know that we are sticking to her like glue.

And that's what we did.

Friends from church had pruned and primped our backyard until it could have won prizes. Although it was a warm, sunny day, extra water had ensured that the late summer roses looked their best. The lawn had *not* been watered that morning, so that the borrowed chairs - and high heels - would not sink into the turf. Daniel and Will, who was the best man, kept tweaking the locations of the chairs, making sure they wouldn't tip over.

Frankie, the maid of honor, had spent the night. Now, she and Bailey prowled around the yard in their jeans, clipping yellow and apricot dahlias for their bouquets. Connie was organizing the potluck brunch, finding places in the fridge, the oven, and coolers for all the tasty things our friends had brought.

Nana had been recruited to babysit Peter until Bailey's mom arrived, at which time, I would take over, and Nana would "stick like glue."

And then it was time.

The bride was beautiful, still smiling as if she didn't quite believe this was happening. Like a flower blossom, she floated across the lawn in lemon yellow chiffon. Her auburn hair, long and straight, glorious in the sunshine, stirred in the breeze.

I turned from her to look at Daniel. The love and delight shining from his eyes drew her toward him. I guess Gary had looked at me that way on our wedding day as well. Breathtaking!

Peter stirred on my lap, pulling on the necklace Bailey had given me that morning. Across the way seated beside Nana and Pops, Bailey's mother, wearing a lavender dress, was behaving herself.

Gary put his arm around me, and Peter crawled onto his lap to try to play with baby Anita, cuddled in Abby's arms next to Gary. Peter finally settled for Gary's tie.

Daniel stretched out his hand as Bailey reached him. She gave her flowers to Frankie, and Eli welcomed everyone to the wedding.

What can I say? It was perfect. I kept crushing down the tears that threatened to overwhelm me. Tears of happiness and relief. Eli talked of marriage and of its perfect picture of Jesus Christ and His Church. Then they committed their lives to each other, slipped rings on fingers, and said "I do."

Their first kiss was sweet - a bit clumsy at first, but as they got used to it, it was plain to everyone that they didn't want to stop. The wedding guests chuckled, and someone shouted, "Come up for air!"

They laughed, both of their cheeks pink with the excitement. Then Eli announced, "May I introduce to you all: Mr. and Mrs. Daniel MacGregor?"

Amid the applause, Daniel came at once to pick up Peter who buried his little face in Daniel's shoulder. The three of them turned to greet the wedding guests and to receive best wishes from their friends. Gary invited everyone to stay for lunch.

For our family, the buffet lunch was like a complicated dance with Josie. "We'll kill her with kindness," Nana had said.

Although it was a shame to have to do it at all, we played our parts well. Nana took the first shift and walked with her as she perused the buffet tables. Then they ate together until Will wandered over with his plate, and Nana excused herself. Gary arrived to ask if he could bring her and Will something to drink. Later Abby was sitting beside her, allowing Josie to hold Anita.

At that point, I noticed Bailey watching her mother with a slight smile on her face. With sudden determination, she handed Daniel her plate, picked up Peter from the grass, and marched over to where the two women were talking. Eli arrived with another chair and placed it on the other side of Josie so Bailey could sit down with Peter. Josie, suddenly all smiles, gave Anita back to Abby and turned to tickle Peter and make baby noises. Stranger-shy at eight-months-old, Peter turned his back on her.

Obviously annoyed, Josie stood, picked up her plate from the grass and flounced off toward the dessert table. Pops joined her there, where they chatted about cake and apple pie. Pops also gave her a brief lecture on babies.

I was proud of Bailey for trying.

My turn came, and Josie asked abruptly what Bailey's dress had cost.

"It was my gift to her," I said.

"But I want to pay for the dress," she protested.

I shrugged. "You can't. If you want to give them money for Peter's college fund, that might be a good idea."

I was surprised to learn much later that she had told Gary she would pay for the wedding.

"The wedding cost very little," he told her. "It was all the work of friends in the church. If you want to contribute to Peter's college fund, I'm sure they would appreciate that."

Daniel and Bailey had decided to time their departure for after Peter went down for his nap. Gary was ushering everyone from the backyard to the front of the house to send off the newlyweds. He stopped in the hallway to give me a kiss. Frankie was handing out little bags of confetti.

Bailey had changed into the red dress we had given her for Christmas. As she and Daniel were coming up the stairs, her phone buzzed, and she stopped halfway up to read a text.

"No time for that now," Daniel told her. "Let's go." He turned to me. "I love you, Mom. Thanks for the lovely wedding. Thanks for everything. And don't stop praying."

We hugged, and Bailey, now at the top of the stairs, joined.

I gulped tears back and said, "We love you and are so happy for you. Have a wonderful time and don't worry about Peter. We'll take good care of him, and we will call if anything happens."

Daniel took Bailey's hand, and together they ran down the front steps under a shower of confetti. At the car, they stopped, and Bailey once more pulled out her phone. Daniel opened the car door for Bailey, but she didn't get in. They talked for half a minute before Daniel grinned at me and shrugged. Resignation, I think. Bailey trotted back up the steps and handed me her phone.

"Can you fix this, Mom? I met Stella at the City Sanctuary while I was there. I won't tell you her story today; it's too sad. But she's pregnant and also has a little girl, I think about two. She's talked to Connie, but she needs, like, a place to live." She cast a glance at Daniel, waiting patiently beside the car. "I'm going on my *honeymoon*," she explained, as if I didn't know. "Can you take care of this for me?"

I took her phone and looked at Gary, who winked at me and laughed.

I hope you enjoyed my novel. If you did, please leave us a review be sending it to us at floyd@thebiblecompass.com.

Thank you!

Other Books by Christine

Christine's Website: www.thebiblecompass.com[1]

~~~~

In the Shadow of the Cathedral

Hammering at the Doors of Heaven

We Never Saw It Coming: Fifteen Years in Austria

Time for Authenticity

Goodness for God's Sake

Lessons in Trust: From Women in Messiah's Family Tree

Understand the Bible Better (workbook)

---

1. http://www.thebiblecompass.com